She was sitting with her back to him looking over a magnificent vista of moor, river, and sky. Randal stood very still. He felt as though he could hardly breathe; the wonder and excitement burning within him were almost too great to be endured. And as he stood there, not moving, not speaking, it seemed as if the intensity of his feelings communicated itself to her wordlessly.

Slowly she turned her head and, and seeing him, rose to her feet. Slowly, Randal advanced, and when at length he stood beside her, he looked down into her small face raised to his. He knew he had come at last to his goal!

THE
PASSIONATE
PILGRIM

Barbara Cartland

▲ PYRAMID BOOKS • NEW YORK

THE PASSIONATE PILGRIM

A PYRAMID BOOK
First published by Rich and Cowan Ltd. 1952
Arrow edition 1970
Pyramid edition published March 1974
Second printing, February 1976

ISBN: 0-515-04063-0

Printed in the United States of America

Pyramid Books are published by Pyramid Communications, Inc. Its trademarks, consisting of the word "Pyramid" and the portrayal of a pyramid, are registered in the United States Patent Office.

Pyramid Communications, Inc., 919 Third Avenue, New York, N. Y. 10022

The Passionate
Pilgrim

1

There were footsteps on the terrace above.

Randal Gray was suddenly tense and began to swear softly beneath his breath:

"Damn! Damn! Damn!"

Despite his most explicit instructions that nobody, however important, should be admitted, he was about to be interrupted.

But French servants were all the same, he thought savagely. If one tipped them enough, they would allow the Devil himself to creep through the door.

"Damn!"

He was so tired, so inexpressibly weary that his desire for rest and solitude had become an almost unbearable craving.

He wanted nothing else in the world but just to lie here in the sun, to enjoy the warmth of it seeping through his naked back, to feel himself drifting away into a dreamless sleep after those interminable days, nights and weeks of noise, music and the chatter of tongues.

It was that more than anything else which had reduced him to the verge of a nervous breakdown.

The incessant talk going on and on ceaselessly and undiminishingly until the time came when, even if he were alone, the echo of those voices still rang in his ears.

There were voices now, voices coming nearer, and Randal realised that his hands were clenched fiercely while a wave of hatred swept over his whole body.

With a tremendous effort of will-power he forced himself to relax.

This was being ridiculous. He was letting himself be theatrical and dramatic.

How often had he sworn never to let himself become temperamentally unbalanced as were so many of those with whom he came in daily contact!

Usually his practical common sense and his unfailing sense of humour were an armour and a safeguard; but now he was so tired, so terribly, terribly tired.

They were coming nearer to him now, the footsteps and the voices encroaching upon him, disturbing him, so that he knew that in a moment he must rouse himself to greet his so-called friends.

For one moment he hoped with a kind of hopeless desperation that, seeing him lying still with his eyes closed, they might believe him asleep and go away; but even as the thought was formulated in his mind, he knew it to be ridiculous.

In his world no one went away, not from him at any rate. They stayed to be bright and cheerful and maddeningly persistent.

It was then that Randal laughed at himself.

"God! I am getting spoilt," he thought.

With what was almost superhuman effort he sat up on the red striped mattress on which he had been lying beside the swimming pool.

Two people were watching him and for a moment he stared at them blankly.

He had expected to see some of his many acquaintances from Cannes or Monte-Carlo.

There were a number of people who he had expected might call when he instructed Pierre to let no one under any circumstances into the Villa.

Even as he gave his orders he had suspected that they would be disobeyed.

Pierre had been too long at the Villa d'Azur as manservant to Madame de Montier not to know and be known by the majority of the socialites who flocked to the Riviera in search of sunshine and cosmopolitan conviviality.

Pierre would doubtless find it more advantageous, Randal reflected dismally, to keep in with someone whose generosity he had already tested.

Someone who was likely to prove a fruitful source of income in the future, rather than with the strange, unaccountable guest whom Madame had left in the Villa when she departed precipitately to America.

Pierre could not understand a young man who did not wish to entertain, who wanted to keep the famous swimming pool to himself, and who could hardly be roused from his slumbers to eat the delicious meals prepared for him.

Yes, Randal had expected that his solitude would be invaded sooner or later.

The only thing that was surprising now was that the intruders should at first sight appear to be complete strangers.

The man was tall, elderly and dressed in the inevitable blue blazer with brass buttons and white flannel trousers as if he had just stepped from one of the luxurious yachts lying in the harbour.

Beside him was a child, an overdressed, rather ridiculous-looking child in a frilled frock of organdie and lace which would have been far more suitable in Paris than in the shimmering afternoon heat of the Riviera.

The visitors stood watching him gravely; at least it appeared to Randal that the expression on the child's face was peculiarly grave;

Then the man held out his hand and began to speak. Instantly he was no longer a stranger, but familiar in that he was one of a type which Randal knew only too well.

"My dear boy, you must forgive us for barging in like this," the man said. "Your man-servant told us you wished to be alone, but I persuaded him that I was one of your oldest friends, one who I might almost say had been a father to you and whom you would not wish to turn away."

9

Randal got slowly to his feet.

He shook hands, trying as he did so to recall where he had heard that deep, gay voice before; where he had seen that somewhat dissolute face which had once been exceedingly handsome.

It seemed impossible that he could have forgotten those deep-set, glittering eyes, which held some strange, almost mesmeric charm within them.

Randal found himself smiling, and without effort as he listened.

"I said to your man," the deep voice went on, " 'No, Mr. Gray won't be expecting us! How in Heaven's name could he be when he had no idea that we were here? It must be nearly twenty years since we met, and twenty years in the life of a young man is a long time.

"Yet I can claim that, if Randal Gray had not known me twenty years ago, he would not have been here today, would not have been taking a well-earned rest after his outstanding and brilliant success in two Continents.

"He would have been . . . well, what would he have been doing? Shall I tell you? He would have been sitting on an office stool adding up accounts.' "

There was a dramatic gesture to accompany the last words and a lowering of the voice for effect which would have told even an impartial listener all too clearly that the speaker had been trained for the stage.

There was a pause, a theatrical pause, and then Randal gave an exclamation.

"Of course, I have it! You are D'Arcy Forest!"

"Got it in one!" The elderly man laughed. "And have you forgotten me?"

"No, of course I haven't ," Randal replied, "but it is a long time since we last met. Fourteen years to be exact, not twenty!"

"What does it matter, my dear fellow?" D'Arcy

Forest enquired grandiosely. "What is of importance is that I believe I was of service to you then."

Randal nodded.

"You are quite right! If it had not been for you I would have gone into a solicitor's office as my father wanted me to do. As it was, I went to Oxford."

"And all thanks to me!" D'Arcy Forest exclaimed. "Well, I often wondered what became of you. I could see that you had great promise even at eighteen, and now you have justified my belief.

"I was reading about you a week ago and of your success in New York, so, when I saw in the *Continental Daily Mail* that you had arrived here, I said to Sorella:

" 'I will introduce you to a very famous young man, my dear, a young man about whom I had a hunch many years ago.' "

Sorella knows all about my hunches, don't you, my poppet?"

He turned to the child standing beside him. Randal also looked at her for a second time. She was not as young as he had thought at first.

"She must be about twelve or thirteen," he decided.

It was her dress which made her look younger. Its ridiculous frilled sleeves, ribbon insertions and lace-edged hem made her appear as incongruously garbed as if she were wearing fancy-dress.

She stared at him gravely. She was not a pretty child, he decided.

She was small and thin to the point of ugliness; her hair, which was nearly black, hung in untidy, straight wisps to her shoulders, and her cheeks, surprisingly untanned, were very pale.

Only her eyes were outstanding; deep-fringed with long, dark lashes, they were green, the colour of the sea before a storm.

Her father threw a big, enveloping arm round her shoulders.

11

"You have not met my little Sorella before," he said. "She was only a baby when I knew you, a baby happy and secure in her mother's love, a mother whom she was to lose in the most tragic circumstances."

He paused for a moment, and although he did not move his hand, Randal felt that figuratively he wiped away a tear from his eye.

"I can't begin to tell you what little Sorella has meant to me," he said a moment later with a sob in his voice. "We have been everything to each other. God knows how I would have survived the blows that life has given me had she not been at my side.

"But we have been together, and that has been enough, and perhaps we have been more fortunate than many."

Randal felt uncomfortable. The man was over-acting and yet there was something so sincere about his emotion that one could not help being moved by it.

With the ordinary Englishman's dislike of a display of feeling Randal turned a little restlessly towards the canopied swings and cushioned chairs set invitingly beneath the flower-hung terrace.

But before he moved he noticed that Sorella was standing stiff and unyielding within her father's embrace. There was, too, an expression in her eyes which almost shocked him.

Randal was not sure that he interpreted that expression correctly.

It might have been shyness, embarrassment or boredom; and yet he knew it was none of these things.

It was something deeper, something perilously near contempt.

But why should Sorella be contemptuous, and of whom? Was it of her father or him? Randal had no idea of the answer and he told himself that he had no desire to concern himself with this rather unprepossessing child.

Yet as he and his guests seated themselves on the

12

cushioned chairs it was Sorella he was wondering about.

He remembered D'Arcy Forest now quite well.

An actor of the old school, Forest had made the acquaintance of his mother over some charitable entertainment at the local theatre.

Randal's parents had been living in Worcester in those days. His father was the Manager of a Bank.

He was a dull man with an inferiority complex which made him both dogmatic and pompous; he was content with the mediocre success he had attained in his profession, and asked nothing further of life.

It was Randal's mother who had ambitions for her son.

She had belonged to a poverty-stricken county family, but was determined from the moment that Randal was born that he should go to a good public school.

It had meant a great deal of sacrifice on the part of both his parents, and Randal had just finished his last term at Marlborough when D'Arcy Forest came into their lives.

Mrs. Gray was on a Committee of benevolent ladies who had persuaded the Manager of the local theatre to make the Opening Night of *A Tale of Two Cities* into a Gala performance, the proceeds of which were to go to the local Children's Hospital.

The Manager, as it happened, did not require much persuading. The Company who were coming to the Theatre were not in his opinion particularly good.

He was also not sure if *A Tale of Two Cities,* revived after many years, was going to appeal to the citizens of Worcester.

The fact that he could charge enough expenses against the Gala Night to prevent his being out of pocket and at the same time obtain a remarkable amount of free publicity appealed to his business sense.

It also appealed to him, although he was by no means a socially ambitious man, that the Lord Lieutenant of the County, the Mayor of the Borough, and a number of titled supporters of the Hospital should grace his theatre in their official capacity.

What was more, he was by no means averse to being publicly thanked for what was considered to be an act of generosity on his part.

The Company were as delighted as the Manager of the Theatre. As the Opening Night in any town was a Monday, they usually played to a half-empty house in an atmosphere of chilly gloom.

So that by the time they came to the third act they were all depressed, longing only for the performance to be over so that they could get back to their lodgings or into the more cheerful atmosphere of the pub round the corner.

D'Arcy Forest looked handsome and had given a blood-and-thunder performance as Sidney Carton.

Mrs. Gray, as had many other ladies present, felt the tears prick her eyes as with a throbbing voice he made his famous speech from the scaffold steps.

When she accompanied the other members of the Committee to his dressing-room afterwards to congratulate him, she had been so carried away by his charming manners that she had stammered an invitation to luncheon almost before she realised that she had given it.

D'Arcy Forest had accepted with alacrity.

Although Mrs. Gray had regretted her impulsiveness several times during the week that followed she had not been able to help feeling a sudden flutter of excitement the following Sunday when she saw him enter her small drawing-room overlooking the High Street.

It may perhaps have been relief too which made her welcome D'Arcy Forest so effusively. For three days before his arrival the household had been torn in two. Father, mother and son had talked of one thing and one thing only until it seemed as if there was nothing more to say on the subject.

14

It was a domestic crisis which affected them far more profoundly at that moment than anything else could possibly have done; not even the imminent danger of war had the power to divert their attention from themselves and the problem which beset them.

It was not an unusual problem. It was one which was likely to crop up sooner or later in practically every middle-class home in the country.

It was, quite simply, what was Randal to do in the future?

His father had had it planned for some time. Mr. Gray's elder brother was a solicitor in Kidderminster.

He had written several years earlier suggesting that when young Randal had finished his education he should come into the office. It appeared to Mr. Gray to be an eminently satisfactory state of affairs.

He had accepted his brother's offer and had spoken frequently to Randal of the future which lay ahead of him.

Now, at the very moment when Randal should have been packing his bags and setting out for Kidderminster, things had been changed.

During his last term at Marlborough Randal had sat for a scholarship for Oxford. He had told his parents about it at the time, but he had not stressed the point unduly and they had paid little heed, as neither of them considered their son to be exceptionally intelligent.

And now like a bombshell had come the news that Randal had won the scholarship. To be honest, no one was more surprised than Randal himself.

He had entered for it chiefly because he had been pressed into it by his Form Master who had a high opinion of his ability.

One of Randal's chief characteristics was that he liked to please. It was so much easier to do what people wanted as long as it was within one's power to give them pleasure.

On this occasion at any rate his desire to give pleasure had far-reaching results.

His mother was determined that he should accept the scholarship.

She had fought courageously that her boy should go to a public school; she had not dared to look further than that, but a University was all that she would have wished for him had she dared to voice such an outrageous suggestion.

Mr. Gray on the other hand declared it to be a lot of nonsense.

The scholarship was not a very large one and there would be a great many other expenses. He considered that he had forked out enough for young Randal one way and another.

It was time the boy earned his own living and there was the job waiting for him at Kidderminster. Randal himself was hardly allowed a voice in the matter.

Being devoted to both of his parents, he found it difficult to side with either the one or the other without inflicting what appeared to be a bitter blow on the one he did not support.

He therefore remained silent and let the tempest rage around him.

"I have asked Mr. D'Arcy Forest to luncheon," Mrs. Gray said at breakfast. "I am glad he is coming for one reason at least if not for any other, that we shall have to talk of something else besides Randal's future. I am sick and tired of that argument. He is going to Oxford and that is the end of it."

"He is going to Kidderminster!" Mr. Gray roared, bringing his fist down on the table so that the breakfast cups jumped in their saucers.

They were still arguing when luncheon time came; and although Mrs. Gray said they would be obliged to talk of something else, D'Arcy Forest had not been in the house more than ten minutes before he, too, was involved in the momentous matter of deciding Randal's future.

He was no half-hearted partisan. He came down with a tremendous force and overwhelming eloquence on the side of Mrs. Gray.

"Can't you see what this means to a young man?" he asked Mr. Gray.

He went on to acclaim for over five minutes on the wonder and traditions of Oxford, its place in civilisation and the part it played in the training and equipping of those standing on the threshold of a fuller and wider life.

He spoke so fervently that even Mr. Gray was impressed.

"You were perhaps at Oxford yourself, Mr. Forest?" he ventured.

"Would that I had had the opportunity," Mr. D'Arcy Forest replied wistfully. "I have earned my own living since I was fifteen; but had I a son I would work my fingers to the bone, I would even starve that he might have the opportunity of learning those things that I have never learned, that he might reap a harvest of what had been sown by all the great scholars of the centuries."

It was undoubtedly due to D'Arcy Forest's eloquence and to Mrs. Gray's incessant nagging that Randal had gone to Oxford.

He had never seen D'Arcy Forest again until this day and he was doubtful if either he or his parents had given him a thought after the company of *A Tale of Two Cities* had left Worcester.

That the actor's visit had been the turning point of his life Randal would be the last to deny.

"And are you still on the stage?" Randal asked D'Arcy Forest now as with cigarettes alight they narrowed their eyes against the brilliant sunshine glittering on the sea and on the water of the swimming pool at their feet.

"No, I left the boards many years ago," D'Arcy

Forest replied. "It is a long story, dear boy, so I won't bore you with it. Sufficient to say that, when my wife died and left me alone with my little baby daughter, I was forced to give up the stage so that I could look after my child.

"There were other reasons too, ill-health amongst them; but although I often regret the footlights, I know I did the right thing in abdicating when I did. There is no room for real acting on the stage today."

Randal gave a little sigh of relief. He had been half afraid that D'Arcy Forest was going to ask him for a part in one of his productions.

It was heart-breaking when one had to say no, and yet how often had he to say it!

He did not mind so much when those who sought his patronage were young.

He could steel himself to tell a young man or a young woman that it would be better for them to find another type of employment rather than the stage; but the pathos of those who were old tore him to pieces and hurt him almost unbearably. They had acted all their lives, so what else was there for them to do?

What was also so pathetic was the fact that they never lost faith in their own ability to act.

Crippled with arthritis or so weak that they could hardly make their faltering tones heard beyond the first row of the stalls, they still believed that they were capable of obtaining and sustaining an arduous part.

Faith was indeed often the only thing they had left; and often Randal knew that, if he took that faith away from them, there would be nothing else left for them to do but to go home and die.

Now he could feel himself sink a little lower in the cushions. D'Arcy Forest did not want a part and he could relax. As he did so, he found himself laughing light heartedly at what the older man was saying.

D'Arcy Forest was amusing, there was no doubt about that, and he had, too, a way of holding his listener's attention.

It was with a genuine start of surprise that Randal realised that it was after half past four and he had been listening to his uninvited guest for over an hour and a half.

"We must have some tea," Randal said, "or would you prefer a drink? I ought to have offered you one when you first came. Do forgive me."

"Don't apologise, my dear fellow," D'Arcy Forest said. "Little Sorella and I had just had luncheon when we arrived, but I won't say no to a drink now."

Beside the swimming pool there was an elaborate, ornamental grotto which contained a house telephone. Randal spoke to Pierre in the pantry.

"Bring down the tray of drinks," he said, "and also some tea for me. Wait a minute."

He turned towards D'Arcy Forest.

"I have forgotten your daughter, what would she like."

Randal looked for Sorella as he spoke, but the child seemed to have vanished. He had not given her a thought this past hour while her father had been talking, but now he saw her at the far end of the swimming pool.

She had her back to them, Randal noticed, and was sitting very still, her legs dangling over the high rocks out of which the garden had been constructed. Below her the waves lapped lazily against the cliff side.

He thought of shouting to her and then decided that the effort was too great.

"Two teas," he commanded Pierre and put the telephone down.

"What does your daughter do down here?" he asked casually as he walked back to D'Arcy Forest.

"Do?" For a moment D'Arcy Forest looked sur-

19

prised at the question; then he smiled. "Oh, she finds plenty to occupy her."

There was something in the smooth easiness of his reply which made Randal suspicious.

For the first time he looked at D'Arcy Forest a little speculatively, regarding him not as an amusing acquaintance and a man of the world whose charm and eloquence made him very easy to listen to, but as a father, a man in sole charge of a young child.

Randal's success as a playwright had transplanted him into the theatrical world.

He had lived to the age of twenty-five without knowing a single actor or actress with the notable exception of D'Arcy Forest. But once his first play *The Cow Jumped Over The Moon* had been a success, he found himself living, eating, sleeping and thinking in the theatrical atmosphere of the theatre.

It was a world so utterly different from anything that he had ever known before, and so excitingly different, that even now after seven years it could still enchant and delight him, as if he were a child at his first pantomime.

He found that the theatre left its stamp ineradicably upon all who came in contact with it.

He would have known D'Arcy Forest to be an actor, he thought, if he had met him in the middle of the desert or in the backwoods of Alaska.

There was something which proclaimed his profession in the way D'Arcy walked, the way he talked, and the very manner in which he set his hat at an angle on his greying hair.

And yet there was something more than "actor" stamped on D'Arcy Forest, and immediately the right word rose to Randal's mind—adventurer.

He was sure he was not mistaken. D'Arcy was a type which went out of date at the turn of the century. Nowadays the Smart Alecs and slick spivs had no charm about them.

D'Arcy would rob you with such elegance, eloquence and good manners that one could almost persuade oneself that it was a pleasure to be robbed.

Perhaps robbery was too harsh a word; a loan which was never returned, an investment which never paid a dividend, a guest who never returned hospitality—that would be D'Arcy Forest's line of country.

Listening to him talk and watching the quick speculative glance of his eyes, Randal guessed that somewhere behind that ingratiating smile his agile brain was at this moment pondering how to turn this encounter to its very best advantage.

There were no signs of poverty about D'Arcy Forest and he certainly did not appear to be impoverished, and yet Randal was sure that he was in need of money. There was for instance something almost too carefully calculated about his appearence.

The rich can look poor and it does not matter; but the poor must always look rich.

As Pierre brought the drinks and set them down on a low table beside the two men, Randal guessed that sooner or later D'Arcy Forest would "touch" him. If it was not to be for a job, then it would be for money.

The moment would come inevitably, as it always did; and yet for once Randal did not feel embarrassed.

Randal had not been rich long enough to find it easy to play the part of a generous benefactor.

He loathed the look on people's faces when they were about to ask him for a loan—a look of greed and hunger and at the same time of resentment because he could give while they must take.

He had sworn at himself a thousand times for being so sensitive, but every time it happened he hated it the more.

Yet now, quite unexpectedly, he found himself not apprehensive, but amused. It must be D'Arcy Forest's extraordinary charm, he thought.

Looking back over the years, he could remember his father listening while D'Arcy had talked that day

21

at luncheon. He could remember his mother's close attention and his own half-reluctant admiration for anyone who had such a "gift of the gab."

Now that he was older and more mature, he could appreciate to the full the effect that this man could create by using his tongue.

And yet he could see as he had not been able to see at eighteen that D'Arcy Forest in many circles would be considered a bounder and an outsider to say the very least of it.

There was something intrinsically wrong about him; one realised that even while one was mesmerised into liking him. Yes, mesmerised was the right word.

Pierre finished arranging the tea things and stood back to look at his handiwork.

"Les gâteaux, c'est assez, *Monsieur?*" he enquired.

"I expect so," Randal replied. "If not, I will ring for more."

"*Très bien, Monsieur.*" Pierre bowed and turned away.

As he did so, he glanced meaningly at D'Arcy Forest. When he was out of earshot, Randal asked:

"How much did you give Pierre to let you in? Forgive my asking, but I am curious."

"Give him? My dear boy, I'm no Croesus," D'Arcy Forest replied. "I never tip if I can help it out here. It is so disconcerting for the French not to receive what they expect as a matter of course. No, I merely talked to your man and if he is disappointed when I leave, it will be a lesson to him in the future."

Randal threw back back his head and laughed. This was the sort of frankness he appreciated.

How few other men in D'Arcy's position would have confessed to their meanness! He took up the teapot.

"I insist on my afternoon tea, even in France," he said. "I suppose it is useless to offer you a sandwich or a piece of cake?"

"I seldom eat between main meals," D'Arcy Forest replied, "and never when I'm drinking."

"What about your daughter?" Randal asked.

D'Arcy Forest raised his voice.

"Sorella, come and have your tea!"

She did not move or pay the slightest attention and he shouted again.

"Sorella!"

Still she sat for a second or two longer and Randal suddenly remembered his own reluctance to move or open his eyes when D'Arcy Forest had come down to interrupt him. But she was not asleep, he told himself, watching her swing her legs slowly over the wall.

And yet he knew that she was experiencing the same reluctance that he had felt when she had to forgo her solitude, to be drawn back by voices and noise into the world of other people.

She came walking towards them, her low-heeled strapped shoes making only a faint sound on the slabbed path. As she drew near Randal could see the expression on her face.

There was a kind of radiance in her eyes, but it vanished when her father spoke to her, and Randal wondered if he had imagined it.

"Mr. Gray, with characteristic kindness, has ordered you a delicious tea," D'Arcy Forest said.

Sorella did not answer and Randal realised that never yet had he heard her speak.

"Are you hungry?" he asked her deliberately.

"Yes," she replied; "for I have not had anything to eat since breakfast."

Her voice was very soft and low.

It had a quietness about it which was very unlike the ringing vitality of her father's tones.

"Nothing since breakfast!" Randal ejaculated. "You must be famished!"

He remembered how D'Arcy Forest had said that they had just finished luncheon and knew him for an old liar. Sorella sat down on a low stool by the tea-table.

She put out her hand, took a sandwich and began to eat it, apparently concentrating on her food to the exclusion of all else.

"What will you drink?" Randal asked. "Tea, or would you prefer a cool drink?"

He waited for her to answer, but her father replied for her.

"Give her tea," he said. "She's English and should like English ways. I am all against the foreign habit they have over here of allowing children to drink wine at meals."

"Do you like wine?" Randal asked Sorella in surprise.

There seemed to be some reason for D'Arcy Forest's remark.

Sorella shook her head.

"No," she said. "Father is only saying that because the waiter poured me out a glass of wine last night and he thought it was included in the price of the dinner, but it wasn't, and he had to pay for it."

She spoke, Randal thought, as a woman might speak of an unreasonable husband. For a moment there was silence, then D'Arcy Forest threw back his head and laughed.

"The serpent's tooth!" he said. "Oh, deliver us from the devastating frankness of childhood."

Sorella went on eating and Randal poured himself another cup of tea.

"Where are you staying?" he asked by way of making conversation.

There was a tiny pause and then D'Arcy Forest said:

"Nowhere! That, my dear boy, is what we really came to see you about."

Randal felt his hand tighten on the handle of the cup. Now it had come! The moment he had been expecting, the moment when D'Arcy Forest would "touch" him.

Afterwards, looking back, he could never quite remember what happened next.

He had come down to the south of France for rest, for quietness and above all other things to be alone.

Alone after all those sweltering weeks in New York when the temperature had soared to the most unnatural and unmanageable heights; when tempers had been frayed and rehearsals had gone from bad to worse.

When Randal had asked himself not once but a thousand times why he had undertaken such a thankless occupation as play-writing.

If the six weeks in America had not been preceded by the three months' solid grind of producing a film at Elstree it would not have been so bad.

But the two things had come one on top of the other and he had known himself to be for the first and only time in his life in a state of collapse.

Finally he had flown home after an exciting and triumphant first night, when he had been fêted and acclaimed in a manner which left him even more tired than he had been before.

It was all too ridiculous, he had told himself not once but many times, that a healthy, strapping young man of thirty-two should go to pieces because he had worked twelve hours a day; but often to be truthful it was more like twenty-four.

It was not only the work on his play which was tiring, but the people connected with it, who expected him to be an inexhaustible source of strength—mental, physical and intellectual.

And if he were honest there was another reason for his weariness.

A feminine reason, or should he put it in the plural? Jane and Lucille were both responsible in part for his lassitude, for his lack of sleep, for an over-tired, restless mind.

There were two women in his life, and most men find one quite enough.

He had run away from both of them—from Lucille in New York and from Jane in England, and he had come down to the south of France merely because on the spur of the moment he could not think where else to go.

He had a sudden longing for the sun, the warm, glowing, comforting sun of the Mediterranean which could soak the tiredness out of a depleted body and bring a tranquil peace and contentment to over-tense nerves.

He had met Madame de Montier only a few times at social functions in London, but he had liked her and he had known instinctively that she liked him.

"Come and stay with me when you can escape from all this nonsense," she had said the last time they met in England. "You can lie beside my swimming pool, look at the sea, and forget everything else in the world. That is what I do—only sometimes I like to remember my past."

Madame de Montier's past was certainly something to remember. She had had four husbands and survived them all.

She had been a spectacular and much-acclaimed, if not a great actress. She had been the mistress of a Grand Duke and the *chère-amie* of a Balkan King.

She had lost in her old age not only her husbands but her looks and her figure; her wit, however, had survived and her sense of humour.

She was one of the few women who made no demands upon the men who surrounded her.

She had known so many in her youth that in her old age she asked nothing more than that they should listen when she talked and be silent when she had nothing to say, which was not often.

Randal had been but a few days at her Villa before Madame de Montier had been called to America.

"I must go," she said, as she had read the telegram. "This concerns my second husband's fortune. It is a very large one. When one is old, Randal, money is a very important thing in one's life. I like money and I intend to keep what I have got. I must go to New York."

He had expostulated with her, but she had brushed his arguments on one side.

Two days later she left the Villa accompanied by two personal maids, a secretary, a chauffeur, twenty-four pieces of luggage and two love-birds in a cage.

The love-birds were the pets of the moment. Once Madame de Montier had a monkey, but it had tormented her guests and escaped one night from the Villa, only to be set on by stray dogs and left mangled and dead.

Madame de Montier had sworn she was heart-broken, but her friends believed her to be secretly relieved. The love-birds were far less trouble.

They sang prettily in their cage and the servants did not mind cleaning them out and feeding them as they had the monkey.

It was typical of Madame de Montier to take the love-birds with her to America and leave behind her valuable pictures, a unique collection of snuff-boxes and some exquisite pieces of silver.

She also left Randal in full possession of the Villa.

"Stay as long as you can," she said. "Pierre and Madelaine will look after you. Make them do some work or they will get fat and lazy and when I want to give a party they will tell me it is too much trouble. It is always people who have nothing to do who find the little more intolerable."

Randal had laughed, but he had resolved that Pierre and Madelaine would have very little to do as far as he was concerned.

All he wanted was rest, sleep and the joy of being alone.

It was strange, he thought, how seldom one was alone in life. At his flat in London there was his secretary, the incessant strident call of the telephone, and a thousand daily interruptions and disturbances.

At his house in the country—a very recently acquired possession—it was much the same. People would motor down just for a word with him. He needed a secretary there as well as in London because the servants refused to answer the telephone, saying that if they did they had no time to work.

It was all the penalty of being a success, Randal knew that, and up to now he had been far too happy enjoying that success to realise that there was another side to it, a side which was unfortunately very human and commonplace.

It was just a case of endurance, he thought, and realised how in his desire to miss nothing and to do everything he had over-stepped the bounds of common-sense.

It had not only been his work but being a social success which had drained his strength. He had not anticipated that in becoming a well-known playwright he would become a social figure too; but that was exactly what had happened.

He had been taken up by a certain coterie with whom he had never in his wildest dreams expected to become *au fait*.

He had met them through Jane Crake, and he had known at once that she was going to matter very much in his life.

She was very attractive and he was sure she was exactly what his mother would have called "the right person" for him.

He had meant to talk about Jane to Lucille when he went to New York, and yet there had never been a moment.

It was ridiculous, he knew, to be afraid of telling

Lucille exactly what Jane meant to him, or rather what she was going to mean in the future; but to be honest, he had funked it.

Then almost before he knew it Lucille had been signed up for his new play to be produced in October and was coming to London at the end of August.

"I can't wait to be with you, darling, in dear, dirty, ol' London," she said when he left New York.

And still he had not told her about Jane.

It was perhaps the thought of Jane and Lucille which had made it difficult for Randal to relax, to rest as he might have rested during those days after Madame de Montier had left for New York.

Even when he slept he seemed to hear their voices, to see their faces, to feel that they were reaching out towards him, one on one side and one on the other.

Afterwards—a long time afterwards—Randal asked himself if it was because he was afraid to go on thinking of Jane and Lucille that he had agreed to D'Arcy Forest's outrageous suggestion.

A suggestion which had left him gasping and astonished, and yet to which he had acquiesced, though why and how he had no idea.

It was against everything he had planned, everything he wanted and yet he allowed D'Arcy Forest to move into the Villa with his daughter because he said they had nowhere else to go.

Randal had not really realised that he had consented, nor believed himself capable of such insanity until bedrooms had been allotted to them and the boxes had been carried upstairs.

Then, coming into the sitting-room from the terrace, Randal found Sorella curled up in the window-seat with her face turned towards the sea.

For a moment she did not hear him; and when she did, she started as if he brought her thoughts back to earth from some far-distant horizon.

For a second she appeared hardly to see him, then she jumped to her feet.

Randal had the impression that she was not frightened of him or anxious to be gone, but was merely withdrawing, as a child might do from the presence of someone who could not be bothered with her.

There was something about this self-effacement which struck him as pathetic, and rather over-heartily because he meant to be kind but was not quite certain what tone to use he said:

"You will enjoy being here, if you don't find it too lonely."

She had half-turned towards the door before he spoke. Now she stopped and her eyes met his.

"I think you are very stupid," she said slowly and distinctly.

Without waiting for his reply she went from the room.

2

There were two letters on Randal's breakfast tray when Pierre put it down beside him.

Sunshine, golden and already overpowering, shone through the window to glitter dazzlingly on the silver coffee-pot and to illuminate the valuable, colourful porcelain, which was characteristic of Madame de Montier's taste throughout the whole Villa.

Two letters were propped against the toast-rack. Without looking at the writing, without even picking them up Randal knew from whom they were.

There was no mistaking the florid blue paper of the one or the neat, created severity of the other.

He lay back among his pillows to look at them; and as he did so, he realised that he felt calm and complacent about both the writers, and that his nerves had, over this, as over his other problems, ceased to jangle.

Randal was not particularly introspective, nor had he ever worried unduly about his health; but the fatigue and exhaustion which had been his a week ago had frightened him, so much so that it was an almost inexpressible relief to know that he was now himself again.

"Believe it or not," Randal said to the letters, "this cure is in many ways attributable to D'Arcy Forest."

D'Arcy and Sorella had been at the Villa now for over a week, and Randal had not only enjoyed their company, but had found in it something which was the last thing to be expected—a relief and a cure for his weariness.

It was obvious, Randal supposed now, that what he had needed was not solitude but a change of company. D'Arcy Forest had certainly been refreshingly different from all the people with whom he had spent his time in London and New York.

In fact D'Arcy Forest was an amazing and unusual character. There was no doubt that Randal's first impression had been correct—he was an adventurer!

But that in itself was an understatement. D'Arcy was also a buccaneer, a pirate and a highwayman.

One needed but to shut one's eyes when he was talking to see him only too clearly in velvet and lace, with high boots and feather-trimmed hat.

He might be a braggart and a swashbuckler, but he had a romantic, dashing air about him which fascinated those who looked into his deep-set eyes or listened to his warm, vibrant voice.

D'Arcy might well swagger about his conquests, for Randal could understand all too easily why few women could resist his roistering virility.

He robbed them, or rather made them pay through the nose for the pleasure of knowing him, but if

31

one judged people by what they received as well as by what they gave, D'Arcy Forest was by no means the only beneficiary.

To be in his company was to find oneself enthralled, amused and entertained.

Randal had found himself this past week laughing as he had not laughed for a long time. He was used to conversational brilliance for he had recently been admitted to a certain set in Society which prided itself on choosing its members for their wit and wisdom rather than for their birth and prestige.

D'Arcy's humour was, however, of a very different brand from theirs. Richer and more salty, it had a Shakespearean quality about it and was often as full-blooded as he was himself.

D'Arcy might have lived the life of the libertine, and undoubtedly he was a liar in that he would elaborate and build up a story or anecdote to make it more sensational, but beneath his showmanship, over-coloured as it often was, there was a foundation of hard, solid truth and experience.

He had lived what he talked about and that was far more important than having a pretty turn of phrase or being able to raise a laugh at someone else's expense.

D'Arcy's tales were not always by any means suitable for the drawing-room.

Sometimes when Sorella was with them Randal would look embarrassedly at the child and then at her father, trying with a warning glance or a raising of his eyebrows to convey the fact that he thought the subject unfit for young ears.

But D'Arcy, catching his meaning without difficulty, would merely laugh.

"To the pure sex is a bore," he would say. "Besides, Sorella is not listening. She never does listen to me. She has heard it all too often, haven't you, my pet?"

Sorella seldom answered such questions, but merely stared at her father with her strange green eyes.

She betrayed so little of her feelings, was so quiet and retiring, that more than once Randal found himself speculating as to what she thought about while he and her father drank, smoked and talked from mid-day to midnight.

He knew very little about children, but he would have been a fool not to realise that Sorella was an unusual child. For one thing, she was completely unobtrusive.

She appeared at meal times, and as soon as they were over, vanished without stating where she was going or why.

At first Randal was delighted, believing her to be excessively tactful out of respect for his desire to rest. Then he became curious.

"Tell me about your daughter," he said to D'Arcy Forest one afternoon.

Having finished a delicious lunch of oysters, baby-lamb and ripe Brie, they stretched themselves out in two comfortably-padded chairs and lit their cigars.

"My poor little motherless Sorella!" D'Arcy said emotionally. "It is hard for me to tell you how much she means to me; not that the possession of her has not required great sacrifice of me. But let such matters pass.

"A child is a great responsibility, my dear boy, a great responsibility, especially when one has to be father and mother rolled into one. However, you must admit she does me credit."

"After your wife died, had you no relations who would look after her for you?" Randal asked.

"No, none at all," D'Arcy replied. "My wife, as I think I have already told you, ran away from home to marry me. Her parents cut her off with the proverbial shilling, believing that she was allying herself with the Devil.

"It was not the first time, nor the last, in my life, that I have been accused of being that somewhat

33

reprehensible gentleman. Nevertheless, I think I made my wife a happy woman.

"She had been trained to dance and became a ballet dancer after we were married. Had she begun earlier in life and had better masters, she might have become famous.

"As it was, she enjoyed a brief if gratifying success and died as a good trouper should, for refusing to disappoint her public. She had a chill and a temperature, but insisted on playing to both houses because it was Boxing Day.

"She died forty-eight hours later and I was not prepared to fail her trust and forsake the child she left me."

Randal glanced at D'Arcy speculatively. He could not accept these heroics at their face value.

If Mrs. Forest had gone on dancing when she should have been on a sick bed, it was doubtless because her husband was out of work and they needed the money.

Randal wondered, as he had wondered before, what sort of a father D'Arcy Forest had made to his motherless child.

It was one thing to listen to tales of adventure and excitement, of love affairs and intrigues, of gambling and roistering, but quite another to remember that this old libertine had been trailing round with him at the same time a child, and a girl at that.

Randal guessed that Sorella had proved an asset in so far as she excited sympathy.

He guessed that the extraordinarily unsuitable clothes that she wore had been provided by D'Arcy's lady friends, who had found it conveniently endearing to pet the poor little motherless child of a man whose embraces and attentions they were all too ready to accept.

It was nice to think that Sorella had enjoyed even that much attention, for when Randal saw her in a bathing suit he was frankly shocked.

34

She looked thin and emaciated in the frilly, extravagant organdie and lace frocks she wore, but without them she appeared to be nothing but skin and bone.

It was true that her skin had that unusual magnolia quality which never seemed to burn or tan and which undoubtedly added to the pathos of her sharp little elbows and pointed shoulderblades.

But there was no doubt in Randal's mind that the child was under-nourished and he suspected that D'Arcy's gay, voluptuous stories of the past held many discrepancies in them.

"How old is Sorella now?" he asked.

D'Arcy hesitated before he answered, and Randal guessed he was debating whether to tell the truth or risk a lie.

"Fifteen," he said at length, rather grudgingly.

"Fifteen!" Randal exclaimed. "I thought she was younger than that."

"Sorella takes an unnatural interest in her birthdays," D'Arcy said drily, and Randal's lips twisted in a smile.

He could well imagine that D'Arcy did everything to keep his daughter a winsome child; a girl budding into womanhood was not likely to be a useful adjunct to his clandestine love affairs.

Women were notoriously jealous of their own sex, and a lover's daughter must be very young to be acceptable.

"Yes, fifteen," D'Arcy said again resentfully. "I tell her she is getting old, and soon we shall have to begin to think about her future."

"Do you intend her to go on the stage?" Randal asked.

D'Arcy shook his head.

"She has not the right temperament for it; besides, a good actress is born, not made, and Sorella has little or no idea of acting and art. She has, too, a devastating habit of being truthful. It was a quality

35

I found particularly irritating in my wife, and in that Sorella takes after her."

Randal laughed. He could not help it.

"What then? he enquired.

D'Arcy shrugged his shoulders.

"I wouldn't say my daughter's education has been neglected," he smiled. "But shall we say it is hardly commercialised enough? Sorella can play a first-class hand of bridge, she is a good poker player and you shouldn't trust her to shuffle the cards if you are playing after her.

"Besides that, she can speak most European languages—enough of them, at any rate, to find her way about a strange town. All useful achievements, you must admit, my dear Randal, but hard to turn into a weekly wage."

"I'm sorry for the child," Randal said.

"Good, then perhaps you can find something for her to do," D'Arcy responded instantly. "We can teach her to type and she can become your secretary."

"God forbid!" Randal exclaimed and wondered, as he said it, what Hoppy would think of Sorella.

The same thought crossed his mind this morning as, reaching across the breakfast tray to remove the two letters which were propped against the toast-rack, he found there was another hidden behind them.

It was a small, unassertive letter, the envelope being inscribed in the neat, unpretentious writing which was more familiar to him than any other writing in the world.

He picked it up, and opening the envelope, took out the letter and started to read it as he poured out his coffee. There was, as he did so, a faint smile on his lips and an expression of affection on his face.

Mary Hopkins had come to him as a Secretary when he first started to make a name for himself in the theatrical world. Hoppy—as everyone called her—told him afterwards that she had accepted a much

36

smaller wage than she had been used to, simply because she believed in him.

Randal was sure this was true, for it was so characteristic of Hoppy, because she was in every way an exceptional and unusual person.

She was middle-aged, gaunt and grey-haired and yet it was impossible to be with Hoppy for more than a short time without both admiring and loving her.

It was Hoppy who had made Randal work until he almost pleaded with her for mercy. It was Hoppy who arranged his life and his publicity, dealt with his managers and agents, and finally even with his love affairs.

As he told her once, in a fit of exasperation, she was far more persistent than a wife, and far more demanding than a mistress.

She had merely laughed at him and continued to drive him on to greater and more outstanding successes.

Yet, while she compelled him into respecting the wishes and demands of the great public for whom he worked, she could nevertheless make him laugh by her own utter indifference to all the things which most people thought so essential.

Hoppy had little use for money and less for people of importance.

She liked men and women for what they were, and her own friends varied from Cabinet Ministers to rag-and-bone men with an utter disregard for what anyone else thought of them or her.

She managed Randal's financial affairs with efficiency and a sharp alertness, refusing to allow him to be diddled out of a single penny or to be battened on by the thousands of hungry vultures who were always waiting to pounce on the bank balance of a successful young man.

At the same time she invariably forgot to write a cheque for her own salary.

More than once Randal had to force her to buy some necessary article of clothing, like a winter coat or new shoes, simply and solely because she could not spare the time for attention to herself and her own necessities.

He had a treasure in Hoppy, and her devotion to him was something for which he was ever-increasingly grateful; and yet he often admitted to himself that he was a little frightened of her.

She was so autocratic when she wanted something. More than once he had asked himself whether he was marrying Jane Crake to please himself or to please Hoppy.

It was Hoppy who had made up her mind that Jane's father, Lord Rockampstead, should finance Randal's autumn production, and in bringing Randal and Jane together she had clinched the matter only too successfully.

Lord Rockampstead was new to the theatrical world.

He had discovered the stage rather late in life, and the fact that he was prepared to sink many thousands of his millions in West End productions made him appear as a kind of Angel of Deliverance to impecunious Theatre Managers and even less-affluent Producers.

"Crake's Flakes" were a household word in nearly every British home. It was Lord Rockampstead's father who had developed the business and had made it the industrial success it was.

A hard-headed Lancashire man, with little education and few social attributes, he had been anxious to do the best for his son, who he was determined should never struggle as he had done for social recognition.

When he inherited his father's barony and enormous fortune, John Crake was already a notable figure.

Despite the fact that his name was plastered on

every hoarding, he was known to the more intelligent public for many different reasons.

His collection of pictures was well known amongst connoisseurs; his racehorses had won the Classic Stakes; his polo team held a formidable array of international cups; his sailing yacht had out-sailed all comers; his time on the Cresta run had beaten all records.

For some years the pursuit of sporting trophies combined with an historic mansion and a fine grouse moor in Scotland occupied the new Lord Rockampstead's mind exclusively; then he became interested in the stage.

He had backed three theatrical losers and one winner before he was casually introduced to Randal at a cocktail party, after which it was Hoppy who managed, in some way of her own, to get Randal an invitation to stay at Bletchingly Castle.

The two men liked each other and Lord Rockampstead intimated that he wished to be the first to read the script of *Today and Tomorrow*.

It was Randal's most ambitious play and a production which required a great deal of money.

His agent had been doubtful whether they would find anyone to finance it, until Hoppy's intrigues had drawn Lord Rockampstead into the net, and from then onwards everything was plain sailing.

But if Randal had landed Lord Rockampstead, he had also landed Jane; and Hoppy reminded him only too clearly of this, when at the end of her letter she wrote:

Jane telephoned me yesterday morning. She was very distressed at not hearing from you, and I told her that I felt sure your letters must have gone astray. However, if I were you, I should not waste time making enquiries about them, a telephone call is far quicker.

Randal smiled as he put the letter down on the bed. It was so like Hoppy. Quite suddenly, he felt gay and young and excessively light-hearted. What did it all matter? London and New York were far away.

Neither Jane nor Lucille could bother him this golden morning for his lassitude and weariness had gone from him and he felt the return of his strength.

He jumped out of bed and walked on to the balcony. A haze of heat hung over the horizon and the sea was very smooth and calm.

He could hear the faint splash of the waves against the rocks, and the palm leaves were rustling in a breeze too faint to be felt, while the bougainvillaea tumbled in crimson and purple confusion over the terrace. In the face of such beauty what could anything matter?

" 'O, world, as God has made it! . . . all is beauty,' " he quoted aloud; and as he spoke he heard a faint movement below him.

A face was turned up towards him, and he saw Sorella standing beneath the balcony.

She carried a great bunch of flowers in her arms and was wearing one of the dresses which made her appear so ridiculous.

It was of sprigged organdie, edged with frills of tulle; but her feet were bare and she looked like a princess playing at being the beggar maid.

Randal put his elbows on the balcony and leaned over.

"Good morning, Sorella," he said; "on a morning like this does anything matter?"

"What sort of things?" Sorella enquired cautiously.

"The boring, pompous things, which people say one ought to do," Randal replied. "You must know the sort I mean; the things that are good for you, the things that help you, the things that enable you to get to the top, the things that will horrify everyone if you don't do them. Do they matter, Sorella? That is what I'm asking you."

"If they didn't matter, you wouldn't be asking me if they did," Sorella replied.

Randal felt a sudden irritation rise within him. It was the truth of course, that was why he did not want to hear it.

"You are the most annoying child I know," he said. "Why can't you laugh and be gay and smash things like other children? Come and jump in the swimming pool with me, for that is what I am going to do."

"All right."

Sorella suddenly flashed a smile at him.

"I'll be down in two minutes," Randal said, and went from the balcony back into his room.

"I'm young, I'm gay, I'm happy," he told himself.

He put on his bathing trunks, conscious as he did so that the two letters were lying on his crumpled bed unopened and with what seemed to him to be an accusing air.

Randal looked at himself in the glass as he brushed his hair.

He would not have been a good playwright if he had not been able to consider his own reflection dispassionately and find the effect pleasing to the eyes.

His skin was burnt the colour of old bronze. His shoulders had a sheen on them and despite the fact that he had little time for exercise, he might have posed for a statue of a young athlete.

He put down his hairbrushes on the dressing-table and turned towards the door. The letters were still lying where he had left them.

"Damn all women!" he said out loud, and ran down the stairs and out to the terrace.

Sorella was waiting for him at the swimming pool. She wore the same dilapidated blue bathing dress which she wore every day.

It obviously had belonged to someone else. A big

pleat had been taken in down the sides and sewn with different-coloured cotton from the original material.

Even so, it fitted nowhere and she wore a piece of black tape tied round her waist to keep the suit from slipping off her in the water.

She was sitting on the diving board as Randal came towards her. Her dark hair fell forward untidily over her cheeks as she stared down into the clearness of the bath.

"What are you looking at?" Randal asked.

She raised her head with a start for she had not heard his approach.

"I was wondering what it would be like to lie on the bottom of the bath and look up through the water," she answered. "Fish must think we are very strange creatures. I think they imagine we are monsters in the sky."

Randal sat down on the edge of the pool and dangled his feet in the water.

"Is that the sort of thing you think about when you are alone?" he asked. "Personally, I believe fish have rather a good life. They have nothing to do but swim about, talk to other fish, and find themselves something to eat. But let us stop talking about fish and talk about you. Why don't you buy yourself a decent bathing dress?"

Sorella hitched the black tape about her waist a little tighter.

"People don't give away bathing dresses," she answered after a moment. "They like buying pretty, frilly frocks for nice little girls, but not bathing dresses or underclothes or winter shoes. People never give things like that."

She spoke with a calm fatality which was far more effective than if she had spoken bitterly.

"Are you really as hard up as that?" Randal asked.

She looked at him then, her eyes reflecting some of the colour of the water beneath them. She said nothing, but he knew the answer and called himself a fool to have asked the question.

"How do you live?" he said at last. "How do you manage? Your father hasn't a job, he told me so himself; perhaps he has not had one for years, and yet you are here; you have recently been in Rome, and last winter you were in Paris. How do you manage it?"

"Oh, we manage," Sorella replied. "Why do you worry about us? You said yourself nothing mattered this morning. I'll race you to end of the pool and back again."

She dived in as she spoke and Randal followed her, forgetting as he followed in the wake of her quick-moving body that she had practically snubbed him for his curiosity.

There was no doubt that she could swim, almost as well as the fish she had been pondering about.

She beat Randal not once, but three times in their races to and fro in the pool; then they sat panting on the warm stones, Sorella shaking her wet hair from her eyes, a little colour in her cheeks for the first time since Randal had known her.

"Where did you learn to swim?" he asked.

"A waiter taught me at Antibes when I was seven years old," Sorella replied.

"A waiter?"

"Yes, a waiter from the hotel. He was a Swede and he was terribly good at all sports. He promised that if we ever met in the winter he would teach me to ski. But we never did meet again."

There was no regret in the calm, matter-of-fact voice. It was just a statement of fact.

"So you and your father were staying at Antibes when you were seven?" Randal said. "Were you alone there?"

"No, there were a lot of people in Antibes at the time," Sorella replied with a little smile.

He knew that she was mocking him for his curiosity.

"Why did you tell me I was stupid the first evening you were here?" Randal asked suddenly.

He had been waiting to ask this question for days, but the opportunity had not presented itself. D'Arcy Forest had always been with them, or else he had felt embarrassed in some extraordinary way at having to ask the question of a child.

"That was rude of me and I'm sorry," Sorella said.

"I don't want you to be sorry," Randal replied. "I want to know why you said it."

She looked at him out of the corner of her eyes. "Why should I tell you?"

"Why shouldn't you?" he replied. "You seem to be on the defensive; do you dislike me, or have I done something to offend you?"

"Neither."

"Then tell me what you meant that night when you said I was stupid."

Sorella let go of her knees, and leaning back, lay flat on the ground.

Her eyes were closed against the sunshine, her arms and legs left wet patches where they touched the white marble. They were thin, and almost emaciated beside Randal's brown well-covered limbs.

He could see the soft swelling of her breasts beneath the badly-fitting swimming suit.

She was growing up, he thought; and yet she was such a child in some ways—a lost child, defenceless, as those he had seen desolate and unprotected in some no-man's-land of a battlefield.

That was what she reminded him of, he thought suddenly—the children who, orphaned and homeless, he had seen crying beside the road in Burma, or sitting amongst the smoking ruins of what had once been their homes.

"Tell me," he prompted when Sorella did not speak.

"I thought you were stupid because you had let us come here and disturb your peace. You were alone and happy. You hated our coming. I saw the expression on your face when we came upon you lying in the sunshine.

"You were polite and pleasant, but all the time you hated us. If we had fallen dead, you would have been glad; and then, when we should have gone away, you let us stay.

"I thought you very stupid at the time, and now I am not sure. Daddy has made you laugh. You are eating and sleeping better. You look quite different."

Randal almost gasped. He had no idea that this child had seen so much or been so perspicacious over what she saw.

"I did not want you when you came at first," he said at last. "One does not always know what is good for one; and there is obviously a moral to the story: 'Never make up your mind too quickly,' or should we say: 'A kind action reaps its own reward'?"

"When are you going away?" Sorella asked.

"I don't know," Randal answered.

Even as he said it, he knew that was not the truth. A line in Hoppy's letter had been a pointer as clear as a searchlight:

"Today and Tomorrow *goes into rehearsal next Wednesday.*" She might just as well have written, *"We shall expect you back on Tuesday."*

The inference was obvious and both she and Randal knew it.

He was not, however, going to tell Sorella this; instead he asked:

"Why are you so anxious to know my plans?"

"We have got to make plans, too."

45

"But you must have some idea of what you are going to do. After all, when your father said that the hotels were full for the yacht racing, he . . ."

Randal's voice died away.

Why bother to talk nonsense? D'Arcy Forest's excuse that the hotels were full had deceived no one. He wanted somewhere to go because he had no money—that was obvious, and he certainly had little more since he had arrived at the Villa d'Azur.

A few hundred francs, won from Randal at Backgammon, would be just enough to keep him in cigarettes.

Of course, there was every likelihood that he would touch his host for a few pounds on leaving, but Randal had no intention of allowing it to be more than a few pounds. He disliked lending money.

Perhaps it was the frugality of his upbringing which made him curiously reluctant to write out cheques for impecunious friends, however fond he might be of them.

"You must have made some plans," he said with an almost querulous note in his voice.

"We seldom make plans very far ahead," Sorella replied quietly.

"But you must know whether you are returning to Paris, or wherever you live. I have to be back in England next week."

He saw the look that came into her eyes and turned his face away to stare out to sea. A racing yacht, with brilliant red sails, was skimming across the water.

"Next week!"

The words were hardly more than a whisper, but he heard them.

"Yes," he said with elaborate lightness, "that was why I was asking your plans."

She did not speak again, and he sat watching the yacht with the red sails until it was out of sight.

3

Lucille Lund signed half a dozen autographs, accepted a bunch of tired roses from a spotty child of fifteen, smiled entrancingly for innumerable Press photographs, at last she reached the sanctuary of the hotel sitting-room, where nobody more formidable than Hoppy awaited her.

She threw the roses and her very expensive mink stole down on the sofa.

Then, without wasting time in conventional greetings, asked the question which had been uppermost in her mind since the aeroplane in which she had come from America had touched down at Croydon.

"Where is Randal?"

Hoppy's repy came smoothly and without hesitation.

"On his way home—I hope."

"Why wasn't he here to meet me?"

Lucille spoke sharply.

Without waiting for Hoppy's reply she walked across to the mantelpiece and stood staring at herself in the mirror as if the very sight of her own reflection gave her some reassurance of which she was surprisingly in need.

What she saw was familiar to millions of film-goers all over the world—the perfect oval face, with its high cheekbones and huge enquiring blue eyes which managed by some extraordinary freak of nature to look both innocent and mysterious at the same time; the perfectly-curved lips with a faint smile lurking at the corners; and the tiny, tiptilted nose that made the box-office receipts of a dozen films soar dazzlingly.

A face which women went again and again to see

and to whom it mattered little what story Lucille appeared in.

Lucille Lund, star of *"Universe Super-Features"*, had managed to retain personal glamour and allure in a world which had turned its back on both such luxuries and acclaimed only the common man and his commonplace needs.

While the demand for realistic stories of real life rang through the studios and other actresses wore jeans, flat-heeled shoes and polo-necked sweaters, Lucille, garlanded in jewels and wrapped in sables, entranced her fans with yet another.

"Lucille Lund drama of splendour, passion and excitement."

Her Publicity Agent found it easy, at a time when film stars went out only at dark or wore sunglasses and slouch hats, to fill the gossip columns and the picture pages of magazines with Lucille looking as romantic in real life as she was on the screen.

"I wonder how old she really is?" Hoppy thought now.

She watched Lucille study her face in the glass, then walk towards the window, the sunlight searching her face mercilessly and finding it flawless.

The sitting-room overlooked the Thames, and Lucille stood for a moment, her eyes on the barges passing down the grey water; but it was obvious that her thoughts were elsewhere.

"Does Randal realise what I have given up to come over here at this moment and play the lead in his play?" she asked at length, and her voice was harsh. "The studio nearly went mad when they heard what I intended to do.

"They offered me another fifteen thousand dollars a month if I would stay in Hollywood. In these days when salaries are dropping, not increasing, fifteen thousand dollars is not to be sneezed at; but I had promised Randal, so I kept my promise."

"He is extremely grateful, you know that," Hoppy

48

said soothingly, "but he was terribly run down. He telephoned me when he arrived in France and he sounded so ill that I nearly flew over with the doctor.

"He will turn up shortly, you can be certain of that. Perhaps his aeroplane has been delayed. It is unlike Randal to be late, either for you or for one of his own productions."

Hoppy was trying to calm Lucille, knowing all too well the ominous signs that her temper was rising; yet at the same time, she could not help a certain coldness creeping into her voice.

Hoppy had never liked Lucille Lund, and to Randal she made no bones about it.

He laughed good-humouredly at her outspoken comments when they were alone, but she was wise enough to conceal her feelings from Lucille herself.

To Randal Hoppy was brutally frank and she spoke the truth as she saw it, telling both him and herself that she was too old for hypocrisies and too wise to pretend.

But to the outside world she would always stand between Randal and anything which might disturb or hurt him, whether it were in big or little things.

That was her job and she knew it would not make things easier or more comfortable for Randal if he returned to England to find Lucille in one of her rages and the rehearsal for *Today and Tomorrow* starting off on the wrong foot.

So, with an effort, Hoppy swallowed her own personal feelings where Lucille was concerned and started to do her best to pour oil on troubled waters.

The women were a strange contrast as they stood there in the flower-filled room with its air of luxurious impersonalness which is so characteristic of any hotel room wherever one may find it.

Lucille, in her dove-grey travelling outfit lined with sapphire blue, her diamond ear-rings and dan-

49

gling charm bracelets, might have stepped straight from the pages of a *Vogue* magazine.

Her legs, which were insured for fifty thousand dollars and which were famous in five continents, were revealed by the shortness of her skirt and were barely covered by chiffon-thin nylons, so fine in texture that they cost over thirty-five dollars a pair.

Hoppy was wearing her inevitable black suit with a skirt which was too long to be fashionable and which was badly in need of a brush.

She had on comfortable crêpe-soled shoes and her hair, grey at the temples, was brushed back from her forehead into a neat roll at the nape of her neck.

She looked middle-aged; a plain woman with no pretensions to looks, and yet there was something extraordinarily attractive about her face.

It was the face of someone whom one could trust, someone to whom one could go in trouble, someone who one knew instinctively would listen to anything one might say.

Hoppy had, when she wished, the charm of a hundred Circes, and she was using this charm now to coax Lucille into a better temper.

"Why did I come, Hoppy?" the latter cried querulously. "I'm asking you the same question that I have been asking myself ever since I arrived. Why did I come?"

"I suppose we both know the answer to that," Hoppy answered quietly.

Lucille looked at her, and then with a sudden change of mood laughed.

"Damn the man!" she exclaimed. "What's he got that we all do what he wants?"

"I thought it was Edward Jepson who persuaded you to play this part," Hoppy said cautiously.

Lucille shrugged her shoulders.

"It was certainly Edward who did all the talking," she replied. "But after all what is Edward but an astute business man? I wouldn't have listened to him or to anyone else if it hadn't been for Randal."

"Randal asked you to come to London?" Hoppy queried. There was a slight doubting note in her voice as she asked the question, but Lucille apparently did not notice it.

"As a matter of fact," Lucille replied, "Randal wished me to stay in New York. As you know, I was having a tremendous success there in his *Green Fingers*. They are talking about making a film of it and he wanted me to play the lead in that, too.

"I wouldn't have refused for I've no intention of staying too long in a stage part. I suppose really I am more at home in the films after so many years of them. But at the same time, the stage has a fascination for me—I like the applause.

"I like feeling the live audience in front of me; but, to be frank, any part, however tremendous, becomes monotonous after the hundredth performance."

"So Randal wanted you to stay on in *Green Fingers*?"

Lucille was too intent on her own thoughts to hear the note of relief in Hoppy's question.

"I often wonder if I am doing the right thing in going back to the stage," she pondered. "It was Edward who persuaded me to do so in the first place. After the tremendous success I made in Randal's first film he wanted New York to see me in his next play and in the flesh. That, by the way, is the reason he gives for bringing me to London."

Lucille did not reveal to Hoppy that Edward Jepson had added.

"It is now or never, Lucille. You're not getting any younger, you know."

She had hated him for that remark.

"I don't know what you mean," she cried, but her eyes narrowed as he replied:

"Oh! yes, you do, my girl. I've a pretty good idea of your real age."

"If you ever say such a thing in front of anyone else," Lucille spat at him, "I think I'll kill you!"

He put back his head and laughed, the fat and comfortable laugh of a successful man who is sure of himself.

"Don't be afraid," he said; "there's honour among thieves. We are neither of us in this for our health, my dear. I believe in you, just as sincerely as you believe in yourself; but that does not prevent our being frank with one another. You go to London now or it will be too late."

Lucille had been sulky and disagreeable for the rest of the day, but it was impossible for her to quarrel with Edward for long. He was too important to her.

He was right when he said they were in it together. It was he who had found her doing a second-rate vaudeville act in a one-horse town in North Carolina.

It was Edward who had seen the possibilities of her high cheek-bones when lit from above, who had realised that her legs were perfect and that her voice was a mistake.

It was Edward who had taken her to Hollywood and groomed her into stardom.

He had made her work for it; elocution lessons until she had cried literally at the boredom of them; lessons in deportment; lessons in practically every god-damned thing that women could do.

She wanted to run away, not once but a dozen times a day, because of the things he said to her.

He cursed and swore at her; he humiliated her by his sarcasm; he made her so miserable that she wished he had left her alone with her vaudeville act and that she could have continued touring dingy, half-empty, little provincial theatres on a salary which left her permanently in debt and often hungry.

But if ever the means justified the end, it was true where Lucille was concerned. She became a star overnight. Edward chose a film story in which she could play the lead, financed and produced it.

It was almost true to say that *Angel Face* swept the world. There was certainly not a country, with the exception of Russia, where Lucille's lovely, glamorous face was not well known.

Her half-shut eyes, her parted lips, the seductive symmetry of her legs graced posters, hoardings, magazine covers, postcards and chocolate boxes.

There were Lucille Lund fans in China and Honolulu; there were Lucille Lund clubs in the Philippines and Alaska. There were offices full of secretaries who did nothing but answer fan letters and post photographs.

There was an army of script-writers working on her next film and the one after that.

At first Lucille would think that it was all a dream and she would soon wake up; and then, too quickly, she began to take it all for granted.

It was only Edward who never let her quite forget where he found her and what she had been like before he changed her from an ordinarily-attractive woman to something breath-taking and almost unbelievably glamorous.

"Am I really as lovely as that?" Lucille had asked naively when she saw the first shots of her first film.

"It is certainly an improvement on this," Edward had answered.

He had drawn from his well-filled wallet a photograph that she recognised as having been sent out by the theatrical agents she had employed to get her bookings.

She had been taken by a cheap photographer because she could afford no one better.

The lighting was wrong, the pose was execrable. It made her look fat and rather common, and only the lovely lines of her legs, despite the cheap stockings, were unquestionably photogenic.

"Where did you get that photograph?" Lucille had cried. "Throw it away."

But Edward had looked at her speculatively and put the photograph back in his wallet.

She had known then that he intended to keep it, not only as a kind of satisfaction for himself, but as a hold over her; a threat perhaps that what he had made he could unmake, what he had done he could undo.

At times Lucille hated Edward Jepson and at other times she admired him more than any other man she had ever known.

She was afraid of him, too, afraid because he had such power over her.

'You will go to London," he had said.

Though she had protested and argued just for the sake of appearances, she had known the moment he spoke that the journey lay ahead of her.

But talking to Edward and talking to Hoppy were two very different things.

To the latter she wished to create the impression that she had made a sacrifice, believing, as many women had believed before her, that every word she said to Randal's secretary would be repeated to him.

"What has he been doing in the south of France?" she asked now.

"Resting," Hoppy replied. "I don't know what you did to him in New York, but I have never known Randal in such an exhausted state. He was too tired to care about anything, and that, you know, is very unusual."

"He should not let himself be knocked up so easily." Lucille said sharply. "Look at what I do, and yet I contrive to keep healthy. It is all a question of planning the day right and not being stupid and exhausting oneself on people who don't matter. I often think Randal is too kind."

"Can one be too kind?" Hoppy asked speculatively.

"After all, Randal owes his success to being able to see the other person's point of view, to being able to understand what other people feel and think.

"If he considered only himself, he might lose the knack of getting under the other person's skin, and that you know is what makes a good playwright."

"Well, he won't be writing plays for me much longer," Lucille said, "if he doesn't turn up."

She walked across the room and opened the door into the bedroom. Her maid was already there unpacking the enormous cabin-trunks that had preceded her by ship and which seemed to clutter up the entire room.

Lucille took off her travelling coat and threw it on the bed, then she drew from her fair hair the little grey felt hat trimmed with sapphire feathers and combed out the soft waves so that they touched her cheeks caressingly.

Hoppy watched her for a moment from the doorway and then, glancing at the paper she had in her hand, she said:

"If you don't need me any more, Miss Lund, I'll go round to the flat and see if there is any news of Randal. I will telephone you if there is."

"Thank you, but I'm beginning to lose interest in Randal," Lucille said indifferently.

She lied, and both she and Hoppy knew it; nevertheless, it was a facade they were both, for the moment, willing to accept.

Hoppy took a taxi and was driven through the crowded streets to Randal's flat in Park Lane.

Here again, there was no sign of his car outside the porticoed front door, and Hoppy, who had sent it to the aerodrome early that morning, began to worry as a mother might worry over a thoughtless and irresponsible son.

She had been certain that Randal would return either yesterday or today.

Everything had been in readiness for his arrival

for over a week; but as the days passed and the time shortened before the moment when the first rehearsal would start, Hoppy had believed she could almost pinpoint the moment of Randal's homecoming.

The porter took her up in the lift to the top of the tall building.

"No sign of Mr. Gray, yet, Miss?" he asked cheerfully.

"I was hoping you would tell me that he had come while I was out," Hoppy replied.

"Not a sign nor sight of him, Miss. Been several callers though. Miss Crake is waiting there now."

"I'm glad you told me," Hoppy said.

She got out of the lift hurriedly as it reached the top floor.

Randal's flat was unique.

What had originally been the attics of a huge mansion in Park Lane had been converted into one of the most charming and unusual flats in the whole of London.

The windows overlooked Hyde Park and there were balconies on which one could sit in the sunshine or stand admiring the magnificent view of trees and roofs stretching away to where, in the distance, one could see the Thames winding its way towards the sea.

Hoppy's office was the only austere and workmanlike room in the whole flat.

Randal had had the place decorated by one of the most famous young decorators in London, who had insisted on giving him what was described as "the right background for a famous playwrite."

The red leather curtains and red velvet chairs were a challenge to the conventional.

The murals which decorated one wall had been a god-send to innumerable gossip-writers in need of copy; and there were some lovely 18th-century pieces of furniture and a few modern French pictures for those who considered themselves connoisseurs.

It was all rather pleasant, if slightly pretentious.

Randal's desk of green looking-glass struck a dramatic note which was all the more effective because he had managed to crack nearly all the drawers by closing them too sharply when he was annoyed.

Jane Crake was sitting on the red velvet sofa, turning over the pages of a magazine, when Hoppy entered the room.

She turned round quickly and the look of excitement on her face was quickly supplanted by one of disappointment when she saw who was there. She managed however to smile before she said:

"I got so restless waiting to hear of Randal's arrival that I came round to wait for him. You don't think that anything has happened to him, do you?"

"No, of course not," Hoppy replied. "He has obviously absent-mindedly forgotten our very existence. He is more than likely in Paris at this moment without a notion as to what is happening tomorrow."

"Has Lucille arrived?" Jane asked.

"Yes, she's at the Savoy," Hoppy replied. "She expected Randal to meet her at Croydon and has taken it as a personal insult that he should not be in England when she is here."

"She sounds thoroughly tiresome," Jane remarked. "I can't think why Father was so keen to have her in this new play. He's having to pay her such an enormous salary that he won't make a penny out of the production, however successful it may be."

"He will get the money back on tour," Hoppy said. "It's going to be a tremendous thing from a publicity point of view to have Lucille open in the show, even if she only remains in it for a month or two."

"I expect you're right," Jane said. "You usually are, aren't you, Hoppy?"

She sat down on the sofa and smiled up rather sweetly, so that Hoppy, looking at her, felt a sudden warm relief flooding over her.

This was the girl for Randal, she was convinced

57

of it. Indeed she had been sure since the very moment she had seen Jane.

If Lucille Lund had glamour, Jane Crake had elegance. Dressed almost entirely in Paris, her clothes had a chic and beauty of line which could only come from a French couturier.

She was not strictly beautiful, but her lovely clear-cut features and her big grey eyes gave an instantaneous impression of beauty. Jane had learnt early in life to accentuate her best points and to conceal or disguise her worst.

Her mouth was too small, but cleverly applied lipstick made it seem bigger; her chin was rather heavy, but she held her head at an angle which defied criticism.

At twenty-four Jane was poised with a polished self-assurance which had a charm of its own.

She looked, Hoppy thought now, not only smart but a lady; and that, indeed, was the one thing which one might question when considering Lucille's loveliness.

"What are you worrying about, Hoppy?" Jane asked suddenly. "And it's no use saying you're not worried, for you're twiddling your pencil, as you always do when something has upset you."

"I was only thinking," Hoppy said simply.

"Stop it then," Jane commanded. "Randal will turn up and make us look silly because we have been fussing about him. Did I tell you that Father has had to put up another £5,000 for *Today and Tomorrow*?"

"Another £5,000!" Hoppy exclaimed. "Whatever for?"

"Well, as far as I can make out, the majority of it goes on Lucille Lund's clothes. Father doesn't mind; he has made up his mind that this is going to be the play of the year, and once he has convinced himself of something, nothing on earth would change his mind."

58

"Well, that's a good thing, at any rate," Hoppy said drily.

She thought then, as she had thought so often before, how lucky Randal was to have the backing of Lord Rockampstead.

Most playwrights had to wait for backers, to go through all the agonies of finding security, to wonder if this sum or that would be enough and whether a further hundred or so could be squeezed from one source or another.

Randal had never had to worry about finance where his plays were concerned.

Although his Manager had cried out in horror that *Today and Tomorrow* would be the most expensive production ever put on the London stage, Lord Rockampstead had come forward at precisely the right moment and the money had been there almost before Randal had realised it was necessary.

And what then, Hoppy thought, could be more suitable than that Randal should marry Lord Rockampstead's daughter?

Jane moved in the most amusing and gayest and by far the smartest set that existed in London. In fact, one might almost say in Europe.

The majority of her friends were cosmopolitans and one found them not only in London and in Paris, but in Rome and Venice and Biarritz and St. Moritz or any other playground that might prove amusing at the moment.

But they were not by any means only dilettantes and social butterflies. They were people who merged together because they had all achieved something in common—success.

There were diplomats and politicians, artists and and authors, musicians and playwrights, those who were famous for wit or wisdom, and women who had made the possession of beauty a profession.

Only the very loveliest and most outstandingly beautiful women of the century were included in this small coterie of the notable and notorious; yet beauty by itself was not an "open sesame", any more than a millionaire could buy an entry into what was very múch a closed circle.

One had to have a special quality and an extraordinary genius for one's chosen medium of expression, and to be outstanding amongst all other competitors.

Randal had never ceased to wonder at his own inclusion among this brilliant and very critical clique.

It was indeed Jane who had taken him first to meet a number of those exalted beings, and because he had been in good form that day, he had made them laugh.

So he had gone again, and yet again, until he found himself one of them, one of the accepted few.

At first he had been inclined to scoff at the whole set-up—the exquisite food, the chatter and conversation which was invariably of personalities, the private entertainments after dinner, the sparkling, extravagant parties which were spoken of in tones of awe by those who were not invited to them.

There was, he felt, something rather pretentious in making such a fuss about getting together so that one might talk and laugh and eat.

Then he found that the "Magic Circle" as he called them to himself, had a charm of their own.

Never once could one say one had been bored in their company, although one might feel worn out from the effort of being on one's toes for a long period of time.

The "Magic Circle" met daily in each other's houses, they went together, not always in a crowd, but paired, to all the most fashionable functions; theatrical first nights, film galas, balls and parties; and slowly and surely on all such occasions the others of their little coterie would gravitate towards them.

It might be the Royal Duchess, who was one of their members, who would arrive with her Lady-in-

Waiting; but within ten minutes she would be surrounded by at least a dozen members of the "Magic Circle".

It was almost like belonging to a Lodge of Freemasons.

"Or the Band of Hope," Randal said once and had been told laughingly,

"On the contrary, we are as exclusive as the Jockey Club and far more expensive."

This was true in a way because only the superlative was good enough. Each dinner vied with the previous one. If the "Magic Circle" listened to music, it was of the very best. If they gave a party, it was a sensation, so that those who did not receive invitations cried because they had been omitted.

Eveything they did, in small things as in great, was gay, sparkling and extraordinarily amusing.

There was also, beneath it all, a steady current of power and influence which could be felt in many and various directions. It was sufficient to say that Cabinet Ministers and Ambassadors were flattered when they were invited to a meal.

Ambitious young Members of Parliament tried their best, by becoming attached to one of the women members of the set, to get themselves included. But it was not as easy as that.

That house that Randal went to most was, of course, Lord Rockampstead's.

At first he was so impressed by Lord Rockampsead's patronage and by the fact that he had been included in the set of amusing notabilities that he did not think of Jane so much as a desirable woman, but as someone whom he liked and who was kind to him.

This was unusual, for Randal had grown used to thinking of all women only from the point of view of their desirability.

Hoppy had told him quite frankly, he was in

danger of growing into a dissolute roué with a roving look in his eye.

This was not Randal's fault, for women found him irresistible, and he was not likely to be austere where no austerity was expected of him.

He had begun to think that he was cynical, that all women were bores unless one was kissing them, when he became a member of the "Magic Circle". It was then he found that women could be amusing as well as seductive.

He learned to listen instead of to talk. He learned to admire as well as to argue; and lastly he found Jane elusive, which intrigued and piqued him.

Then, just when he was beginning to wonder about her, to find himself thinking about her when she was not there, to know that he was pursuing her because she was by far the most attractive woman he had seen for a long time, he became aware that Jane had fallen in love with him and the chase was at an end.

Looking at Jane now, Hoppy wished she was not so obviously in love with Randal.

A little anxiety on his part would have been good for him. If he had been made to speculate, to wait, to be more in love with Jane than she was with him, how much easier things would have been!

But Jane, who had refused half a dozen eligible and distinguished suitors, had fallen for Randal from the first moment she set eyes on him.

She had seen him standing in her father's drawing-room in Belgrave Square—a long grey room, exquisitely decorated and hung with some of his famous collection of pictures.

Randal's eyes had gone to a Turner over the mantelpiece immediately after he had shaken hands with Jane. He had stood looking at it, and after a moment he had said, almost reverently:

"It's lovely, isn't it?"

It had given Jane time to notice the extraordinary

attraction of his face, the way he managed to look smartly dressed and yet give the impression of being comfortable and at ease in his clothes.

She liked his well-kept hands, their long thin fingers, which contrived to be artistic while yet retaining a strength and virility about them.

She had liked the way his hair grew back from his temples and the smile at the corner of his lips that made him appear as though he were watching the people around and finding them amusing.

"Yes, it is lovely," she replied. "My father has a great many treasures. Would you like to look at the jade?"

She led him across the room to where there were cabinets of exquisitely carved jade discreetly lit from behind, and told him a little of the history of the very old burial jade, and all the time she felt he listened to her as if she had been the moth-eaten curator of a museum.

They had gone down to luncheon, and Jane found herself sitting by two entirely different people, while Randal was at the far end of the table.

She watched him being a success with her friends— Diana, the most beautiful woman of the century, acclaimed him as delightful, and Jane felt something which was suspiciously like jealousy within her heart.

She had talked to Randal again after luncheon; and when he left she was determined to see him again.

There was something about him which drew her as surely as though he were a magnet, something which made him appear entirely different from the other men she had known.

"That was an extremely clever young man," her father told her. "They tell me he is the best playwright we have produced in the last twenty years. Have you seen his last play?"

"I've been once," Jane replied, "but I'm going again."

She did, and found herself setting a very different value on what before had been merely a theatrical performance. The play was outstandingly clever, there was no doubt about that.

The characters were all brilliantly drawn and there was a touch of cynicism about the whole thing which gave it an unusual quality.

Jane saw Randal the next day, and the day after that. It was hard to know the precise moment when she fell really in love with him, because at first she would not admit it to herself.

She had always imagined that love was a rather over-rated thing. One had a discreet and amusing affaire, or one got married because it was the sensible and practical thing to do; but only in popular novels was one's whole being utterly submerged in loving another person.

That sort of thing, Jane had long ago decided, would not happen to her. And yet it had!

She was in love, madly, crazily and hopelessly in love with a man about whom she knew nothing except that he was a good playwright.

Hoppy had known it before Randal did, and she had been delighted. Randal had known it himself as they drove home from a party which had gone on to the early hours of the morning.

Jane's car had been waiting for her.

He had helped her into it, and then, as they drove back towards Belgrave Square, he took her hand and raised it to his lips with what was to him a familiar gesture.

"A lovely evening, Jane," he said, "and I was proud to be with by far the most attractive woman there."

It was one of the things Randal said so nicely. He knew all the answers, and he had expected Jane to thank him prettily as most women did.

Instead her fingers tightened on his so fiercely that he could feel her nails digging into his flesh.

"Don't," she said. "Don't talk like that."

He looked at her in surprise.

He could see the outline of her head against the street lamps, but her eyes, which were raised to his, were only dark pools of mystery.

"Don't say things you don't mean," Jane continued in a surprisingly emotional voice, "I can't bear it, Randal."

It was then he had taken her into his arms and kissed her and felt her respond with a sudden quiver of her whole being. Her hand had first touched his cheek to creep round his head and hold him closer.

For them both it had been a moment of excitement and quivering desire, but the car had drawn up outside Jane's house and the chauffeur got down to open the door.

"I'll see you tomorrow?" Randal questioned.

"Of course."

She left him then and the car had driven him back to his own flat.

They met again the next day and Randal knew then that Jane was in love with him.

He had been flattered. He told himself that he was excessively fortunate; and yet something was gone, something that he had been seeking and which he had half thought he had found.

Jane was experienced enough to know how to entertain a man, to prevent him from ever being bored, to make certain that he was never completely and absolutely sure of what she would either say or do.

Randal spent a good deal of time with Jane, all the time he could spare from the production of his new play and the alterations and corrections he must make to his autumn production *Today and Tomorrow*.

The play that was being produced that summer was only a light comedy, but even so it took a great deal of his time, a great deal of his energy.

If Jane grew impatient of his preoccupation with everything but her she was too clever to say so.

It was only Hoppy who knew how she was feeling, Hoppy who sensed the rising flood of impatience behind the calm serenity of her smile.

But not even to Hoppy would Jane confess that Randal was making no effort to decide the date of their marriage.

He thought their understanding was an absolute secret, not knowing that her father already spoke of it as an accepted fact. Randal clung insistently to his idea that "no one must know".

He would of course change his mind very shortly, there was no doubt about that, Jane told herself, and she guessed he was waiting until after the production of *Today and Tomorrow*.

She had no idea of the real reason for Randal's reticence, but instinctively she resented that his elation at winning her did not apparently make him want to clinch the bargain.

She was sure of him—no one was more sure. She knew there had been many women in his life before her; but she was confident that she could hold him once he was hers.

Yet somethimes he was unaccountable; sometimes she was afraid, as she was afraid now, when he had gone away to the south of France and had never written to her, not once.

It was Hoppy who had told her where he was and when he was coming home.

It was Hoppy who had assured her, over and over again, that Randal never wrote a line unless he was paid for it. Letters were an absolute bugbear to him.

"He will be back tomorrow," she had said, and now tomorrow had come and he was not there.

"What has happened to him, Hoppy?" Jane said, getting up from the sofa again, as if she could not bear to keep still.

"Supposing he left at twelve o'clock," Hoppy said, "he should arrive any time now."

"Why couldn't he come by an ordinary air service?" Jane asked.

"He likes flying himself," Hoppy answered. "He was in the R.A.F. in the war, as you know, and if there is one thing he really enjoys, it is being up in the clouds. When he gets really disagreeable and things go thoroughly wrong, I say to him,

"For Heaven's sake go and take a flight, and you will come back a different man," and he always does.

That is why I encouraged him to buy an aeroplane. It was so complicated trying to hire one that they would let him fly alone. It isn't as easy as the "Drive Yourself" Motor Service."

"No, I suppose not," Jane said.

She was not listening, Hoppy knew that. They were both talking for the sake of talking.

"He is one of the safest people I know," Hoppy went on. "He never takes any risks and he never tries any silly stunts, like some young fools. Being flown by Randal is like being driven in a Rolls-Royce—steady and sure, you never think how fast you're going."

Jane looked at her watch. It was gold, studded with rubies.

"Well, I suppose I'm being ridiculous to worry about him at all. I hoped we could dine together tonight, but I suppose it's unlikely if Lucille Lund is ramping about. I'd better go home. Tell him to ring me when he arrives. I must speak to him, even if I can't see him."

"Yes, of course," Hoppy said. "I'm certain he will be here before dinner time. It's no use our getting in a fuss."

"Of course not."

As Jane walked towards the door the telephone rang. Hoppy snatched up the receiver.

"Hello."

Automatically she had assumed the polite, mechanical voice of a perfect secretary; it was changed in an instant.

"Hello . . . Randal! Thank goodness. . . . Where are you? . . . We've been worrying ourselves sick as to what had happened to you . . . An accident! Are you all right? . . . What?. . . Who? . . But I've never heard of him. . . . Yes, yes, of course. . . . Yes . . . . Yes, leave the papers to me. . . . You're sure you're all right. . . . Thank God!"

Hoppy replaced the receiver even as Jane put out her hand towards it.

"Let me speak," she cried. "Let me speak."

"He's cut off," Hoppy replied. "You don't want to speak to him now. There's been an accident, a bad accident."

"But he's all right, I heard you say so."

"Yes, Randal's all right," Hoppy said soberly. "But someone who was with him has been killed."

"Who was it." Jane asked.

"A man," Hoppy replied. Someone I've never heard of. I think Randal said the name was D'Arcy Forest."

"I've never heard of him, either," Jane said. "But how was he killed?"

"They had engine trouble and had to make a forced landing. The aeroplane crashed into a tree. Randal is all right except for a few bruises. But Mr. D'Arcy Forest, whoever he might be, was killed."

"But Randal's not really hurt!" Jane gave a deep sigh of relief.

"No, Randal's all right, and also the other passenger in the aeroplane, Mr. Forest's daughter. He's bringing her back with him tonight."

The two women's eyes met. They were both wondering the same thing. They were both asking wordlessly the same question.

Who was D'Arcy Forest's daughter, and why was she travelling with Randal?

4

Sorella was sitting on the red velvet sofa, snipping a dress with a pair of scissors, when Hoppy entered the room.

There were yards of lace flounces lying on the floor, and Hoppy looked at them in surprise for a moment until she realised what Sorella was doing.

"Oh! but you are ruining that lovely dress," she exclaimed.

Sorella looked up at her for a brief second and then returned to her snipping.

"You wouldn't think it was lovely if you had to wear it," she said.

"But you are not to . . .I mean it's a very pretty dress for a child, and it must have been very expensive."

"It was," Sorella agreed.

She picked up the dress as she spoke and held it up as if to inspect it. It looked forlorn and limp now that it was shorn of its lace frills.

"You have ruined it!" Hoppy cried.

"I suppose I have," Sorella replied ruefully. "It will be too short for me now. It always was too short anyway."

With a gesture of disdain she flung the dress down on the floor and said:

"I've got to have some money."

For clothes?" Hoppy asked.

Sorella nodded.

"I suppose that is not an unreasonable request," Hoppy said.

She remembered the night that Sorella had arrived and how fantastic the child had looked in a coat of yellow satin and a little poke bonnet of the same material.

She was expecting somebody so very different.

She had even steeled herself to be angry with Randal because he had frightened them so much; and she had been quite certain, knowing him, that he would arrive suave and smiling with a beautiful and attractive young woman.

She had been wrong about everything. Randal had not been suave or smiling.

He had been worried and apparently quite genuinely unhappy at having been the cause of D'Arcy Forest's death.

And with him had come Sorella—a strange, unpredictable child Hoppy had thought from the first moment she set eyes on her.

Sorella had, indeed, seemed unnatural in that she had shed no tears at her father's death.

Pale and unsmiling she ate a good supper in silence, while Randal interviewed Press reporters and the police.

It was by no means his fault.

He could not be held accountable for engine trouble, and not even the most skilled pilot could have landed that machine any better or prevented a crash.

But Randal seemed to blame himself for what had happened, and Hoppy found herself almost resenting this unknown D'Arcy Forest who was causing such a commotion just when Randal was required to concentrate on very different matters.

And now on top of these there was the problem of Sorella.

Hoppy had prepared, on Randal's orders, the little guest room with its comfortable adjacent bathroom, and had helped Sorella unpack her suitcase.

She had thought then that the clothes Sorella had brought with her were extremely unsuitable for the chilly autumn weather they were already experiencing in London.

She had expected that the child would have other things arriving in a day or two, coming by sea, as they would have been too heavy to bring in the aeroplane.

This was obviously not the case. D'Arcy Forest's clothes arrived and were sent by Randal to a charity which cared for out-of-work and impoverished actors.

Nothing arrived for Sorella and Hoppy was forced to the reluctant conclusion that the contents of that one small suitcase were all she possessed.

Hoppy had to admit that the elaborate frilled and lace-trimmed dresses were unsuitable and that Sorella's pale yellow coat, which had obviously been bought in the Rue de la Paix, could have been worn only by a film star or a child with a large and varied wardrobe.

Now Hoppy bent to pick up the discarded dress and the frills which had once given it a fragile, doll-like prettiness.

"I expect someone is dealing with your father's estate," she said. "We will ask Randal to find out what money you can expect, and then you will be able to buy what you want."

"If you think Daddy has left any money," Sorella replied, "you are much mistaken. When we left Cannes, he had exactly a hundred francs left, because he told me so."

"You mean that was all the money he had in francs?"

"No, all the money he had in the world," Sorella corrected. "Did you think we were rich?"

"No. I mean . . . well, I don't know what I think," Hoppy stammered.

She stared at the dress she held in her hand. It must have cost thousands of francs.

She looked down at the one Sorella was wearing. Tucked and embroidered, it was the kind of useless extravagant bit of nonsense one would see only in a shop window.

Any normal child would be horrified at being asked to wear anything so ornate and impractical.

Sorella got up from the sofa.

"You don't understand," she said quietly.

She walked across to the window. Hoppy noted the lithe grace of her movements. Her dress was far too short, it barely reached her knees, and her white ankle socks and black strap shoes looked absurd.

Yes, Sorella needed some new clothes. There was no doubt about that. Something would have to be done for her, and Hoppy realised that this was another of her jobs.

"I'll speak to Randal about getting you some new clothes," she said kindly. "He'll agree to help you, I'm sure of that."

"Tonight? You'll speak to him tonight?" Sorella asked, turning eagerly from the window.

"If I get the chance," Hoppy replied with a smile. "He's gone to rehearsal now, as you know; and if they stop early, I expect he'll go out to dinner with one of his friends."

"Jane, most likely," Sorella said.

"Don't you call her Miss Crake?" Hoppy asked.

"She told me to call her Jane," Sorella answered. "It doesn't matter to me; I can call her anything, if it comes to that."

"No, no, of course call her Jane, if she asked you to," Hoppy said hastily. "Everyone in the theatrical world is always talked of by their Christian names. I felt Miss Crake was different. But of course you must do as she asked."

Sorella said nothing and Hoppy looked at her enquiringly

The child had an extraordinary habit of being silent when one least expected it. It was disconcerting and almost had the effect of making one feel embarrassed.

"You like Jane Crake a lot, don't you, Hoppy?" Sorella said suddenly.

"Yes, of course I do," Hoppy replied. "She's a very nice person."

"And you don't like Lucille Lund."

Hoppy started.

"What makes you say that?"

"The way your voice alters when you talk about her. There's a cross expression in your eyes, too."

"I hardly know Miss Lund," Hoppy said repressively. "She's made a great name for herself, and I admire her acting. It's really not a case of whether I like her or dislike her."

Sorella's lips twisted in a little smile, which told Hoppy as clearly as if she had said it aloud that she did not believe a word of this prevarication.

As if the conversation no longer interested her, Sorella turned towards the window again and stood looking out.

Hoppy felt a sudden irritation surge up within her. The child could be exasperating at times, and this was one of them.

Still carrying the mutilated dress, Hoppy turned towards the door.

"If you want a walk," she said, "I've got to go to the library in about ten minutes' time."

"Are you going down to the theatre after that?" Sorella asked eagerly.

"No, not this afternoon," Hoppy replied.

She sensed, rather than saw, that Sorella's eagerness had gone. The child turned towards the open window again, and Hoppy left the room.

Sorella's eyes were on the trees below.

Yellow, gold and russet with the tints of autumn, the leaves were beginning to fall with the insistence of a wind blowing sharply from the river.

There was a glint of sunshine between the clouds, yet even so the horizon was misty blue and there was that strange, secretive haze hanging over London which gave it an air of mystery and enchantment.

Directly below there was the noise of traffic, strident

73

and insistent, a klaxon occasionally seeming to cut the air with a strident shriek.

Sorella seemed not to hear it; her eyes were on the trees and to where between them was the sudden glimmer of the waters of the Serpentine. She stood there for a long time, then was suddenly aware that the wind was cold on her bare arms.

She shivered and came back into the room.

Over the mantelpiece there was a portrait of Randal painted by one of his artist friends.

It was a clever picture; his charm and good looks exaggerated, while one was conscious at the same time of the slightly ironic expression in his eyes and the cynical twist to his lips.

It was Randal as the world saw him.

It was Randal as he believed himself to be when his upbringing and early environment did not seep through the worldly veneer and make him far less complacent and far more human.

Sorella stood looking at the portrait. She did not turn round when she heard the door open behind her for she expected it to be Hoppy who had come into the room.

Then quickly, as if some instinct told her what to expect, she turned to find Randal standing there.

His expression had been one of worry and strain when he first came into the room, but now he grinned.

"Are you admiring me," he said, "or making up your mind to fling something?"

"Why have you come back?" Sorella asked, ignoring his question. "I thought you were at the rehearsal."

"I was," Randal replied.

He moved to the table in the corner, which held a tray of drinks, and poured himself out a whisky-and-soda.

"Lucille has gone temperamental! We've had to postpone rehearsals until tomorrow."

"What upset her?" Sorella asked.

"Heaven alone knows," Randal replied. "I don't."

He threw himself down in an armchair with what was almost a petulant gesture.

Sorella sat down at his feet on a long tapestry-covered stool.

"You do know," she said very quietly.

Randal stared at her.

"What makes you say that?"

"Because it is the truth," Sorella replied. "You do know what has upset Lucille Lund, but you don't want to admit it even to yourself."

Randal met her eyes with a glint of irritated defiance in his own, and then he shrugged his shoulders.

"All right," he capitulated, "I know; and as you know so much, perhaps you would like to explain what I can do about it?"

Sorella folded her hands in her lap and sat very still.

She had the way of being serenely still at all times when it mattered, Randal thought suddenly. He couldn't have borne her to fidget at this moment.

He would have hated her to appear embarrassed or restless after what she had said.

Instead she was still. Her green eyes, grave, yet somehow extraordinarily sympathetic, were fixed on his face.

"Well?" he said at last, as she did not speak. "What is your remedy?"

"There isn't one," Sorella said. "Lucille is jealous of Jane. You know that. She is angry today because you took Jane out to dinner last night."

"That's true enough," Randal exclaimed, "but how did you know this, you extraordinary child?"

"I was in the theatre all yesterday afternoon," Sorella answered, "and I heard people talking. They didn't pay much attention to me. I don't think they even knew I was there.

"There was a Mr Jepson who had just arrived from America. He didn't like the way Lucille was doing the third scene.

75

"He said it was not what you meant when you wrote it. She said that in that case you could tell her so yourself. And she added that you seemed to be more interested in breakfast cereals than in stage production these days!"

"And what did Edward Jepson reply?" Randal asked.

Sorella pondered for a moment, as if she was trying to remember the exact words.

"He said, "Now, now, honey," in a very American voice—I expect you know how he talks. He tried to smooth her down and it seemed to make her worse. At last she said.

"You know I wouldn't have come to this lousy dump if it hadn't been for Randal; and if you think that he's going to stand me up for some milk-faced Society dame, even if she's hung with gold nuggets, you are much mistaken.' "

Sorella gave a little chuckle and added:

"When Lucille gets angry, she talks exactly like an American comic paper."

Randal gave a laugh and finished his whisky-and-soda.

"Lucille suits herself to her company," he said. "Edward Jepson started life as a cowboy, but nobody would believe it now! Well, I suppose I'd better take your advice."

'Have I given you any?" Sorella enquired.

"Oh, yes, you've told me that if I want this play to be a success, Lucille has got to be kept in a good temper. The question is, what sort of temper will Jane be in, if I stand her up for Lucille?"

He smiled at Sorella, the irresponsible, mischievous grin of a schoolboy who is about to do something he knows quite well is going to cause trouble.

He got to his feet and walked across to the telephone.

Sorella did not reply.

As he lifted the receiver, he noticed a strange

expression chase itself across Sorella's face. He would have asked her what it meant had he not been intent on dialling Jane's number.

Actually, his words had evoked a memory, a none-too-pleasant memory, for Sorella. She could hear her father saying the same words, five years ago, as he strode up and down the bedroom floor.

"Women are the devil, Sorella," he had said, "the very devil. I've tried all the tricks I know; now it's up to you."

'But what can I do?" she had asked him.

"You've got to do something, and quickly," D'Arcy Forest replied. "I've got exactly a fiver left, and there's a fortnight's bill to pay. The manager spoke to me about it yesterday. I told him I was expecting a cheque from England.

You know as well as I do that that cheque is sitting here in the hotel, sitting in the best private sitting-room, with its own car waiting at the front door."

"But, Daddy, quite obviously Mrs. Lazard does not wish to know you. When you spoke to her in the lift last night, she just gave you a cold stare; and this morning, when she saw you coming into the hall, she quite deliberately walked the other way."

"That doesn't say she doesn't want to know me, Sorella," D'Arcy Forest replied; "women are strange creatures. If one pursues them too openly, they pretend they don't want you. Walk away and they will walk after you. The point is that we haven't got time to play about, to stalk the creature cautiously, as one might do in other circumstances.

We have got to act quickly, my poppet, and this is where you come in."

"How?" Sorella enquired briefly.

D'Arcy Forest stood still and tapped his teeth with his finger-nails. It was a habit he had when he was thinking. Sorella knew it only too well.

"Now let me see!" He scratched his chin.

Suddenly he flicked his fingers together with an untranslatable ejaculation.

"I've got it," he said. "The dog is the passport to Madame's affections!"

"I don't understand," Sorella said.

'Yes, you do. Mrs. Lazard will come in from her drive about quarter past four. You will wait about in the hall while she is asking for her letters. She usually goes to the reception desk for them.

'As she does so, you start making a fuss of the dog. Pat it, stroke it and talk to it—baby nonsense— it's a little beast and will probably bite you, but that can't be helped.

"You'll say in sweet, child-like tones what a darling little dog it is and how you wish you had one of your own. Be persistently affectionate to the little hound, and when Mrs. Lazard gets into the lift you must ask her if you can go too.

"'Please may I come and play with your dog a little while?' you must say. 'I'll be very good, I won't cause you any trouble!'"

"Oh! Daddy, I can't do that!" Sorella exclaimed.

"It's a perfect, a fool-proof scheme," D'Arcy Forest went on, ignoring her protest. "You'll go with her into the sitting-room. If she tries to refuse you must cry, make a fuss, cling to the dog, kissing and hugging it. When you have been there a few minutes, I'll come and fetch you, and then you can leave the rest to me."

Sorella went very pale.

"I can't do that, Daddy, I can't," she repeated. "Mrs. Lazard won't let me. It is quite obvious she doesn't like us. How can I insist on going into her sitting-room?"

"You can and will," D'Arcy commanded. "Put on your prettiest dress, the one that Florence Erskine gave you in Paris. And for God's sake try to make yourself attractive. If only I'd been blessed with a pretty child, what might I not have achieved?

"You don't try to make the best of yourself. You don't try to make yourself pleasant. I've not forgotten that Florence said you glowered at her. I would like to know how much money your glowering has cost me, one way and another."

"You told me to call her 'Mummy' and kiss her." Sorella said. "She was a nasty, fat woman, and I didn't want to touch her."

"Good heavens, do you think I wanted to?" D'Arcy Forest shouted, "but she was rich, my child, rich! Look what we got out of her. A fortnight's comfort at Torquay, a week in Paris, and enough money to enable us to come here.

"There would have been more if you had played your cards decently. I swear she began to get wise as to what I was up to after you had made yourself unpleasant."

"I hated her," Sorella said sulkily.

"If we have to study your likes and dislikes all the time, we'll starve," D'Arcy Forest snarled; "and it's pretty nearly what we're going to do now, if we're not careful. A fiver is all I've got left, and the bill will come to almost £20. Have you got that into your stupid little head?

"If you have, go and change, and do what you can to help save the sinking ship."

"I won't; I can't do it."

For a moment her father looked at her and then he slapped Sorella sharply across the face.

'You'll do as I tell you," he said, "or I'll beat you within an inch of your life. I've had enough of your airs and graces, young lady. We've got to live.

"If you don't help me, I'll find someone who can. It was a damn' sight easier when you were a baby and didn't have to do anything but look stupid, I can tell you that."

"You certainly made the most of it," Sorella said. She did not flinch when he struck her again, although the first imprint of his fingers was red and angry across her white face.

"It's ten minutes to four," D'Arcy exclaimed suddenly. "Hurry up, and change. If you don't, I swear I will dump you in the next orphanage I come to."

For a moment longer Sorella had contemplated resisting him. Then he had put his hand on her shoulder and shaken her.

He was getting angry and she knew she was afraid of him.

He had spoken truly when he said that he had beaten her before, and she remembered all too vividly how helpless she could be within his grasp and beneath the force of his anger.

She had done exactly as he wished. It had not been as hard as she anticipated to get into Mrs. Lazard's sitting-room; and once there, everything had been plain sailing. Her father had come to fetch her and began the heartrending tale of his poor, little, motherless child.

Sorella had heard it so often that she almost knew the words off by heart.

Yet she could not fail to appreciate the way he conjured a note of genuine emotion into his tones and a hint of real tears into his eyes.

It was an artistic and even brilliant performance, and as usual it evoked exactly the result D'Arcy intended.

Within a week they had moved with Mrs. Lazard to another hotel, a hotel where neither she nor D'Arcy Forest was known, and where they could register themselves as man and wife.

Widowed women with money were D'Arcy's speciality. Sorella was a stalking horse whom he found extremely useful at the outset of his campaign, but rather a bore once he had achieved his objective.

From the earliest years she could remember Sorella had played in hotel corridors and sat for long hours alone in hotel bedrooms.

She was fed at odd hours when anybody remembered her, or when her hunger was so acute that she was forced to ask the floor waiters for scraps from other people's meals.

It seemed to Sorella then and ever after in life that all hotels were exactly the same.

Whether they were big or small, mean or luxurious, interminable, dimly-lit corridors, the same impersonality, which to her so often seemed prison-like in its uniformity.

Whether the hotel was in England, France, Italy or Germany, to Sorella the routine of her life remained unchanged.

Her only playmates were the page boys, who would sometimes allow her to shoot dice with them or join them in a game of cards.

Her only playthings were favours left over from some gala night at the Casino, or for a short space of time the elaborate toys which some woman, infatuated with D'Arcy Forest, would buy her, in the same way as they bought her expensive and impractical clothes.

The toys she was allowed to keep so long as the giver of them was the recipient of her father's favours. But the moment they started off on their travels again, when the lady in question had either returned home or had found D'Arcy too expensive a luxury, the toys would be disposed of to the highest bidder.

Sometimes they received only a few shillings for a doll which had cost as many pounds, and Sorella would cry with misery at being forced to part from her plaything.

"Now, listen, you little idiot," D'Arcy would say.

"If someone sees you with an expensive toy like that, they're going to suspect that someone has extended us a kindly hand. Don't you understand that you have got to look forlorn, a little motherless misery whom nobody loves?"

81

"That's true enough," Sorella had once said defiantly.

In reply D'Arcy Forest had flung his arms around her and covered her face with kisses.

"I'm a rotter," he said with dramatic intensity. "I'm a bad father to you, but I love you my poppet. This may not be much of a life for you, but it is the best I can contrive. You stand by me, and I'll stand by you. Here's my hand on it."

Even she was not proof against D'Arcy's eloquence when it was turned on her; and even though she knew he lied, she found herself smiling tremulously at him, as weak as the women he seduced so easily.

As she grew older, she realised that his threat of sending her to an orphanage must have had some foundation in it. He had considered it.

It had appeared the only alternative to taking her about with him, to living the strange, unusual life of adventure which they enjoyed together; and in some ways Sorella did enjoy herself.

She liked, for instance, being in Paris.

The loveliness of the city fascinated her, and she would wander for hours beside the river, or sit in the Tuileries Gardens, watching other more fortunate children playing with their friends. When she was eight, she could find her way about London and Paris without getting lost.

When she grew older, she would often disappear for a whole day, returning at nightfall to the hotel where they were staying, to find that no one had even noticed her absence.

Her greatest difficulty was that she had no money. Her father never gave her any, and the women who paid for him, usually after the first flush of generosity, grudged even the food she put into her mouth.

They had a convenient habit of even forgetting that she must be fed, and her breakfast usually consisted of the scraps left on the trays after her father and his paramour of the moment had finished.

Her luncheon was, more often than not, an act of kindness on the part of a waiter or one of the chefs.

From hotel to hotel, from town to town they journeyed, year after year, till Sorella began to find it increasingly difficult to play the rôle that D'Arcy demanded of her.

As a lisping child of eight or nine, an air of naieté and a look of ingenuousness was not difficult; but at fourteen, she found herself not only appearing gauche and uncomfortable in such a rôle, but feeling even to herself that she was being unconvincing.

Women began to look at her with suspicion, rather than to exclaim over her motherless state.

Despite all her protests, D'Arcy insisted that she should continue to be a little girl.

He liked to see her in frocks, frilled and be-sashed, which had been the fashion when he was young and which had always been worn by any child who appeared in a melodrama.

He absolutely refused to see that children's clothes had altered and that children nowadays wore shorts and a sweater rather than starched party frocks.

Nothing Sorella could say would convince him that he was wrong or that he was over-dressing one of his chief characters.

As she had no money, she was forced to wear what he wanted her to.

Once she stole some money from his wallet, when he was absorbed, went out and bought herself a cheap, severely-tailored dress, and walked into her father's room to confront him in it.

He stared at her for a few seconds, and then, white with fury, dragged the frock from her and threw it into the fire. After that he had beaten her for stealing.

Later when she lay sobbing on her bed, she had decided that it was hopeless to defy him.

It was not so much that she minded the pain of being beaten; she had grown used to knocks and blows; it was just that the physical humiliation seemed to do something to her spirit.

She felt herself shrink and wither, not so much physically, but mentally, beneath D'Arcy's hand; and after that one desperate act of defiance she had never again defied him openly, where her appearance was concerned.

It was fortunate for D'Arcy that she was so very smallboned. Her mother had been a ballet dancer and she had inherited not only her stature, but her grace.

Music would make Sorella long to dance.

She could feel it animating her, causing her feet to stir restlessly; but she knew that she was not born to be a dancer, so she never spoke of training for the ballet or even going on the stage.

She had other aspirations, but to herself she could hardly translate them into words. She had been so much alone that she peopled an imaginary world of her own.

It was a secret, very precious place in which she could enter and forget entirely where she was or even the hunger and loneliness which were her daily lot.

She had no idea where such imaginings came from. They were added to by every book she read, by every lovely thing she saw, by every note of music she heard.

These were her treasures, these her possessions which no one, not even her father, could take from her.

Her education was certainly unconventional.

She had learned to read from the newspapers and the racing calendars which D'Arcy left scattered about in whatever room was their home at the moment.

She learned to add by being made to total up the bill and find how much short they were of it in funds.

She learned languages because they went to places where different languages were spoken and also because nearly all the servants in hotels were foreigners; and if she did not make herself understood, she must often go hungrier than she was already.

Indeed if she had not learnt to talk to them, she would have starved altogether.

That was the beginning, and from such sources she learned many things which were denied to more fortunate children.

At first she read her father's papers because she was bored and had nothing else to do.

Then she began to enjoy reading for its own sake and would go around the hotels looking at musty, forgotten volumes in old bookcases, or borrowing glossy, colourful magazines from an adjacent bedroom when the occupant was out.

She was not very old when she discovered the free libraries; and a year later, when they were in Paris, she had learned that one could enter without paying an entrance fee an art gallery where there were pictures for sale.

A well-brought-up, cared-for child of the same age, in either a French or an English home, would not have known that the candles at the shrines of a Catholic Church give out a decent amount of warmth on a cold day, or that a piece of soap, pilfered from a hotel bathroom, can be sold in the Paris market for a few centimes.

Not that Sorella stole often. She had some inner revulsion against it, which made her refrain even from taking food when she was ravenously hungry.

She was quite used to her father's easy way of making himself comfortable.

He never travelled in a railway train without helping himself to a towel, if there was one. He never waited in someone's sitting-room without filling his cigarette case from the box on the table.

If a woman gave him money to pay a bill, he automatically kept most of the change for himself.

Sorella accepted all these things; but for her own part she preferred not to pilfer. There were other things she preferred not to do.

Not because anyone had told her not to but simply because her own instinct warned her against them.

She had, at times, an almost grown-up dignity about her, even when she was quite small.

Sometimes the page boys would call her impertinent names; but she never cried, and as a general rule they liked her, because, as they told her, she was so unlike other girls.

It was a compliment which she could not appreciate, for she had no chance of comparing herself with girls of her own age.

Women she saw in plenty.

Mostly middle-aged women, whose eyes would light almost pathetically at the sight of her father, women who would be gay and kittenish and suddenly much younger than they had seemed the day before they met him.

Sorella had got her own standards by which she lived, just as she had a world of lovely fantasies which at times seemed to her more real than anything else.

One thing she had acquired in her years with her father, and that was a philosophy.

She accepted things as they came, she made the best of every situation, no matter how dreary or unpleasant it might seem.

She had learned not to worry about the future, not to scheme or intrigue for anything she wanted for herself, but merely to be grateful for anything, however meagre, which came her way.

She seldom criticised people. She only noted what

they did and was usually certain of their motives, or the secret reason for their actions.

She could at times, with a clairvoyance which was startlingly correct, know exactly what people were thinking.

Randal was talking now on the telephone; and as Sorella listened to him, she knew what Jane, at the other end of the line, was feeling.

"I can't dine tonight, darling," Randal was saying; "Lucille is being quite unbearable. If I don't make her see reason, she will go back to America and then where will my production and your father's money be? . . . Yes, yes, I know it's madly disappointing; I was so looking forward to it, and as you say, we've not had a chance to be together since I got back from France. . . ."

Jane was obviously asking something of him and for a moment his eyes flickered over the room, as if he considered it. Then he replied:

"No, not now, dear, I wish I could, but I've got to go out at once. . . . Yes, I'll try to telephone tonight or if not, first thing tomorrow. . . . You are a wonderful person to be so understanding. . . . Good-bye, and bless you."

He put down the receiver with a little sigh, then made a grimace at Sorella.

"I haven't got to go out," he said. "I'm going to talk to you and relax. Did I make the remark just now that women are the devil? I think that is almost an understatement."

He was dialling a number as he spoke.

"Hello, put me through to Miss Lucille Lund's room, please."

There was a pause, as he listened for a petulant voice at the other end of the telephone.

"Is that you, Lucille?" he asked. . . . "My sweet, I'm sorry if you are upset. I could not understand better that things get on top of one. . . . Yes. . . . Yes, yes I know. I've cancelled everything until tomorrow

. . . . I'm going to take you out to dinner tonight, just you and me alone. We'll talk things over. You tell me what you want, and if it's in my power, I shall give it to you. . . . Yes, that's a promise. Do you doubt me? No? . . . Well, eight o'clock then . . . . shan't be late, I'm far too impatient to see you; and let's talk about ourselves, not the damned play. . . . But of course, why should you think I don't? . . . You want me to say it? . . . Very well then, '*Je t'adore.*' Is that right? I'll say it again tonight when we meet. *Au revoir.*"

He put down the receiver and stood for a moment looking at it.

Sorella knew that he had forgotten her very presence, and was lost in his own thoughts, concerned only with some inner turmoil.

She sat still, and after what seemed the passing of a long time, but which was actually only a few minutes, Randal came back to his chair beside the fire.

He sat down, put up his feet on the tapestry stool and looked at Sorella.

"I'm in a mess, Sorella," he said quietly.

She nodded.

"I know."

"It's the sort of thing one can write about so glibly. My second play, *Duet for Three Hearts,* was written about just such a predicament as I find myself in at the moment. Two women, and I love them both. Do you understand that?"

"Yes, of course, one can love a lot of people, and all at the same time."

"Well, if you realise that, you realise one of the difficulties most men have to face. It is only women who, finding a man, cleave only unto him until death them do part."

Sorella smiled.

"Not all women," she said. "Many of them would

love a different man every week if they could find enough men to love them in return."

Randal gave a sudden shout of laughter.

"Is that your experience of your own sex?" he said. Then suddenly, before she could answer, he looked serious.

"You ought not to be talking like this; you are much too young. I keep forgetting you are a child and talk to you as I would talk to your father."

"And why not?" Sorella asked. "I lived with him long enough to know that I could talk like him if I wished. Actually, I don't like talking very much. Father did. I'd rather listen. Tell me about Lucille. Do you really love her?"

"No, I suppose I don't," Randal replied.

He forgot once again that Sorella was so young, and concerned himself only with his own difficulties.

"But I did love her—I loved her three years ago when we first met in Hollywood. She's a very sweet and a very lovely person. I was flattered that she singled me out for such special attention.

"We were together for only a short time. It was a year before I could go back. Last year, I made a film there, where before I had only sold the story.

"Lucille has a house in Beverly Hills. I wish you could see the swimming pool and her garden.

"One seems to live in a kind of fantastic dream all the time, and while nobody is quite human, everyone only wants to be pleasant and carefree. I was very happy last summer with Lucille.

"But the winter came. I returned home, and then I met Jane. Damn it all, I ought not to be talking to you like this!"

"I wish you'd stop saying that," Sorella said. "I'm the most sensible person for you to talk to, because I'm the an outsider, someone who has no axe to grind and no favourites."

Randal caught on to the inference.

You mean Hoppy and Jane?" he asked.

"She wants you to marry Jane," Sorella said. "Are you going to?"

"Shall I?" Randal questioned with a smile.

Sorella shook her head.

"No?" he enquired. "That's a new point of view. Why not?"

Sorella didn't answer, and after a moment he went on:

"I should imagine you are the only person in the world who would tell me not to marry Jane. She's very attractive, no one could deny that; she has masses of money, which doesn't matter one way or another, but it's always useful stuff to have about the house; and she has an impregnable social position, a position which I admit freely to you intrigues and amuses me.

"I like her friends, I like the ambitious witty people whom I meet at her father's house, and of course, we must not forget Jane's father.

"He's God's gift to the theatre, which has long needed a divine intervention to keep it going. Is there anything else I should add?

"Yes, of course, Jane herself. A sweet, exciting, unforgettable person. Now, do you still say I shouldn't marry her?"

Sorella's green eyes met his with some expression in them which he could not fathom.

Then, as he looked at her enquiringly, she said quietly:

"If you do marry her, you'll be disappointed."

5

Lucille put the receiver down and there was a smile on her lips as she walked across the room. Her ill-temper was forgotten for she had gained what she intended to gain by it.

She knew only too well how much Randal disliked outbursts of temperament and how badly they reacted on the other members of the cast.

She had got her own way in everything that mattered for so many years now that it was inconceivable to her that the time would come when it might not be so easy to subdue and bully people into accepting what she wanted rather than what they wanted themselves.

Edward Jepson was always warning her against overplaying her hand.

She laughed at his gloomy forebodings and had only to look at herself in the glass to believe herself invincible.

It was Edward, however, who had made her make a tremendous decision while she was flying over in the aeroplane.

It was not often that Lucille had time for thought. Her days were one long whirl of work and gaiety, of beauty treatments and social parties. She thought incessantly about herself, but never had time to think seriously, never had time to plan further ahead than the next day or the next Contract.

The long hours in the aeroplane had given her time to consider herself from a different angle from that of looking at her reflection in the looking-glass.

Besides this, Edward Jepson's last words to her had somehow held a warning.

"I'm quite nervous of making my first stage appearance in London," Lucille had said as he saw her off at La Guardia airport.

She had not really been nervous. It had just been something to say and she knew, too, it was the type of thing men like Jepson expected her to feel.

She thought he would reassure her with a few flattering words. Instead he had replied ponderously:

"You must make a success of it, Lucille. It is always

91

wise to have two strings to your bow, especially a bow that has played the same tune for a long time."

She would have been very obtuse not to hear the warning behind his words; and when she was alone, being carried swiftly and efficiently over the Atlantic, she began to think harder than she had thought for a very long time.

It was then that she had known what she must do, known it as clearly as if it had been written on the wall of the aeroplane in letters of fire.

For a moment she had gasped almost breathlessly at her own idea, and then she had accepted it, warmly and whole-heartedly, knowing that subconsciously it was what she had been wanting.

It all seemed so simple and so satisfactory; and once she had made up her mind, Lucille had no doubts, no hesitation. She would marry Randal, she decided.

It was years since she had thought of marriage.

She had, of course, received innumerable Hollywood proposals; most film stars do; and being more glamorous, more exotic than most of her contemporaries, Lucille's appeal to the other sex was not, for once, exaggerated by her Press reports.

She had been far too pleased and elated with her own success to wish to share it with anyone else. She wanted only to soar higher and higher, a comet climbing so brilliantly in the sky that the other stars paled in comparison.

She took lovers when she had the time for them.

She discarded them as easily, and without consequence, as she would discard the clothes she wore in a film or the costume jewellery which had to be effective only for the short time in which it was required.

Lucille was in love with success during those first years in Hollywood when Edward Jepson produced her and she knew for the first time in her life the heady, exciting quality of praise and applause.

Like Narcissus, she became enamoured of her own beauty and had little time to notice attraction or good looks in other people.

Men seemed to her shadowy figures, whose love was no more real than the emotions that were expressed in front of a camera.

It was part of one's success to have men clustered around one, just as one had sables and orchids, French perfume, and jewels from Tiffany.

But as individuals the men who made love to Lucille never seemed to her to have any substance, to be anything but escorts and dance partners, good hosts and equally good benefactors.

She accepted presents as she accepted their homage, as if she were entitled to them. And because she expected so much, she received practically everything she expected.

There were, of course, a few men to whom it was not only policy to be charming and to make oneself attractive, but also pleasure.

For three months Lucille became the mistress of a Mexican millionaire.

She had thought before that she knew something about luxury; but even she was wide-eyed and astonished at the magnificence to his entourage, the splendour of his houses and the money he would spend on a party and forget next morning that it had ever taken place.

But even the millions that might have been hers for life, or at least for a very long time if she had been prepared to give up the films and live in Mexico, had not tempted her from Hollywood.

It was not money she wanted, but success. It was an elixir more wonderful than anything she had believed possible.

She never grew tired of seeing her name in lights, of signing autographs, receiving bouquets, or appearing in public places and talking to reporters.

Lucille had no complex about wishing to be alone, or living her private life in private.

She liked the limelight, she sought it. And because she was an extremely beautiful person, she could bear its cruel, merciless scrutiny far longer than many other stars.

It was only recently that Lucille had begun to suspect that it was not quite as easy as it had been.

She was still one of the most famous names in the film world; and yet other, younger, more sensational rivals were catching up with her. She could sense far more clearly than her agent or manager could do the slight falling off of her popularity.

It was nothing tangible; nothing could be noticed as yet in the box office receipts, and yet Lucille was aware of it. It could not be her looks; they for the time being at any rate, were impregnable.

It could not be the films in which she appeared, for the stories underwent the fiercest and most exhaustive scrutiny and criticism before she even saw them.

After that she would often turn down a good part simply because she felt it was not as glamorous and sympathetic as her public would expect.

No, it was something more subtle than that; at the moment, something as difficult to pin-point as the moment when summer ends and autumn begins; but in her heart of hearts Lucille knew that was exactly what it was.

Soon the leaves would turn yellow, soon the sun would lose its warmth and the first signs of middle age would alter her face, her figure, and perhaps even her famous legs.

Edward knew, as surely as she knew, that the sands were running out.

Soon her technique must change or she must either disappear from being the centre of her lovely, superficial, celluloid world or be content to play a secondary part in it.

That, she swore to herself, she would never do.

Never! Never, while there is breath in my body, she said will I be humiliated into taking anything but the lead!

She saw how subtly and cleverly other actresses were relegated to the part of the "other woman"— the rival for her hero's affection, the part which everyone described as requiring "real acting ability", but which did not figure in the last tumultuous close-up.

How well she knew those parts and the flattery which accompanied them!

"You can make something really big of this, darling. You wouldn't want to be the ingénue. After all, your part has some real beef in it. You'll head the bill of course with . . ."

Then would come the other name, the name of the girl or woman who was playing the part that you would have played ten years ago.

In the aeroplane, Lucille had clutched her hands together and felt herself go tense and stiff.

So this was what Edward was planning for her! She could not believe it; it was impossible.

She thought of the bags of fan letters which were delivered at her house every morning.

It was a well-established rumour that she read them all; a rumour based on a certain amount of truth, for she read a large number of them. How sweet they were, those letters of affection and admiration and youthful hero-worship!

No, the moment when she must abdicate was not yet upon her; and yet for the first time she saw a dark cloud on the far horizon.

It was then that she decided to marry Randal.

She had been in love with him now for three years. In love as Lucille had never known love before.

He was so different from the men she had met in Hollywood, from the actors with whom she had played a part, from Edward Jepson and all the other friends who surrounded her.

There was an elegance about him which at first she had half suspected of being effeminate; but there was, too, a virility which she had found, as many other women had found before her, irresistible.

She was uncertain what it was about Randal that made him so different from any other man.

At times she thought that it was his handsome face, with that faint cynical twist to the lips; and then she remembered how many handsome men she had known, and knew it was not that.

She delighted in the firm, athletic strength of his body; and yet Hollywood was full of athletes only too anxious to prove themselves, either by day or by night.

He was English, of course, and Lucille had known few Englishmen, but enough to know that Randal was unique among them.

She was in love with him almost before she began to puzzle about him; and even after they had been lovers for some months, she was no nearer to having her questions answered, for she found him difficult to understand.

Lucille had known few clever men with the exception of Edward Jepson and it was to her a new experience to feel that she could not always dominate the conversation when Randal was there.

Her ignorance made it easy for him to master her; and somehow, for the first time in her life, she liked being mastered.

She had, too, never had an affaire before with someone who was creative, someone who, caught up with an inspiration, would forget her very presence and often come back to a consciousness of it with a dazed expression on her face and no idea that he had been in the slightest abstracted or rude.

"I love you, of course I love you," Randal had said to her once. "But can't you understand that I have to write at this moment? What I have to put down on paper is far more important than any party or first night.

"It wouldn't matter if we were going to the opening of Paradise, I should still have to stay and write down what is surging within me."

Lucille had been incredulous at first, and then she accepted it, because, though easy-going in many ways, Randal could be adamant when it concerned his work.

And yet, because of these things rather than in spite of them, Lucille fell deeper and more headlong in love with Randal every day they were together.

In the past, it was always to dictate to her men-folk what should be done, where they would go, what they would do and when they might make love to her.

Now, Randal gave the orders and expected her to obey them; and to her own astonishment she did.

One night, after dinner at her house in Beverly Hills, they had walked into the garden; Randal had bent to kiss her, and at the touch of their lips a flame of passion had ignited them both, creeping higher and higher, burning, consuming them with its own warmth, until Lucille clung to Randal, her eyes half shut, her lips parted.

She was very lovely in the light of the moon; and then, as he raised his head to look down at her trembling within his arms, she said:

"Come indoors. I want you. Oh! Randal, darling, I want you so."

He had stood looking down at her for a moment and then roughly, because of the urgent need within him, he had lifted her in his arms and carried her into the shadow of a magnolia tree.

She had cried out in surprise at his impetuousness, and yet somehow it had been a new experience and one which had thrilled her.

She had grown so used to silken sheets, scented

pillows, and satin-draped beds; and now being pleasured as if she were only a peasant girl being made love to in the ditch on the way home from a village dance was something she had never anticipated.

It was perhaps the unexpected things that Randal did that appealed to Lucille more than anything else.

Once he had driven her out to the country, and because the sunset was so lovely and he found her attractive, he had refused to drive her back home for a large and important dinner party.

Another time he had taken her away from a dance almost by force, because when they were dancing together, her nearness had excited him and he wanted only that they should be alone together.

For these, if for no other reasons, Lucille would have loved him because he was so different from all the other men who had toadied to her, who had been grateful for any small favour she might bestow upon them.

But her love for Randal took possession of her, and later she knew that it was nothing he said or did, but something about himself which held her.

She would marry him. She wondered now why she had never thought of it before.

After all, what could be more suitable? she asked herself.

Already Randal was a name in the theatrical and film worlds. He was young, he was just at the beginning of his career. She would help him to soar to dizzy heights, higher than any that he had as yet dreamed about.

She would act in his films until the day came when she would know herself too old, and then she would produce them.

She saw herself as the Mary Pickford of the future; a brilliant executive, a chairman of a great company, the genius behind each succeeding success.

That was what she would do; and now because

98

she had decided her future, she need fear nothing, not even her first grey hair.

Lucille had stepped from the aeroplane at Croydon, flushed and thrilled with the decision she had made, only to find that Randal was not there to meet her, and to feel instead a chill wind blow away her flushed joyfulness.

The next few days in London had been very different from what she had planned. For one thing, she never saw Randal alone.

They were together most of the day, and yet there were always other people with them—rehearsing, lunching, dining, planning the scenery, furnishings, costumes and all the other thousand and one intricate details of the production—talking.

"Yes, talking all the time, so that never for a second can I have a word alone with Randal," she thought.

She had expected that he would come back to her suite at the hotel at night; but he had not suggested it, and she would not humble herself to invite him.

She told herself there were reasons for his reticence.

He had been shaken by the accident in which he had killed a man whom he openly avowed was a great friend; he was thinking of her, of her health, and the fact that she must be tired after flying across the Atlantic and embarking straight away on the arduous and exhausting intricacies of the first rehearsals.

She made every excuse for him; but the fact that she was jealous of Jane had set a match to her anger.

Jane had come with her father to the first rehearsal.

She had said very little, and Lucille had not noticed whether she spoke to Randal or not, but she had not been foolish enough to miscalculate or underestimate Jane's attractions.

She was not by any means as beautiful as Lucille,

but the latter was honest enough to know that Jane's clothes from Paris surpassed anything she had been able to buy in America.

Lucille did not miss, either, Jane's air of elegant good breeding or her poise and easy cosmopolitan grace, which seemed to make her a vivid, outstanding personality, even when she sat and said nothing.

In brief, Lucille had disliked Jane on sight; and when finally they were introduced, she had been gracious and condescendingly charming, with a viperish hatred in her heart.

To her credit Jane had appeared supremely indifferent to Lucille.

She had watched the film star link her arm through Randal's and raise her lovely face to his, with an overaccentuated air of possession.

She had heard Lucille order him to fetch her coat from where she had laid it at the side of the stage, and she had heard her thank him with a soft "Bless you, darling" as he wrapped it round her.

The expression of Jane's face had not altered in the slightest.

She appeared not to notice that Randal looked a little uncomfortable. But Lucille's hatred had not gone unrequited from that moment.

It was after that that Jane, too, began to play the part of the "woman in possession". She came to the rehearsals and insisted on Randal's coming out to luncheon with her father and herself.

If he liked to bring Lucille with him, that was his business; but she made it difficult for Randal to refuse the invitation.

"You've got to eat somewhere," she would say when he protested, "and Daddy has lots to discuss with you."

"Things to discuss" was the excuse for luncheon, dinner, and any free time that Randal might have between rehearsals. Lucille knew, for Edward Jepson had told her, the exact amount of the very large sum that Lord Rockampstead was putting up for *Today and Tomorrow*.

"The man who pays the piper, calls the tune," he had said more than once with a smile.

Lucille was well aware that no one, however important, however famous, could afford to quarrel with her bread and butter, or rather with her weekly salary.

If Lord Rockampstead wished to talk to Randal or to anyone else in the company, they were obliged to listen to what he had to say, and Jane would have been a fool not to use such a weapon to gain her own ends.

It was war to the knife; both women knew that as they faced each other across the table at the Ivy or dined sumptuously at Belgrave Square.

Lucille was not aware whether Randal knew what was happening, or whether he was supremely ignorant. She was certainly not going to tell him. She knew all too well that this was the sort of thing which would appeal to his sense of humour.

He would laugh and make her feel extremely foolish.

What was more, to be told that she was jealous of him would, she knew, merely make him feel more confident himself, and just at the moment she did not wish him to be too confident.

She wanted him to feel unsure about her, to grasp at her because he was afraid of losing her. In the years they had been together, he had never mentioned the word "marriage"; and as Lucille told herself, that was doubtless her fault.

It had been so far from her mind that never for one moment had she anticipated that it might be necessary to bring Randal to the point of proposing.

She had always believed, deep within herself, that he wished to marry her. She was conventional enough to think that the desire for marriage should be a prelude to physical connubiality.

A European had once said to her:

"You Americans are so middle-class. You always want to marry your lovers."

She had laughed at the time, but afterwards she began to see that there was a certain truth in what he had said.

She had always a sense of guilt about getting into bed with someone without a wedding ring on her finger. She wondered now whether it was her American upbringing or her German ancestry that was responsible for that.

Her father had been a Lutheran, a son of a shopkeeper from Hamburg. He had come out to America because he had quarrelled with his family over his marriage.

His name was Hans Schmidt, and his first child, born a month after he set foot in the Land of Freedom, had been christened Maria.

Maria Schmidt had been a lovely child, with fair hair which was obviously inherited from her father, and big, liquid blue eyes, which also echoed in colour, if not in shape, his small twinkling ones.

There the resemblance to her father ended; for the rest Maria was in temperament, as well as in figure, extremely like her mother. As she grew older, Maria used to wonder about her mother, and wished she had known her better.

Unfortunately she died when Maria, later to be re-named Lucille, was only fifteen.

Drascha Schmidt came from Poland, but there was Russian, Jugoslavian and Lithuanian blood in her veins, and as her husband told her often with deep affection, she was a little mongrel.

She came from the peasant class, with no money and no family to make her acceptable to the Schmidts of Hamburg.

But directly one looked at her one knew that she had more spirit in her little finger than they had in the whole of their fat, blond bodies.

Drascha had no dowry, but she had character.

102

She had few talents for home-making, but she could make a man crazy about her by merely looking at him and moving her hips a little, as if she were about to dance.

Half-gipsy, half-autocrat, was how Lucille remembered her mother; and even then it was difficult to know where one began and the other ended, or whether indeed she had imagined both things.

But undoubtedly it was her mother's blood in her which induced Lucille to throw up the good, sensible job which her father had found for her in a shop, and made her haunt the theatrical agents until she got a part in the chorus.

She hated now to remember those years of struggle and difficulty. Years when she had longed to confess herself a failure and to go home.

That she had not done so was due in one part to pride, and in another to the fact that her father had married again and that she was far too pretty to be tolerated by a stepmother.

But some of her father's teaching and strict code of behaviour lingered in her mind.

She would always feel a pang of conscience on Sunday morning when she awoke to hear the church bells ringing and knew that she was going to lie in bed when she should be walking sedately in her best clothes into the nearest chapel.

She would find herself remembering his ideas of fair play and decency, when she was storming and raging until a few dozen lines in another person's part were cut or given to her.

Hans Schmidt had not been a successful man, but his daughter found it hard to forget him.

Lucille was thinking now that marriage was a Holy institution, that in marrying Randal she would be doing the good and right thing.

There was an almost childlike smile of simplicity on her face a few hours later when Randal came up to her suite before dinner.

She had spent the time since their telephone call preparing herself for him. She had been massaged from top to toe. There had been a woman to work on her thin, supple body, kneading and slapping till it tingled with a youthful elasticity.

There had been another to cream and smooth her face, and yet a third to manicure her nails and tint her ten small toes.

She looked lovely and not a day over twenty-five as Randal stepped into the sitting room to find her waiting for him in a gown of frosted lace, sprinkled with diamonds.

There was a necklace of rubies round her neck, and she wore a bracelet and ear-rings to match. They had been the present of the long-forgotten Mexican millionaire.

Seeing her run to him with both hands outstretched, he thought then as he looked at her that she was quite the loveliest person he had ever seen.

She had a breath-taking quality which was quite indescribable, whther one was watching her moving across the screen or seeing her alone in a conventional hotel sitting-room.

"Randal, dear Randal, I'm so looking forward to this evening."

Lucille's face was raised to his. Randal bent to kiss it, not her lips, but her cheek.

"You look very magnificent," he said. "Where are we going? Buckingham Palace?"

"We are going to be alone," Lucille answered.

"That is just what I like," Randal said gallantly.

He was conscious as he said it of the bedroom door at the far end of the room standing invitingly open.

In the soft, shaded light he saw the satin-covered bed in the other room; he could see the soft lace pillows which Lucille took everywhere with her. He could see the white ermine bedspread, which kept her warm both winter and summer.

He could scent the fragrance of her exotic perfume;

everything in her bedroom always seemed to be impregnated with it.

It was alluring and disturbing, as Randal knew only too well.

It came to him faintly now, as she moved away from him, the silken petticoats under her full dress rustling as she walked.

"I've ordered a cocktail for you," she said; "your favourite."

He took it from her hand and raised it almost mechanically.

"To the loveliest woman in the world!" he said.

The same words he had said to her so often, and the words she had used the very first time they had drunk together.

How often they talked of that moment when they had both known that something momentous was to come of their meeting.

They had known it in the tingling of their pulses, in the sudden dryness of their lips and the leaping fire of their eyes as they gazed at each other.

"To the loveliest woman in the world," he had said in a very low voice.

"No one had ever spoken to me quite like that before," Lucille said afterwards—meaning that his voice was unique, not his words.

"I meant it, every word. I did not believe that such loveliness could exist."

"But you had seen my films," Lucille smiled.

"I always suspected them of being a fake, and now I know that they fall very far short of the reality," Randal answered.

They had dined together that first evening, and the morning had found him standing at her bedroom window watching the golden fingers of the sun thrusting the sable darkness of the night from out the sky.

"Randal," she had called from the bed.

He turned towards her, and she roused herself from sleep to admire the clean, young energy of him.

"I must go," he said.

"Why?" Her voice was surprised.

"It's nearly six o'clock," he answered. "I mustn't be found here. Your servants will be waking."

She laughed at him then, the low amused laugh of a woman who is old enough to be sure of herself.

"But, darling, do you think it matters what the servants think, or what anyone else thinks for that matter?"

She had held out her arms, two perfectly-moulded white arms, and he let her draw his head down to her lips—eager and greedy for his kisses.

No, they had not minded what was said about them or what happened in those first halcyon days in Hollywood.

But how, Randal wondered, could he explain to Lucille that he minded now? He set his cocktail glass on the chair.

"Another one?" Lucille asked, picking up the shaker.

"We neither of us can drink much tonight," he said. "The rehearsal is called for 9 a.m. tomorrow morning and we mustn't be late."

"Have you ever known me late?" Lucille asked. "You have often said yourself that I am the only punctual woman you have ever known."

That was true enough, for when Lucille was working she had a punctiliousness which put many of her contemporaries to shame.

"All the same, we've got to work very hard tomorrow," Randal persisted. "We wasted a lot of time this afternoon. We should have finished reading that second act by now. As it is, we've got to try to get those two scenes and the beginning of the third in tomorrow. We haven't got any too much time, you know."

"I don't think you need to worry yourself," Lucille said. "I shan't let you down."

"Do you suppose that I think you would?" Randal said, a little hastily. "You're wonderful, Lucille, you

106

know that, but we've got to remember the rest of the cast. It's no use skimping rehearsal so far as they are concerned. I heard today that we definitely open on October 25th."

"If you know the date, then we must drink to it," Lucille said, picking up his cocktail glass and her own.

She handed the glass to him and then touched it with the rim of hers.

"To the greatest success and . . . happiness you have ever known, Randal, my very dear," she said.

There was some meaning in her voice which he could not quite understand. He drank, looking at her a little speculatively, while Lucille reached up her hand to touch his cheek.

"You're looking thinner than when I last saw you," she said softly. "That sunburn is particularly becoming, but you are thin. I shall have to try to keep you as young and strong as you were when we first met."

"That was three years ago," Randal said; "I didn't work nearly as hard then as I work now, Lucille."

"We seemed to have so much more time to be together, didn't we?"

Randal looked a little uncomfortable as he set down his glass.

"Let us go and have dinner," he said. "I expect you're hungry, and I know I am."

"There is something you've forgotten," Lucille said quietly.

He knew only too well what it was.

In the past when they had been going out to dinner, he always kissed her before they went, giving her, as he had phrased it, an armour against the envious glances of other less fortunate men.

It had been a little ritual such as lovers delight to invent.

He would kiss her forehead and her eyes, her cheeks and her ears, her mouth and then the little hollow at her throat, where a pulse would beat maddeningly because he excited her.

Sometimes when they kissed, they would forget the party or the occasion for which they had dressed and stay loving each other until the night was far spent, all else forgotten save their bodies' need—one of the other.

Just for a moment Randal hesitated, and then, as if he steeled himself to a sudden resolution, he said quietly:

"You mustn't tempt me, Lucille, tonight. I want to talk to you; and if I start kissing you now, we may forget that dinner is waiting."

She searched his face with her eyes, as though she knew that he was making an excuse; and then, as if she accepted an unexpected situation gracefully, she gave a soft laugh.

"Are you really afraid or only being cautious?" she asked. "Well, if you won't kiss me, I must kiss you."

She raised herself on tip-toe; drawing his head down towards her, she pressed her lips against his forehead.

For a moment he resisted her.

Then as her mouth rested warm and inviting against his, he put his arms round her and held her close.

6

Randal sat in the third row of the stalls and watched the rehearsal.

There was an air of heavy gloom about the theatre; the seats were empty and shrouded; the smell of stale tobacco mingled with that of disinfectant.

There was also that inevitable, chilly draught which

blew from behind the scenes and contrived to penetrate even the warmest fur coat or thickly-padded boots.

It wasn't cold outside; in fact, when Randal entered the theatre he had wished he could stay out in the autumn sunshine, where to brace himself against the wind, which came roaring round the street corners, had been an exhilarating rather than a distasteful experience.

But there was no exhilaration about the cold inside the theatre.

He could feel it creeping round his ankles and he noted that it seemed to chill even the most passionate words before they could be spoken.

Only Lucille looked warm, comfortable and entrancingly lovely.

She was wearing a short sable coat over a wool dress of periwinkle blue which accentuated her fragile fairness and made her shine like the star she undoubtedly was against the gaunt, bare background of the unfurnished stage.

Rehearsals, Randal thought, were often unnecessarily depressing.

Lack of scenery made the stage itself seem like an empty tooth. There was the flicker of two or three lights instead of a whole barrage of them.

There were the hard wooden chairs which had to serve as furnishings, and there was, above all, the dismal appearance of the actors and actresses themselves.

It was so wise of Lucille, he reflected, never to appear looking commonplace and ordinary, without make-up or attractive clothes, and also, as seemed the case with many of the younger actresses, without any charm or good manners.

If the women were open to criticism, the men were certainly no beauty chorus.

The hero, who could look quite dazzling in his perfectly-cut Savile Row suits and double-breasted dinner jackets, wore for rehearsal an ancient high-necked polo sweater and baggy old corduroy trousers which would hardly have done credit to a roadmender.

Two effeminate-looking youths had kept on their tightly-belted mackintoshes; another older man was wearing a dilapidated homburg and a woollen scarf.

Women in slacks, with shiny noses and uncombed hair, were poring over their lines in the background.

Lucille, already almost word-perfect, and looking like a fashion-plate, moved elegantly about the stage, taking an immense amount of trouble to do exactly as the producer told her.

"There is no doubt that she deserves the success she has achieved," Randal thought.

She would never be a great actress, for the fire of genius was not in her; but she was not prepared to rely only on her looks. She worked, and worked hard, and the result certainly did her credit.

Only when she was temperamental did she become impossible to deal with and then there was nothing to do but to give her time to get over it.

To give Lucille her due, her outbursts of temperament were not unduly frequent.

Randal had a sneaking suspicion that they were more often a calculated means to an end than an uncontrollable exhibition of nerves.

Watching Lucille now, seeing her as pliable and manageable as any producer could wish, he wondered, as he had wondered so often before, what would be the ultimate end of her so-successful career.

He was not certain why the question so often presented itself to him, but perhaps subconsciously the idea had been transmitted to him by Lucille herself.

There was certainly nothing in her present appearance to suggest that she was growing old, and it was impossible to imagine that her public could ever grow tired of her as long as she looked as she did.

Yet Randal would find himself speculating about her.

Lucille's age was something they never discussed, but he guessed her to be much older than the thirty-two years to which she admitted in her Press interviews.

"I was eighteen when Edward Jepson gave me my first big part," she would say, her eyes as candid as those of a child.

There was no difficulty in believing that she spoke the truth, except that Randal noticed strange discrepancies when she spoke of the places she had visited and of the life she had led before she became a star.

But now, watching her on the stage as she contrived to create an atmosphere even in the cold bareness of the empty theatre, Randal told himself that she was superb and that her future would be as rosy and golden as the present.

And then, even as he reassured himself about Lucille, he felt vaguely apprehensive. He had a feeling that she was leading up to something, but what it was he had no idea.

There was, he thought, something she wanted of him; but she had not told him directly what it was, and now for the life of him he could think of nothing he might give her other than further years of devotion.

That, although Lucille did not know it yet, was impossible, for he had not forgotten Jane.

Last night while Lucille was in his arms and he had found himself responding almost automatically to her endearments, he had been conscious that Jane was also in his thoughts, in many ways an unwelcome third.

It was a situation, he told himself in the early hours of the morning, which could not continue.

Yet he had not had the courage to tell Lucille the truth, for he knew that to break with her at this moment would be fatal to the success of the play.

The part of the leading lady in *Today and Tomorrow* was a heavy and arduous one. It required someone clever enough to carry it off, someone who must look outstandingly beautiful and also, if possible, be a stranger to London audiences.

There was so much that they had to believe about the heroine, so much that had to happen because of her beauty, her glamour and her magnetism.

Randal knew that, if as a man he was bored with Lucille, as an author and co-producer of *Today and Tomorrow* it would be suicide so far as the play was concerned to find a substitute for her now at the very moment when rehearsals were starting in earnest.

To be truthful, Lucille did not bore him—she had never done that.

It was only that his thoughts and his mind were set on marriage with Jane, which made him less eager to respond to her affection and all that she required of him.

He had been for nearly three years very much enamoured of Lucille.

She had haunted his waking hours and had coloured his dreams to the exclusion of all else; but now he found himself left with only an admiration for her, and a very genuine affection.

It was more than remained after the majority of Randal's love affairs.

He found women an inspiration, a spur and an entrancement, until he possessed them; after that, some elusive and exciting quality vanished and he discovered that they could be irritatingly possessive and usually far too persistent.

At the back of his mind there was some ideal which as yet he had never found. Often he had reached out towards it, but always it eluded him, like a note of music which could not be recalled.

Randal's wandering thoughts were recalled to a realisation that the scene on the stage was going badly.

He was not certain what was wrong with it; but the dramatist in him was all too aware that the actors appeared stiff and unnatural, and that the words they were speaking did not ring true or sincere.

He knew that Bruce Bellingham, who was working with him, was worried, knew it by the note of desperation in his voice, by the way he ran his fingers through his hair.

Bruce had already spoken to him about this scene, but Randal had pooh-poohed his fears.

He had thought everything would work out when once the actors got into their stride; but he could see now that he had been over-optimistic.

He felt a rasping exasperation rising within him —an invariable reaction when something went wrong with his work and he was not certain how to correct it.

Randal had the script on his knee and he stared at it, searching each sentence.

Where had he gone wrong? Surely Lucille could make those words seem more alive? Was she deliberately mistaking the timing, or was Bruce at fault? He was not yet prepared to admit his own discrepancies.

Suddenly, he was aware that someone was sitting beside him.

For a moment his annoyance was extended to the intruder, and then he realised that it was Sorella.

She was not looking at him; she was not trying to speak to him; she was staring ahead at the people on the stage.

He had seen her at rehearsals before, but she usually sat far back in the darkness of the stalls and made no attempt to contact him until he was going home.

Then she would insinuate herself at his side, so

113

that automatically he became aware of her presence and they would go out of the theatre together in search of his car.

He wondered now for a fleeting moment why she was departing from her usual procedure; then, as he continued to frown at the written script, Sorella spoke.

"She wouldn't walk to the window at that moment," she said very softly; "she would go on doing the flowers, and when he spoke to her, she wouldn't answer."

"What do you mean?" Randal asked almost roughly.

"She wouldn't want to talk after what had happened," Sorella replied. "That would come later; but now, at this moment, she would be silent. He would go on talking, quickly, nervously, because he is embarrassed and upset by what he has said. She would be quiet, so quiet that he becomes frightened."

"I've never heard of anything . . ." Randal began, and then stopped. "You're right, of course you're right! That's exactly what she would do. By Jove, I shall have to change the rest of this scene!"

He got to his feet almost excitedly and walked down towards the orchestra pit. He spoke to Bruce.

They were in consultation for only a few minutes, but Bruce's irritation vanished, and he smoothed down his hair instead of ruffling it.

"You've got it, Randal!" he exclaimed. "We'll go back and do Scene II while you re-plan this."

It was many hours later when Randal got back to his flat, tired but triumphant. He had re-planned the scene, and though there was a lot more writing to be done the skeleton outline was there, and he knew it was good.

As he came up in the lift, he suddenly remembered that he had had nothing to eat since breakfast. He had been rewriting since about noon, and he had no idea how quickly the time had slipped by.

Now he was aware of being ravenously hungry,

besides feeling unusually elated and pleased with himself.

Things were going well. This was undoubtedly not only the most ambitious, but by far the best, play he had ever written.

He let himself into the flat with his latchkey. Hoppy was in the office. He could hear the tap of the typewriter, but he did not wish to speak to her at the moment.

He opened the door of the sitting-room. A stranger was sitting with her back to him. He could see a sleek, dark head, elegantly balanced on a long white neck.

Then the stranger turned and he saw it was Sorella.

"Hello," she smiled. "Was it all right?"

He stared at her for a moment before he replied.

"Yes, quite all right; but what have you done to yourself? I didn't recognise you."

"I've had my hair cut," she answered, "and bought myself a new dress. Hoppy said that you had told her I could get myself some clothes."

"Yes, of course," Randal said absently, "but you look quite different."

It was hard to explain why two such simple things should alter her so completely. The straggly, untidy tresses, which had fallen to her shoulders, were gone. Sorella's hair was now parted in the middle to frame her white forehead and tiny oval face in big, smooth waves.

She was no longer so thin as when she first came to the Villa.

With regular meals her body had filled out and her skin had lost that unhealthy pallor which had first shocked Randal into thinking her a very unprepossessing child.

Now he noticed things about her which he had never noticed before. She was, he supposed, in her own way, really lovely.

115

It was not the breathtaking beauty that one found in Lucille or the elegant loveliness of Jane.

It was something far more subtle, far more distinctive. It was like turning from two vivid oil paintings to a small but exquisite etching.

The darkness of Sorella's head seemed to hold gleams from the flickering flames in the fireplace.

Randal had never noticed before how perfectly moulded her head was or how well set upon her long neck.

There was a poise and a grace about her which made him remember that her mother had been a ballet dancer.

It was easy to see what she had inherited in the unconscious way in which she sat, in the way her arms were bent to leave her hands lying loosely in her lap.

"Pretty hands," Randal thought, "with thin, pointed fingers."

She had not moved or fidgeted under his scrutiny, and he wondered how many women of his acquaintance could attain such tranquillity and quietness.

Her eyes were still unnaturally large, as they had been when, as he now knew, she was under-nourished almost to the point of starvation; but her lips had grown fuller, and her tiny, straight nose might have been moulded by a sculptor.

Sorella had bought herself a dress of deep green wool. It was very plain and strictly tailored, with a narrow leather belt as its only ornament. It made her look much older.

Randal noticed, too, for the first time since he had known her, that she was wearing stockings and shoes with high heels.

"I congratulate you!"

She flushed at his praise.

"I asked Hoppy who was supposed to be the best hairdresser," she said. "He said I was always to part my hair in the middle, and that I looked like an

Italian picture he had once seen, but he couldn't remember what it was called."

Randal knew then exactly what Sorella did look like.

She resembled, he thought, many of the early Italian painters' pictures of the Madonna—the child-like Madonna who seemed far too young to have a Baby and who gazed at Him wide-eyed, not only in adoration, but in sweet astonishment.

There was something serene and restful in the faces of those little dark-haired Madonnas, too, something sacrosanct and celestial which the masters had caught and transmited on to the canvas to retain a permanent wonder to each suceeding generation.

"The young Madonna!"

Randal did not say aloud what he thought, merely watching Sorella as she sat still in the firelight, her green dress revealing the soft curves of her breasts and the smallness of her waist.

Then with a start he recalled his wandering thoughts. Sorella was speaking to him.

"Tell me about the play," she said.

Still watching her, he sat down in the chair opposite and began to talk. It was only when he had told her exactly what he had planned that he remembered to ask:

"But how did you know? How were you sure that that was the right thing? I've read the scene a hundred times, and so had Bruce, Edward Jepson, Lucille, and a dozen other people; and not one of them had spotted what you did. How did you do it? What do you know about the stage if it comes to that?"

"Whenever he had nothing else to do Daddy would go either to a show or a rehearsal and usually I went with him," Sorella replied. "He always got in free, of course, one way or another, and the stage-door keepers got to know me, so they would let me into the theatre when I was alone."

Sorella paused a moment; and then, as if she was telling Randal a secret, she continued in a low voice:

"When I see a play or read a book I always imagine that I am the chief person in it. I think that it is I who am experiencing all that happens—the happiness and unhappiness, the excitement and danger, the thrills and disasters.

"If the book is well written, it is easy to identify oneself with a fictitious character; but if it is written badly, then I know something is wrong and that I wouldn't have done this thing or that, or have felt that particular emotion."

"Yes, yes, that's the right approach," Randal agreed; "it's what I try to do myself, but so often I fail. In this case, how did you know that Marlene, the woman in the play, wouldn't have reacted as she did?"

"I just felt it," Sorella replied. "I can't explain it any better than that. I just felt that I would have said nothing."

"It seems incredible that you should have spotted my mistake," Randal said, "and I wonder you were not afraid to tell me."

Sorella's eyes opened wide.

"Why?" she asked. "It's the play that matters, surely?"

Randal thought there was nothing to say.

The child was right, it was the play that mattered, and only a very obtuse person would think otherwise; and yet he knew that the majority of his friends and acquaintances would think twice before venturing a criticism of anything he had written.

It was so much easier to agree, so much easier to praise and applaud, and criticism was seldom accepted in the spirit in which it was offered.

He looked across the hearth at Sorella.

The ill-fed, untidy, ridiculously-dressed child with whom he had spent ten days in the south of France had vanished. Instead, he was watching someone he had never met before.

A very unexpected young woman, who had a beauty of her own, and a poise and dignity that he had not suspected beneath the frills of lace and organdie.

He wondered what D'Arcy Forest would have thought of her now, and he knew that this new Sorella was the very last thing that D'Arcy had wanted to find in his daughter.

This was not a child—a child who could be patted one moment and sent to bed as a nuisance the next. This was not an accommodating little actress who would lisp pretty things in return for pretty presents.

This new Sorella was a personality who could think for herself, who had decided opinions and an intelligence far beyond the average.

"Sorella, you're a genius!" Randal exclaimed. "Now give me the script and for God's sake go and get me some food!"

He went towards his writing-desk as he spoke. He sat down with the play in front of him, and everything else was forgotten.

He was aware a little later that a tray containing some sandwiches and a pot of black coffee was at his side. He ate mechanically, hardly taking his eyes from the play and having no idea what he tasted.

Hoppy came in much later and slipped a piece of paper in front of him. On it was typed:

"Jane wants to speak to you. She says it's very important."

Randal did not even look up.

"Tell her to go to Hell," he said, "and for the love of Mike leave me alone."

Hoppy went from the room, quite unperturbed. She knew what Randal was like when he was working, but she had not really believed Sorella when she said that Randal was busy altering the play.

She, like Randal himself, had believed that not even a comma or a full stop need be added or changed.

She spoke to Jane, changing and altering Randal's message in something charming and pleasant, and telling her, as an excuse for his absorption, how busy he appeared to be.

"Tell him to telephone me whatever time he finishes," Jane said. "He's got to go to bed sometime, and the telephone is beside mine. I don't suppose I shall sleep; and if I do, I don't mind being wakened up."

"It may be very late," Hoppy said warningly.

"I don't mind that," Jane replied.

"Well, I'm going home, but I'll leave a message for Randal," Hoppy told her.

"Be certain he gets it," Jane commanded. "I wish to speak to him tonight. As I said before, it's very important."

"I'll do my best; you know that."

Hoppy put down the receiver and turned to find Sorella standing beside her.

"How much longer do you think Randal's likely to be?" she asked the child.

Not because she expected an answer, but because it was something to say. She herself was worried and perplexed at Randal's sudden decision to change the play after it had gone into rehearsal.

"A long time," Sorella answered. "The whole of one scene has got to be rewritten."

"Good gracious, did he tell you so?" Hoppy exclaimed. "I expect it's that tiresome Lucille Lund. She always wants something different from what has already been decided. It gives her a sense of her own importance."

"It's not her fault this time," Sorella said.

"I wouldn't be too sure of that," Hoppy muttered ominously. "What I can't understand is why Randal should change the play for anyone, whoever it might be. In my opinion it can't be improved upon. It's the best thing he's done—the best by far."

Sorella said nothing. She said good night to Hoppy, and picking up an armful of books, prepared to take them to her own room.

"You'd better go straight to bed, child," Hoppy said; and then, as if her attention was suddenly diverted to Sorella herself, she added, "Did he notice your new dress and the way your hair had been cut?"

"Yes."

"And he liked it?"

"Yes, I think he liked it."

"Then that's all right." Hoppy gave a sigh of relief. "One never knows with Randal. He tells one to do something, and then, when one's done it, it's quite wrong."

Her tired, middle-aged face, was suddenly full of trouble, as if she remembered the many times when Randal had been angry or displeased and they still had the power to haunt her.

Sorella, on an impulse, stood on tiptoe and kissed her.

"You're tired," she said. "Go home and forget about Randal. He's perfectly happy. He's going to make the play far, far better than it's ever been before, and you'll be pleased when it's done, I know you will."

For a moment Hoppy looked surprised at her gesture of affection. Then she returned Sorella's kiss and the worry vanished from her face.

It was after three in the morning when Randal finally put down his pen and stretched his cramped fingers, rubbing them together to get the circulation back into them.

He stared at what he had written; and then, as the words danced before his eyes, he rose to his feet and walked across the room to pour himself out a drink of soda-water.

121

It was done, and he knew it was good, very good. He drank off some of the soda and turned towards the fireplace; and then for the first time he saw that he was not alone in the room.

The only light was on his desk, a specially adjusted reading-lamp which flung a circle of brilliance just over the writing-pad.

There was, however, still a flicker of light from the fire, and crouched on the hearth in front of it he could see a small figure, her face turned towards him.

"Sorella!" he exclaimed. "Are you still here? Why ever aren't you in bed?"

"I was waiting for you to finish," Sorella answered. "I thought you'd be hungry. I've got some coffee ready for you in the kitchen, and I'll make you some scrambled eggs if you would like some."

"I can't imagine anything I'd like more," Randal replied; "I'll come and help you make them."

"Yes, do," Sorella answered: "it's much warmer in the kitchen than it is here."

It was like Sorella, Randal thought, not to ask him about the play.

When he had just finished writing he felt depleted and he had no wish to discuss what he had just achieved.

Tomorrow, or even in an hour or two, it would be different; but at this moment he wanted to talk of anything in the world rather than that last scene.

But how few women of his acquaintance would have understood this, Randal thought, as he followed Sorella down the passage which led to the small modern kitchen with its cleverly-fitted walls, electric stove and steel sinks.

It was deliciously warm, for the electric fire was switched on, and Randal sat down at the table with its gaily-checked red tablecloth while Sorella poured out the coffee.

She was still wearing the green dress which he

had seen for the first time earlier that evening, but she had rolled back the sleeves till they were above the elbow, and he noted the whiteness of her arms and the delicate turn of her wrists.

"You'll grow into a very pretty young woman if you're not careful," he said impulsively.

"That would be only fair," Sorella exclaimed with a sudden chuckle, "I was such a very plain child."

"Who said so?" Randal asked. "Or did you guess it by yourself?"

'Daddy told me how ugly I was at least a dozen times a day," Sorella answered, "and I wasn't blind, I could see myself in the looking-glass. Oh, Randal, you don't know what it is to be rid of those ghastly frilly dresses!"

"Is that the only dress you've bought yourself?" Randal asked.

"No, I've got two others coming tomorrow," Sorella replied. "I've spent rather a lot of your money: do you mind?"

"You can have a hundred dresses if you like," Randal said with a reckless generosity. "That's because I'm feeling guilty at not having thought about what you should have or what you should do. My only excuse is that I've been pretty tied up since we got back to England. We shall have to come to some decision about your future sometime, I suppose."

"Why?" Sorella asked.

"Well, it's got to be decided by someone."

Do you mean what sort of work I shall do and where I shall live?"

"I suppose so; those are the usual things to consider, aren't they?"

Sorella set her lips for a moment, and then she took up the saucepan containing the scrambled eggs and scooped them out onto a warm plate.

"I don't mind telling you I'm extremely hungry," Randal remarked, diverted for a moment from what he was saying. "I don't know who made this coffee, but I swear that it's better than we have ever had in the flat before."

"I made it," Sorella smiled. "One day I'll cook you a proper dinner. I used to watch the chefs at the different hotels we stayed in and I'm sure I can cook nearly as well as some of them."

"I'm not going to ask you to become a cook," Randal laughed.

"Why shouldn't I be your cook?" Sorella enquired. "Hoppy's always having trouble with the servants. They don't like the late hours you keep and the changes you make at the last moment.

Tonight they expected you to be out to dinner, and they were awfully annoyed when you came in and wanted something to eat. If I was your cook, I wouldn't mind what time you came in and wanted a meal."

"It sounds like a good idea from my point of view," Randal remarked with his mouth full, "but what about yours? You've got to enjoy yourself, have fun and go out dancing with the smart young men."

"Without being able to pay for my dancing shoes, I suppose?" Sorella said with a touch of sarcasm that he hadn't heard before in her voice.

He laughed.

"I hadn't thought of that. What sort of job do you want to do? I asked your father and he had no idea. He thought you were fitted for nothing but card-sharping. Actually we needn't begin to think about jobs just yet. You've got to finish your education for the next two or three years."

"I can't see why," Sorella replied. "And if you imagine I'm going to a boarding school or anything like that, you're mistaken."

"I hadn't thought of a boarding school as a matter of fact," Randal answered; but now you mention it, I suppose it would be the right thing to do."

"I'm not going to one."

"Why?"

"Because I should be out of place. Do you imagine the type of life I've lived would go down well with girls who have always been sheltered from the world by loving parents? No, of course not!"

"Then what can we do with you?" Randal asked.

Sorella did not reply for a moment. She took some toast from the electric grid and placed it in front of him. He helped himself to a pat of butter and spread it thickly.

"Well?" he enquired after a moment, as she did not speak.

"Can't I stay here with you, at least until you get married?" Sorella asked.

"That's an idea, at any rate," Randal replied. "There's just one thing I want to make clear. I feel a definite responsibility towards you. I want you to look on me as someone who will always take care of you. I shall never forgive myself for what happened to your father.

I know that directly it was not my fault; and yet perhaps, if I had taken a little more trouble over the aeroplane before we left, he might never have been killed."

"I don't think Daddy would have minded dying as he did," Sorella said. "He was always afraid of getting old, having no money and not being able to coerce people, women especially, into giving him what he required. More than once he said to me:

'If I have to die, Sorella, I would like to die quickly. A bomb or bullet is not the worst way of encountering death.' "

"I wish to Heaven then it had been a bomb or a bullet, and not my aeroplane," Randal exclaimed.

He put down his knife and looked at Sorella.

"Tell me," he said after a moment, "are you sorry at losing your father?"

Sorella met his eyes levelly.

"No," she replied. "I never loved him; and when

125

he used to beat me, I think I hated him. It wasn't the life we lived—I had known no other, so I grew used to it. I disliked having almost to beg my food from the kitchen and having to plead with hotel servants to let me have a piece of soap, or a bath, or any of the things which Daddy wouldn't buy me.

I wouldn't have minded any of them if he had been really fond of me, but he wasn't. He wasn't fond of anyone except himself.

I was rather like one of the babies the women in the East End of London hire out for the day so that they can take it begging. A child to excite sympathy—an easy way of raising money."

Sorella spoke with such bitterness that Randal stared at her in astonishment. Then unexpectedly she laughed.

"Am I being dramatic?" she asked. "I'm sorry; it's ridiculous really, because there were many things I enjoyed. If I hadn't gone about with my father I should not have seen Paris or Venice or Rome. There were so many things to learn about the big cities, so many things to love in the countries we visited.

Once, only once, we went to the country—to a little hotel in Yorkshire. It was the loveliest place, with an old mill near the hotel and the moors stretching away behind it.

"We only stayed there a week but to me it was Heaven. I used to walk out on to the moors and lie hidden in the heather until it was dark.

I never felt alone. I seemed to be very close to God, as I listened to the peewits calling from the sky, and saw the grouse winging their way over the heather.

"I was happier there than I've ever been in my life before, but all too soon we had to come back to London.

The woman's husband turned up unexpectedly,

knocked Daddy out of bed and threatened him with the police.

"He had a black eye and a cut on his mouth for three weeks, which meant he couldn't get hold of anyone else to keep us until they were healed."

"You poor child, what you have suffered!"

"I'm not telling you this to gain sympathy," Sorella said sharply. "I don't want any pity or sympathy; but I do want you to understand why I can't go to a respectable boarding school with a lot of well-brought-up, respectable boarders.

Besides, I feel too old, much too old in myself, to do lessons at a desk. I have read a lot, and I know enough to know how ignorant I am. I know how much more there is for me to learn, but not that way.

I wouldn't fit in. I should be unhappy and miserable among a crowd of elegant young ladies who one day would grow up to look like Jane."

"Then what do you want to do?" Randal asked. "It is a bit of problem, isn't it?"

"I've told you that I want to stay here," Sorella replied.

Randal finished his coffee and sat back in his chair. He felt at peace with the whole world.

He had finished the alterations to his play; to-morrow he would take them down to the theatre and everybody would be delighted.

He could already sense their delight; but what really mattered was that he himself was satisfied with what he had done.

A feeling of well-being came over him; nothing mattered very much at this particular moment when there was only Sorella and himself talking in the tiny kitchen and all the problems of tomorrow seemed far away.

He felt he wanted to do something big and generous. So he smiled at Sorella and said:

"You shall stay here with me, if that's what you want to do."

"You promise?" Sorella asked.

He was surprised at the hard determination in her voice.

"I promise," he repeated.

He saw the happiness in her eyes.

It was like a sudden light, rapturous, enchanted and strangely moving.

7

Sorella awoke with a smile on her lips; and then, as she opened her eyes, she gave a little exclamation of delight.

The sun was shining! She had known that it was going to be a wonderful day when she went to bed last night.

It would have been wonderful even had it been raining and the skies had been overcast; but that it should be sunny too made everything seem perfect.

She sprang out of bed and ran to the window.

Her room overlooked a side street and she had no glorious view of the Park as the windows had on the other side of the flat.

But it was high up and she could see over the grey roofs to where the towers and turrets of Whitehall rose from the green embrace of St. James's Park like a fairy palace from beneath the waves of the sea.

Beyond these were more roofs, mile upon mile of them, until at last they seemed to merge into the very horizon itself.

London was large—too large, Sorella had often thought—and now today she was going to leave it.

That was why she was so excited. That was why she had looked forward to this morning with such a passionate intensity that it had been hard to go to sleep the night before.

After a long week of rehearsals Friday afternoon had brought mistakes, misinterpretations and inanities to a climax. Randal had suddenly thrown his script down on the stage and exclaimed:

"We're getting stale—all of us! We'll rest over the weekend."

There had been no mistaking the relief of everybody from the scene-shifters to Bruce Bellingham. They were all tired, and as Randal said only too truly, they were growing stale.

They were rehearsing the main character parts intensively to start with, because he and Bruce, his co-producer, had decided that once they started on the crowd scenes and the minor parts the whole thing would become unwieldy, unless those who carried the bulk of the story on their shoulders were to all intents and purposes, word-perfect.

Lucille had been extremely good at her part from the very first rehearsal.

Randal had often stared at her in amazement, thinking that he had never before appreciated what a hard worker she could be if she really put her mind to it.

He was also beginning to believe, almost against his better self, that Lucille could, if she wished, become a really great actress.

He didn't know, and only Lucille could have told him, that she had a reason for what she was doing, and that reason was himself.

Lucille welcomed the holiday as much as the others. It was only when they were leaving the theatre that Randal realised she intended them to spend it together.

"I want so much to see the Olivier's new play, darling," she said.

She slipped her arm into his and pressed herself against him with a caressing movement of her body, which always reminded him of a cat.

"It would be impossible to get in at the last moment," Randal said, knowing that was but an excuse.

"Nonsense," Lucille smiled. "A place will be found for you—and for me, if you ask nicely. Let us have a box if possible. I love your boxes over here, they have such an Edwardian air about them."

"I'll do my best," Randal replied reluctantly as if the words were dragged from him.

He hadn't realised how tired he was till he reached his own flat. Hoppy was waiting for him with a sheaf of letters in her hand.

He gave her what was almost a comical look of dismay as he threw himself down on the sofa and put up his feet.

"Go away, woman," he said. "If you think I'm going to do any work, you're much mistaken. I won't sign a letter, won't sign a cheque. I'm dead beat, finished and flattened! It's no use arguing with me."

"Do we ever argue with you?" Hoppy asked, with a humorous note in her voice. "And you do look tired. I'll get you a whisky-and-soda."

She brought him a strong one and watched him drink it.

"That's better," he said with a little sigh. "My head was beginning to whirl. I felt that if I had to say 'Speak up a little, darling,' once more, I should go raving mad. I've given everyone a holiday for the week-end. and that includes me."

"Good!" Hoppy exclaimed, "and what are you going to do? Stay here or go to the country?"

"Lucille wants a box for the Oliviers' new play," Randal answered. "She also wants me to sit in it."

"That won't be much of a rest," Hoppy remarked tartly.

"That's what I thought," Randal said wearily. "But see if you can get it for her, there's a dear."

Hoppy went from the room with something that was suspiciously like a snort. Randal settled himself more comfortably and closed his eyes.

He must have been asleep for nearly twenty minutes before he had the feeling that someone was in the room.

Slowly, as if he dragged himself back from a very long distance, he looked to see who it was.

Jane was sitting in the chair opposite. Drowsily he smiled at her.

"Hello, beautiful. I wasn't expecting to see you!"

"So it appears," Jane answered a little drily and then added, "Randal, you're terribly tired."

"I know," he replied. "Can't you tell me something more informative?"

Jane gave him a little smile, intimate and secret. He had never seen her look smarter or more elegant, Randal thought, than she looked this afternoon. She was wearing a coat of deep mulberry-coloured velvet, with a little hat of the same material. There was a tie of Russian sables round her neck, and there were diamonds in her ears and on her fingers which played with her handbag of crocodile skin dyed to match her shoes.

"I've got a plan," Jane said softly.

"What is it?" Randal asked.

Despite the effort he made to be interested there was a note of caution as well as of weariness in his tone.

"We will spend the week-end together," Jane answered. "We'll go racing tomorrow at Hurst Park. In the evening we'll dine at home and then go on to Diana's party. She's giving a very special one, as you know, for the Crown Prince.

He arrives in England today, and incidentally, she told me she hasn't had an answer from you, although she sent you an invitation almost a week ago."

"I shall have to sack Hoppy," Randal said feebly.

"I asked Hoppy," Jane answered with mock severity "and she told me that, as Diana had written you a personal letter, you told her you would answer it yourself."

"Very well, I'll be honest and say I forgot all about it!"

"And nobody will blame you at the moment," Jane said soothingly. "You should have given it to me and I would have answered it for you. Never mind, Diana will understand—we all know how busy you are. Now, don't you think that's a good plan for tomorrow?"

"It's wonderful," Randal agreed, and he sounded singularly unconvincing.

"I've got to go now," Jane sighed, getting to her feet. "Don't move, darling. I know it's no use asking you to go on to a cocktail party, so I won't waste my breath. And I wish you were coming to the American Embassy with me tonight. I shall miss you, but we'll have tomorrow.

"Will you pick me up about twelve o'clock? We might as well go in your car, unless you prefer one of ours?"

"Twelve o'clock," Randal replied, as though he was trying to remember the hour.

Jane stood looking at him for a moment, and then she bent down and laid her cheek against his.

"I shall be glad when this rehearsing is over," she whispered very softly; "then we'll be able to talk about ourselves."

Instinctively Randal's arms went round her.

The scent she was using was sweet and fragrant and he could feel the softness of her furs against his neck. He had a sudden feeling of compunction—he felt guilty about Jane.

"Once the show is opened, everything will be different," he said fervently.

She sat down on the edge of the sofa, her hands on his shoulders, her eyes searching his.

"You promise me that?" she asked a little wistfully.

Taking one of her hands in his, he carried it to his mouth and kissed the palm.

"I promise," he said.

"We've told no one we intend to get married," Jane began; "but, Randal, keeping it a secret isn't really as pleasant as I thought it might be. I never see you, and when we do meet, there is always someone else there. Let's announce our engagement. I can't for the life of me think what we're waiting for."

Randal kissed the palm of her hand again with a slow deliberation which gave him time to think.

"What sort of engagement would we have, darling, if I had to be perpetually at the theatre?" he asked at length. "Besides I couldn't cope with the Press and all the other horrors which will descend on us like a swarm of hornets. You mustn't forget that you are a very important young woman. And if I have to hit the headlines at this moment, it will be on a stretcher."

"Poor Randal! You do take it out of yourself, don't you?" Jane responded tenderly. "I do understand really that this is not an opportune moment. It's just that sometimes I get bored with having to pretend we are only friends—and you may be sure there are quite a number of curious people trying to find out exactly what we do mean to each other."

"We'll have it written in electric lights in Piccadilly Circus," Randal said, "but after the opening of the play! Please, darling, remember that—after the opening of the play."

"Should I be jealous?" Jane asked, and Randal knew that this question was important.

"Of what, or of whom?" he enquired. "If you're

jealous of my work, I'm delighted. After all, you're only marrying me because I'm a famous playwright."

Jane put out a finger to touch his cheek.

"Do you really believe that is the only reason?" she asked.

"I can't think of another one," he replied.

"You're fishing for compliments," she smiled. "You are conceited enough as it is. I've no intention of pandering to your vanity."

She spoke lightly, but her eyes were to his mouth and her breath came a little more quickly through her red lips.

The clock on the mantelpiece chimed the half hour. Jane glanced round with a start of surprise.

"I must go," she said. "Gerald will be furious with me. I promised I'd be there early to help him receive the guests."

"Kiss me good-bye."

Jane bent forward.

"I shall cover you with lipstick," she said, warningly.

Randal seemed not to have heard her. He held her close in his arms, and his mouth was on hers.

It was a long kiss, which gradually grew fiercer and more possessive, until there was something almost desperate about it, his lips hungry and insistent as if they demanded some response which she could not give.

At last Jane drew away from him.

"Darling you're hurting me," she complained;

But her voice was low and deep, her cheeks flushed, her eyes very dark.

"I'm sorry," Randal muttered.

"I've never known you so brutal before."

She didn't look as though she really minded his brutality, and after a moment she bent towards him again.

But the fire and strength seemed to have gone from Randal.

His head was back once more on the velvet cushion; his eyes were closed. He looked, Jane thought suddenly, utterly deflated.

She waited for a moment, for once undecided what to do or what to say; and then, as he did not speak, she rose to her feet and crossing to the mantelpiece stared into the looking-glass which surmounted it.

She straightened her velvet hat and, taking a gold-and-diamond vanity case from her pocket, powdered her nose.

It took her a few minutes to reapply her lipstick, to brush away the grains of powder which had fallen on to her velvet coat and to replace everything in her bag.

Randal did not speak or open his eyes, and when at length Jane had titivated herself to her satisfaction, she turned round to look at him.

"Go to sleep, dearest," she said. "What you need is a good night's rest. I'll be waiting for you at twelve o'clock tomorrow."

She did not wait for his reply, but turned towards the door. As she reached it, she said:

"Don't forget that Daddy is dining with you at eight o'clock tonight. I'll tell him not to keep you up late."

"Thank you," Randal replied faintly.

The door shut behind Jane and he was alone. He lay for a long time, not sleeping, nor dozing, but thinking. No one came to disturb him; the light outside began to fade; the room grew dark.

The curtains had not been drawn, the fire in the hearth sank lower and lower until there was only the warm, glowing red of the cinders.

Then the door opened softly, and Randal heard someone come into the room. There was only a momentary hesitation before he realised who it was.

"Sorella, is that you?"

He knew the answer before he heard her voice.

"Yes, are you asleep?"

"No; not now at any rate. What do you want?"

"Everybody's in a terrible state because they think

135

you are going to be late for dinner; but they were all too frightened to come in to see if you were asleep or dead, so I braved the lion in his den."

Randal laughed and sat up.

"What's the time?"

"Nearly a quarter to eight."

"Good Heavens! Rockampstead will be here at any moment."

"That is what Norton keeps saying and wringing his hands. Hoppy gave him strict instructions that you were not to keep his Lordship waiting."

There was laughter in her tones and her voice seemed to lighten the darkness which encompassed them both. For no reason that he could think of, Randal found himself chuckling.

"Put on the light," he said; "if anyone comes in, they'll think we're lunatics talking to each other through the gloom."

He heard the click of the switches at the door and the room was flooded with a glowing pink light. Randal found himself blinking.

"Hoppy gave me a message for you," Sorella said, coming towards him.

He saw that she was wearing another new dress.

It was very plain and straight—a teen-ager's frock like the one she had bought before. But this was a blue wool, the deep blue of the Mediterranean sea.

It made her skin seem very white, and her neck seemed to rise from the severity of the bodice like a column of ivory, so young, so lovely in itself that Randal found for the moment he could think of nothing else.

He realised that Sorella was waiting for his attention and with an effort he recalled his wandering thoughts.

"A message from Hoppy?" he asked vaguely. "Well, what is it?"

"She said that she had got a box for the play. The ticket has been left in Lucille's name at the box office."

"Good."

Randal took out his cigarette case and lit a cigarette.

"I shouldn't have thought there was a chance in a million of getting a box as late as this," he said. "But, let's face it, Lucille always gets what she wants!"

"Does she?" Sorella enquired. "I wonder if that's nice?"

"Always to get what you want?" Randal questioned. "Charming, I should think."

"I'm not so sure," Sorella said. "Things would cease to be exciting if one was quite sure one was going to get them."

"I wish just for once I could get what I want," Randal said. "And that, I would have you know, is peace! But as I can't have it I must go and change."

He threw his cigarette, from which he had only taken a few puffs, into the fireplace.

"You're looking very smart," he remarked, stretching himself a little. "What are you going to do with yourself tonight."

"I'm having a tray in my bedroom," Sorella answered, "because Hoppy told me you and Lord Rockampstead want to talk business. Don't eat all the chocolate soufflé, will you? It looks delicious, and I shall only get it after you've finished."

Randal laughed.

"Let's hope my guest hasn't a big appetite," he said.

"I'll let you have as much as you want," Sorella offered generously, "but I grudge every mouthful Lord Rockampstead eats. Hoppy says he has wonderful food at home, so I don't know why he should bother to come here and eat ours."

Randal laughed again.

He had moved across the room while Sorella was talking, and his hand was actually reaching towards the handle of the door when it opened and Norton, his valet, stood there.

"They've just rung up from the House of Lords, Sir, to say that Lord Rockampstead is extremely sorry, but he can't dine with you tonight. His Lordship has been

137

asked to attend a special meeting of the Committee of Ways and Means. He sends his apologies, but feels sure you will understand why he is unavoidably prevented from coming to dinner."

"Yes, of course," Randal said, and turned to Sorella. "There'll be some chocolate soufflé for you after all."

"I can dine with you?"

The question was almost breathless.

"I shall be honoured," Randal replied.

He walked out into the hall.

"Tell Cook we shall be ready for dinner as soon as I've had time to have a bath and change," he said to Norton. "I won't be more than quarter of an hour, at the outside."

"Very good, Sir."

Norton opened the door of Randal's bedroom for him with the expressionlessness of a perfect servant.

Then as he shut it, he turned to Sorella with a grin and something suspiciously like a wink.

"Nicer than having a tray in your bedroom, eh, Miss?"

"Much nicer," Sorella replied solemnly. "I'm very grateful to the Committee of Ways and Means."

Norton chuckled.

"I've often wondered what use that sort of Committee was," he said. "Now we know."

When Sorella told Randal what Norton had said he put back his head and laughed.

The lines of worry and irritation disappeared when he was laughing, she thought; and almost as her father might have done, she set to work to amuse him.

She tried and for a short while succeeded in making him forget the production of *Today and Tomorrow,* in keeping his mind from wandering either to Lucille or to Jane, in forcing him to remember that the world is an amusing place with a lot of amusing things in it.

They talked for a long time in the dining-room, and then went back to sit in the sitting-room. There seemed to be so much to say, so many things which made Randal laugh.

He settled himself comfortably in a big armchair, his legs stretched out in front of him, a glass of brandy at his side. Sorella sat on the hearth-rug at his feet in a pose which was instinctively and quite unconsciously graceful.

Her little face was raised to Randal's, the firelight echoed in her eyes.

He knew she was happy, knew it by the gay lilt in her voice, in the smile at the corners of her soft mouth.

"She has never known before what it is to be at her ease with someone she trusts," Randal told himself as he watched her.

They hardly heard Norton's murmured "Miss Crake" before Jane was in the room, a resplendent, beautiful Jane, dressed in a gown of shimmering silver, with a tiara set in her hair and a cape of white ermine round her shoulders.

"I came to show you my new dress on the way to the Embassy," she said. Then she stopped, "But, where's Daddy?"

The question somehow had the effect of making both Randal and Sorella feel guilty.

They started to their feet, and now Randal had the feeling that he was a child who had been caught in the pantry stealing the jam.

"You father couldn't come to dinner, Jane" he explained. "He's been kept at the House."

"Oh! Randal! And you didn't telephone me. You could so easily have dined with us. We were a man short as it happened."

"I didn't know till the very last minute," Randal replied, somehow annoyed at having to make the explanation.

"Well, you're changed and you've nothing to do," Jane exclaimed; "what's to stop your coming on to the party with me?"

"I can't, Jane, I can't really," Randal protested. "I

was only resting for a few minutes before Sorella goes to bed, and then I'm going to start work. It isn't often you catch me being idle!"

"But you hadn't planned to work tonight," Jane pointed out, and her voice was hard.

"It's got to be done sometime," Randal said, "and quite frankly, I don't feel like a party."

Jane turned petulantly on her heel.

"It's after ten o'clock, Sorella, and time you were in bed," she said sharply.

Her words seemed to awake in Sorella the realisation that she was not wanted.

"I'll go to bed at once," she said quietly. "Good night, Randal; good night, Jane."

She went from the room before they could answer her. The door closed behind her and Jane whirled round again, faced Randal with something suspiciously like anger.

"You're making a fool of that child," she said accusingly; "and as it happens, I've wanted to talk to you about her for some time. Hasn't she any relations?"

"None, as far as I know," Randal replied.

"Well, she can't go on staying here."

"Why not?"

"Because she's much too old for one thing. When she arrived I thought she was about nine or ten; but she's practically grown up. You can't have a young, not unattractive girl living alone in your flat with you."

"Who says so?"

"I say so, for one person," Jane retorted, "and I'm only saying it before everybody else begins to talk. You're not a fool, Randal, and you know exactly what I mean."

"I only hope, Jane, that you don't mean what your words imply," Randal said slowly. "Sorella is a child— the child of a man I killed. If the people you know have such filthy minds as to infer that I can't have her live under my roof, then, quite frankly, I don't care two

140

damns what such scandalmongers say or what they think. I shall do the right thing as I see it."

"But is it the right thing?" Jane asked. "And it's obviously ridiculous to take up that attitude, Randal. No famous young man of thirty-two can have a girl living with him without creating comment and very unpleasant speculation."

"Obviously from very unpleasant people," Randal snapped.

"Whatever you think at the moment, this can't go on," Jane retorted. "You're not suggesting, for instance, that when we are married we should have Sorella stay with us indefinitely? I don't intend to start my married life by adopting a girl of fifteen!"

"To tell the truth I haven't thought about it," Randal said wearily. "I'm responsible for D'Arcy Forest's death and I'm obviously going to do what I can for his daughter. At the moment she wants to stay here with me."

"I expected you would turned her head. I suppose the poor child thinks she's in love with you," Jane suggested sarcastically.

"I don't think she thinks anything of the sort," Randal replied. "Sorella has had a peculiar and what most people would think a wretched upbringing. For the first time in her life she's staying somewhere where she's wanted, where people are kind to her, and where she has regular meals at regular times.

I don't think Sorella has looked beyond these immediate creature comforts, and I certainly haven't."

"Then it's about time you did."

"I think I am the best judge of that," Randal answered angrily.

There was a sudden silence between them, and then Jane stepped forward to put her hands on his shoulders.

"Darling, we're quarrelling!" she said. "It's the last thing I want to do. I came here really because I love you, because I wanted to show myself off. When I looked in the glass tonight, I thought,

'This is how I'd like Randal to see me';

When I went down to dinner a lot of people were very complimentary, and again I thought, 'There's only one person whose admiration I need.'

That's why I came here, letting the others go on ahead! And now we're quarrelling!"

"I'm sorry, but I feel responsible for Sorella."

"Of course you do, darling," Jane smiled soothingly, "and I tell you what we'll do. We'll find a nice school for her, a school where she'll meet charming girls and make really nice friends."

"She doesn't want to go to school," Randal protested. "Oh, don't let's argue about it, Jane. I'll decide what's to be done about her later."

"Very well. We won't talk about it any more. It's obviously a controversial subject."

Randal flicked his cigarette ash into the fire, his eyes on the flames.

"Won't you come to the Embassy with me?" Jane asked pleadingly.

"I should only be a wet blanket, or whatever the expression is," Randal replied. "I don't feel like a party tonight. Forgive me, and go and enjoy yourself."

Jane put her cheek against his with a little gesture which was peculiarly individual.

"I won't tease you to come if you really don't want to," she said. "We'll have tomorrow together."

She pressed herself against him for the moment.

"Don't crush me," she said quickly, as his arms went round her.

She moved away from him, leaving a fragrance and an impression of soft, warm femininity behind her.

Seeing that she meant to go, Randal walked with her to the front door and rang for the lift.

"You're not angry with me?" he asked. "But I couldn't face a crowd when I feel like this."

As he said it, he thought how very recently he would have been thrilled and excited at having such an invitation. It was extraordinary how easily one tired even of the most amusing and scintillating people.

"Of course I'm not angry," Jane replied softly. "I understand. You've been through so much these past weeks."

She raised her face to his, but the lift came up more quickly than she anticipated. She blew him a kiss through the glass doors as she descended out of sight.

Randal went back into his flat and shut the door.

He felt restless and disturbed by Jane's visit. A sudden wave of irritability swept over him. He was at peace until she came, but now . . .

He stood looking at the messages on the hall table, which had been neatly typed out for him by Hoppy. At the top of them was a slip which read—

"Notify Lucille Lund that there is a box for her at the Empress Theatre for the matinée tomorrow afternoon."

Randal suddenly felt very tired indeed. The idea of telephoning Lucille was too much to be endured. Then he remembered who else would be expecting him tomorrow afternoon, Jane and Lucille.

It was quite hopeless, he thought, to try to plan one's life when there were two women both demanding one's attention, both assuming that they had the right to his affection.

He crumpled up the slip of paper and chucked it on the floor. Then he walked a little way down the passage and knocked on the door of Sorella's bedroom.

"Come in."

He entered to find she was already in bed.

The room was small, but exquisitely decorated with a pink-and-white wallpaper, shell pink hangings, and the bed covered in silk rose petals under a corolla of god angels.

It was one of the flights of fancy of Randal's artistic friend, and it made, he thought, a perfect background for Sorella's white skin, dark hair and strange green eyes.

She was sitting up in bed reading a book.

143

Her nightgown of sprigged lawn had tiny puff sleeves and a sash of blue ribbon at the waist. She looked very young and very sweet, and the smile she gave him was one of sheer, untrammelled joy.

"Has Jane gone?" she asked. "I felt certain she intended to take you to the party."

"I hate parties," Randal replied and sat down on the bed.

"I think the only nice party," Sorella said, "would be to be alone with the one person whom one wanted to be with."

"How do you know that's the sort of party you would like?" Randal enquired. "When you get a little older you'll want to dance, drink champagne and listen to a lot of fools talking at the top of their voices.

"The noise, the lights and the bands will go to your head, and you'll be quite angry if anyone wants to take you home before dawn."

"I don't like that sort of thing at all," Sorella protested. "I've seen lots of parties, as it happens. I used to watch them when I stayed in hotels.

"Once I crept under a table and sat through the whole evening listening to the people talking and watching them dance. They looked awfully silly, most of them."

"I expect they were silly, too," Randal said, "but the trouble is that people at parties never think they're silly. They're so terribly pleased with themselves for being there that the only people they are sorry for are those who have not had an invitation."

"Well, I'm glad you didn't go with Jane," Sorella announced. "Are you going to bed or shall I come back into the sitting-room and talk to you?"

"I'm going to bed," Randal replied, "and Jane is right. It's high time you were asleep."

Sorella smiled faintly and made no reply, but Randal felt as though both Jane's remark and his own were too fatuous to need an answer.

144

"What are you reading?" he asked, to change the subject.

He bent forward to take a look at the book she held on her knees. He saw that it was *English Saga* by Arthur Bryant.

"Do you like it?" he enquired.

Somehow it was not at all the type of book he expected to find Sorella reading.

"I want to learn about England," she answered, "and this tells me so many things that I don't know about the English people."

"Why do you want to know about England?" Randal asked.

"Because I'm going to live here," Sorella answered. "I've been abroad so much, I'm tired of other countries. I want to learn to love my own."

She took the book from him, and turned over the pages.

"I've been reading about the great country houses," she went on, "and the English countryside. Arthur Bryant describes it as it was a hundred years ago. I feel it must be much the same today. The countryside can't have changed so very much. That is the England I want to know."

"That's the England you shall see," Randal announced positively. "I have a house in the country. It's not very big, but it's very beautiful. We'll go down and stay there. At Queen's Hoo you will see England at its very best."

"Oh, Randal! How wonderful! When can we go?"

There was a note of excitement in Sorella's voice that he had never heard before.

The desire to give pleasure made him forget to be cautious and sensible.

"We'll go tomorrow," he replied. "We'll get up early. Queen's Hoo is not more than an hour's run from London. We needn't come back until late on Sunday night. Would you like that?"

"It would be more wonderful than anything I've ever dreamed of," Sorella answered.

Then her expression changed. It seemed to Randal as though a cloud passed across the face of the sun.

"What is it?" he asked.

"They won't let you go," she said unhappily, "Hoppy, Lucille, Jane. They're all expecting you to do other things tomorrow. You can't run away like that."

Randal got to his feet.

"I can and I will. Am I a mouse or a man? It's about time I asked myself that question. Hoppy shall ring everyone up in the morning and say I'm dying. On doctor's orders I've got to take forty-eight hours' rest. We'll be up and away before anyone else is awake. Can you be ready by nine o'clock?"

"Of course I can," Sorella laughed, and the sun was shining again in her expression. "But are you sure, quite sure, there won't be a terrible row?"

"I'm quite sure," Randal said, "and if there is, I don't care. Good night, Sorella, sleep well."

"I'm too excited to do that," Sorella answered. "Oh, I wish tomorrow had already come!"

He left her hugging her knees over the bedclothes. The lights from the bedside lamps illuminated the dancing excitement in her eyes.

As Randal fell asleep, he thought they had shone like stars, and he laughed to himself because the expression was so banal, so hackneyed.

He was barely awake before Hoppy came bustling into his room.

"I'm sorry to disturb you so early," she said, in a tone of voice which told him that she was not at all sorry. "Sorella tells me that you're leaving at nine o'clock. The child has ordered the car to be round and is in an idiotic state of excitement. What's it all about?"

"I'm very ill," Randal replied sleepily. "I've got to rest today and tomorrow. You'll have to telephone Lucille and Jane and tell them what a very serious view the doctor takes of my condition."

"And what if I refuse to tell such nonsensical lies?" Hoppy asked.

'Then Norton will have to ring them, and he won't do it half as well as you."

"I think you're crazy," Hoppy exclaimed. "This is nothing more or less than a schoolboy prank. This isn't the moment to play truant, and well you know it."

"It's the most sensible thing I can do," Randal said with a yawn. "Apart from my own inclinations, you know perfectly well that if I go to the theatre with Lucille, I shall annoy Jane. If I go to the races with Jane, I shall annoy Lucille.

My dear Hoppy, I am really an extremely sensible and, if you like, calculating young man."

Hoppy capitulated.

"All right," she said grudgingly. "I only hope I sound convincing. You don't look very ill to me."

"For Heaven's sake don't tell them where I've gone," Randal called out as she reached the door.

"I wasn't born yesterday," Hoppy retorted as she went down the passage.

"I've telephoned Queen's Hoo and told them to expect you," she said, as Sorella and Randal said goodbye to her half an hour later.

"I hope you've ordered some decent meals," Randal said. "What time will you arrive?"

"Not till after dinner," Hoppy replied.

"Does Hoppy always come down to the country with you?" Sorella asked, as, seated in Randal's silver Bentley, they threaded their way through the traffic in Park Lane.

"I can't do anything without Hoppy," Randal replied. "I used to try going to the country without her. The result was I spent all the time answering the telephone, or dictating reply-paid telegrams to tiresome little girls on their mothers' bicycles who had trundled three miles from the village with a message which could quite easily have waited until Monday."

"Hoppy's a darling," Sorella said; "but it must be nice sometimes to be entirely on your own."

"I don't believe it's possible," Randal answered. "People always turn up. Even when one flies to the south of France, one still can't find any solitude!"

He was teasing her, and Sorella gave a little giggle.

"You were very angry when Daddy and I came down the steps to the swimming pool."

"I was furious," Randal agreed. "But you were very persistent. Remember—if anyone finds out that we've gone to Queen's Hoo, they'll be down tomorrow in their hordes; cars screeching up the drive, people tumbling out of them into the house, switching on the radiogram, rushing to mix cocktails and open champagne."

"Oh, they mustn't find us, they mustn't!" Sorella said, with a cry that was almost a prayer.

"We can trust Hoppy to keep them at bay," Randal reassured her. "She likes to come to Queen's Hoo, too. She has her own little flat at the top of the house, and I don't go near her unless it's really important, and she doesn't come near me, unless she has to."

"Then we'll really be alone all the time," Sorella said, ". . . unless they find out."

"We won't let them."

Randal accelerated, letting the car out a little as the traffic thinned and they came into the less-frequented streets round Regent's Park.

It wasn't long before they were out of London and on to the by-pass.

Then the Bentley swept forward like a greyhound on a race-track. Sorella stared breathlessly ahead as the miles slid past and the houses and villas gave way to open fields.

Randal felt a sudden urgency to reach Queen's Hoo.

He had not owned it for very long, but for years he had longed for a country home, as like most men he hated to spend the week-end in London.

As soon as it had become known that he wished to

148

buy a house, he had been sent details of innumerable estates of all sizes by the agents, who were only too anxious to please the much-publicised young play-wright.

But from the moment Randal saw Queen's Hoo he had known it was the one house he wanted, the one house he felt must, under any circumstances, be his.

He felt now the same thrill that he had experienced the first day that he saw it.

It was almost like the thrill of going to a woman one loved, or better still, returning home. That was what Queen's Hoo really meant to him. He knew it now, if he had never known it before.

He knew, too, that he wanted, with an almost surprising urgency, to take Sorella there and show her his home.

8

Queen's Hoo had been built in the reign of Queen Elizabeth I and had remained, to all intents and pur-poses, untouched since.

Of red brick, with diamond-paned windows, it was small and compact, looking over a garden divided by walls and dark yew hedges into small exquisite squares of colour and fragrance.

The house stood slightly on a hill and from it one could look for many miles over the fields and woods of Hertfordshire.

Randal had fallen in love with Queen's Hoo from the first moment he saw it, and he was used to people giving exclamations of delight when they saw his country home.

Sorella, on the contrary, said nothing, she just sat in the car and looked as he drew up at the front door.

But there was something so expressive in her eyes that there was no need for her to speak or to find words to express her admiration.

Randal watched her for a moment; then he leaned across her to open the door.

"Why don't you get out?" he said. "It's even lovelier from the other side than this."

She turned to look at him.

"How can you bear not to live here always?"

He smiled at that.

"You mustn't forget that I've got to make the money to keep it up."

"You could write here."

"I do," he replied. "I wrote the whole of the first draft of *Today and Tomorrow* in the garden. Come, I'll show you exactly where, if you're interested."

He stepped from the car, and walking round to the open door on Sorella's side he held out both his hands to her.

"Come and inspect Queen's Hoo," he invited, "the home of that famous playwright, Randal Gray."

She laughed a little at that, and some of the awe with which she was regarding the house vanished from her expression.

But it returned as she stood on the door-step, looking back at the courtyard with its ancient well, the big wrought-iron gates and heraldic stone newels astride the arched entrance through which they had just driven.

Randal slipped his arm through hers as he opened the heavy, nail-studded oak door which led into the house.

As he did so, there was a noisy, tempestous greeting from two cocker spaniels who were waiting inside the hall.

Almost shrieking with excitement, they circled round him, jumping up, trying to lick his face, whining and barking in the manner which indicated without any possible doubt their delight at seeing him.

"Down, boys" Randal commanded.

He added to Sorella, as soon as he could make himself heard.

"These are part of the household and are known, for no apparent reason, as Moss and Tweed."

"What lovely names!" Sorella exclaimed, patting the dogs.

Then, with Moss and Tweed at their heels, Randal led Sorella into the sitting-room.

It was a long, low room, overlooking a formal garden on one side, with a door opening on to the lawn on the other.

There was a big log fire burning in the open fireplace, but the sunshine was coming through the open door, and, without waiting for Randal, Sorella ran ahead of him out into the garden.

There she stood looking first at the view and then at the house behind her.

The warm, weather-beaten bricks seemed to give the house an air of happiness and of kindliness which she had never known in any house she had seen before.

It was so exquisitely correct in its period, and yet, at the same time, so small and compact that inevitably it radiated a cosy, homelike atmosphere.

It managed to be beautiful without being the least bit frightening or awe-inspiring. It was old without being antiquated.

There was, too, some indescribable magic about its age, a sorcery which made one think that here one would learn secrets that one had long sought to hear, or would make discoveries for which before one had sought in vain.

"Do you like it?" Randal asked quietly.

Sorella did not realise that she had stood for several minutes saying nothing, and now, as if Randal could bear her silence no longer, he must ask a question and thus recall her attention to him.

To his surprise Sorella did not answer him.

Instead, she moved along the paved path, bordered

151

with an ancient box hedge, to stand at the edge of a flight of steps which led down to the rose garden.

Where she stood she was silhouetted against a low brick wall, her hand resting on a curiously-fashioned wrought-iron gate, swung open so that she could reach the steps beyond.

She was wearing the green dress which she had bought a few days earlier; she had thrown down her coat on entering the house, and no hat covered her dark head.

The wind came blowing up the valley and whipped her hair around her little face; and suddenly, as he watched her standing there at the top of the steps, Randal felt something stir and move within him, and he knew that in that second Sorella had given him a plot for a new play.

It always came to him like that, a tiny incident, a fragment of conversation, a glimpse of a scene, a character of the story, which he knew, in that instant, was was the foundation stone for a whole plot.

Sometimes there would be nothing more for a long time, and yet the seed was there, sown and ready for the ultimate harvest.

Sometimes Randal would almost despair when he knew that something must be written and yet an idea would not come; and now, with *Today and Tomorrow* finished already, far sooner than he expected, the embryo was in existence for his next play.

What it would be, or how it would develop, he had, at this moment, no idea.

He only knew, looking at Sorella, that she had awakened that creative impulse within himself which so often lay dormant and still when he most needed it.

There was, in his imagination as he looked at her, an impression of waves, of a rough wind blowing from off the sea. Perhaps it was her green dress which made him think of this.

But already he could see, quite clearly in his mind,

the woman who would be the heroine of his play and the man to whom she gave her love—a man who would come to her in a ship.

Always when he had a new idea, Randal felt a strange, almost breathless excitement within himself. The beginning was always exciting, like this.

Afterwards there would be the hard, often boring work of setting everything down, of invoking craftsmanship and technical knowledge, writing, revising and re-revising, until the finished product brought him not the elation that might be expected, but more often than not only a sense of relief that the task was done.

Now he could remember none of this, he only knew the thrill and a sense of joy that the curtain was rising.

It was then, at last, that Sorella turned towards him.

Her eyes were shining in her face, her lips parted with delight. She walked back down the flagged path to where he was standing and slipped a small hand into his.

"Now show me the house," she said.

It seemed to Randal quite perfect that the idea for his new play should have come to him at Queen's Hoo and that he should be with Sorella.

She had, he thought, that quality of silence and of quiet that was more valuable than anything else to someone like himself—who found such things so rarely.

For a fleeting second he remembered the other women he had brought to Queen's Hoo, whose high voices, exclaiming in parrot-like tones over the charm of the house, had jarred upon him until he even welcomed the music from the radiogram as a relief from their ceaseless chatter.

Sorella was so different, he thought.

She said very little as they went from room to room, but he knew that she appreciated, perhaps more than anyone else had ever done, the trouble and care he had taken over the house.

His artistic friends might furnish his flat in Park Lane for him, but Queen's Hoo had been his own production from first to last.

He had chosen the colourful chintz in the bedrooms, the old rose velvet hangings in the the sitting-room, and the ruby-red brocade up the twisting staircase.

The furniture, too, he picked up, piece by piece, in antique shops.

Some rooms were still unfinished, while he waited for an oak table which would fit exactly into an alcove or for a high-backed needlework chair to stand against the dark oak panelling.

If Randal had loved Queen's Hoo when he first bought it, he loved it infinitely more now when he had practically finished furnishing it. Every piece of furniture was a part of himself.

There had been no mass buying, no order given to a professional decorator, and no unnecessary expense.

It was in fact, Randal felt, home; and more than once he wished there could have been someone belonging to him to live there with him.

The house demanded a hostess, so he brought down his women friends, feeling they would ornament and grace the house and somehow fill the empty blank that he so often felt there.

Yet their visits were not always an unqualified success.

Jane, it was true, seemed to fit in better than anyone else had ever done. Yet she made Queen's Hoo seem so small.

It was, Randal admitted, tiny in contrast to her own home in Derbyshire—a huge, magnificent mansion which Lord Rockampstead had bought soon after his father's succession to the title, and which he kept up with a splendour which might have been equalled but never surpassed by the first owner, for whom the house was built by Robert Adam.

Yet Jane loved Queen's Hoo, she had told Randal so over and over again.

"It's a little gem of its kind," she said.

While Randal wanted to be pleased with the compliment, he yet resented the qualification.

He felt that Jane was comparing Queen's Hoo with Bletchingly Castle, with the homes of her friends, so many of whom accepted their historical mansions and national monuments as a matter of course.

Queen's Hoo was unique to Randal in that he owned it. It was, he thought, more especially his than anything he had ever been able to buy and own in his life before.

He had known, when the title deeds were handed over to him and the final contract was signed and sealed, a thrill greater than anything he had ever felt even at the first night of his first play.

It was not only because he had worked for the money which had bought him Queen's Hoo. It wasn't only because he had furnished and decorated it himself. It was something more important that both of these things.

There was something which told him that he and Queen's Hoo belonged to each other.

Now, as he went round the house with Sorella, Randal felt that he could never be tired of going from room to room, of seeing the shine on the old furniture, of straightening the rugs on the floor, rearranging the ornaments on the stone mantelpieces, moving a chair nearer the fire, or pulling back a curtain from the window.

He wanted to touch the things and make himself part of them; to know that they were his and he was theirs.

Now, when their tour of the house was finished, they came slowly down the stairs and back into the sitting-room. Randal realised that Sorella had hardly said a word.

He had talked all the time, and yet he had known

155

what she felt and had been as sure of her delight as he was of his own.

She sat down on the long stool in front of the fire and held out her hands to the blaze.

Once again there was something in the movement of her hands, something, too, in the grace of her bent head, which made Randal think of the sea and the story that was gradually awakening within him.

The dogs, realising that for a moment they need follow their master no further, flopped down on the hearth-rug and Moss laid his head against Sorella's knee.

She bent to pat him, and then her arms went round him, and being as sentimental as most spaniels, he shut his eyes as if in ecstasy and wriggled a little closer to her.

"Don't encourage him," Randal said, watching, "he always wants to be loved."

"And I have never had anything to love," Sorella said quietly.

She was not complaining or seeking sympathy. She was merely stating a fact.

"But, surely, there must have been someone. . ." Randal started to expostulate.

Then, thinking of what Sorella's life had been, felt how fruitless his words were.

"No, no one," Sorella replied. "You see, we never stayed very long anywhere. Once, when we were in Venice, the chef's cat had kittens and he gave me one. For three weeks it slept in my room and I looked after it. I shall always remember how happy I was because I had something of my very own to play with, something to love; and then we had to go away.

"The chef promised me he would keep it, but I knew he had too many already. I expect as soon as I was gone it was drowned."

Randal wanted to say something comforting, but he could find no words. To have been happy in Venice

156

because of the kitten, to have gone through all one's childhood without love!

He could see the pathos of all that without elaborating it further. It was not only that children want to be loved. They also want to give. Love for their Mothers, love for their Nannies, love for their playmates, for their homes and their animals, and even for their toys.

This is part of their growth and upbringing, an essential and very important factor in their development.

Sorella had had none of this.

"And yet I liked your father so much," Randal said.

He could not help himself; he felt that in some obscure way he must defend D'Arcy, whose death lay at his door.

"I know, nearly everybody liked him," Sorella replied, "and women always loved him—for a time, at any rate. I think I loved him when I was a baby, and I tried so hard to go on loving him; but, you see, to love somebody properly one has to admire them, one has to believe in them. I couldn't admire Daddy.

"He lied always, not always because it was necessary, but because he liked lying. He even liked pretending to dislike the life we led. I expect he told you that he couldn't get a job.

"That was quite untrue. He was a good actor when he wanted to act; but it was much too much trouble to go on making it his profession."

Randal threw his half-smoked cigarette into the fire.

"It was a damnable life for a child," he said.

"I'm not complaining," Sorella said. "Some children must have a far worse time. All I was saying was that I have always wanted something of my own to love, and there just hasn't been anyone or anything. Shall I tell you what I used to dream about at night?"

"Yes, do," Randal said.

"I used to dream that I had a home of my own and someone to love and someone to love me. There would always be a dog in it, and a cat, and horses—although I never had much chance to ride, I'd rather ride than do anything else in the world, and I would stay always in the house I imagined as my home. I would never go away from it, I would just stay there, making it beautiful for the people I loved."

"I suppose we all of us dream about a home," Randal said. "I've wanted one, too, but I didn't know how much until I saw Queen's Hoo."

"The moment you saw it you were sure?" Sorella asked.

"Absolutely."

"I felt like that, too, as we came in at the gate," Sorella said. "Queen's Hoo has a feeling of surety about it, hasn't it? You feel it has stayed here so long that it could never fail you or anyone else."

"That's exactly what I felt," Randal agreed.

He was silent for a moment, thinking of Queen's Hoo, of himself, of his new plot stirring deep down within him, and lastly of Sorella.

"Luncheon is served, Sir," the butler said from the door.

Followed by the dogs, they crossed the hall to the dining-room.

Looking back on the afternoon that followed, Randal could never quite remember what they had said or what they had done.

The day, which had started with sunshine, clouded over, a wet grey drizzle hiding the view from the windows.

It hadn't seemed to matter.

The flames from the big logs in the fireplace cast a golden glow on the ceiling as the afternoon drew on. The sitting-room looked warm and cosy. Sorella sat on the hearth-rug and played with the dogs, while Randal lay on the sofa and talked.

It was all very quiet and restful, and Randal was

soothed and rested as he hadn't been for a long time. He found himself talking about his early life.

He told Sorella about the house in Worcester to which her father had come so unexpectedly and changed the whole course of his life.

He told her about his Mother and how proud she had been belonging to a County family, and how once she had taken him out to see the old Manor house in which his grandparents had lived.

It had long been empty, and it had seemed to him only an ugly, dilapidated place, smelling dank and mouldy.

But to his Mother it had been her home, and now he owned Queen's Hoo. Randal felt he could understand better than he had ever understood before what a bleak house and overgrown garden had meant to her.

She had not seen the broken windows with the shutters swinging in the wind. She had not seen the peeling wallpaper, the piles of soot sprawled over the hearth, or the cobwebs joining the banisters together with a lace-like pattern of dirt.

She could picture the place as being full of life and laughter, echoing still with the voices of her family; a place where she had been happy and carefree.

That is what a home should mean, Randal said to himself, and remembered that Sorella had never had a home and could only remember hotels, an endless line of them, varying only in their size, each in its turn being as meaningless and as unimportant in her life as the last.

"Some day you'll have a home of your own," he said impulsively.

Sorella looked up at him.

Tweed's head cuddled against her breast, while Moss lay half in her lap, his tail thumping on the floor with pleasure at the touch of her fingers.

"I should like a home like this," she said.

"Oh, in a year or two you'll want a home much

159

bigger and better than this," Randal teased her. "This is only a small place. I love it because it's mine; but Jane's home is fifty times the size, and Diana's home—you haven't met her yet—is of the same period as Queen's Hoo, yet it's so big that it requires a complete army of retainers to keep it clean."

"I don't want a big house," Sorella protested, "and I don't want to be rich."

"You don't want to be rich!" Randal cried. "Not after you've been so poor! Why ever not?"

"Rich people seem to look at life in an entirely different way from ordinary people," Sorella said seriously. "I met a lot of rich people with Daddy. They were mostly women, but sometimes we met their friends, and they were rich, too.

"They all seemed so pleased with themselves because they had got money, and yet at the same time they seemed to know very little about life as it really is.

"They talked as though they were watching everyone else from behind a plate-glass window. The cold couldn't get at them, they couldn't quite hear everything properly.

"I can't explain what I mean. It's rather like watching a film. The things that affect the people on the screen can't really affect you.

"You feel sorry for them, you even feel pleased, because it is all part of the story; but when it's over you suddenly remember that none of it is real and there's no reason to upset yourself, whatever happens."

"I know exactly what you mean," Randal said, but absently.

In speaking of the screen, Sorella had reminded him of Lucille, and he wondered what she was doing now.

He supposed she would have gone to the matinée. She'd have found someone to take her. There was always a mass of hangers-on round Lucille.

Young men who paid her compliments and bought her flowers. Women who lionised her, and who flattered her to such an extent that Randal would feel vaguely disgusted, not only with them, but with Lucille for listening to their gush.

At the same time, whether she had an escort for the theatre or not, Lucille would be angry. He knew her well enough to know that.

He suddenly felt guilty. He had run away from both Lucille and Jane; and yet in doing so he might have jeopardised so much—the production of his play, Lord Rockampstead's money, the whole harmony between himself and Lucille that he had created so carefully and withal so calculatingly on the night he had taken her to dinner at the Savoy.

Randal sighed. For a moment he had forgotten Lucille.

Now the thought of her had come back to trouble him, to worry him, and to make him ask himself whether he would have been wiser to stay in London and keep Lucille happy, whatever the cost to himself.

And yet to escape, even for a short while, had been wonderful.

He could not remember when he had enjoyed a day more. It had been an inexpressible relief to be with Sorella.

She might be a child; but she was, in many ways, wiser and easier to talk to than any older women he knew, and what was more, she made no demands upon him.

If Lucille or Jane had been here, he would have had to make love to them.

He would have had to tell them, not once, but a thousand times, in a dozen ways, how much he loved them, how much they meant to him.

Sorella had just listened. She had talked when he wanted to talk, and if he sat silent as he was doing now, she was silent, too.

He looked at her. The room was nearly dark, but the light from the flames illuminated her.

She had seemed like an elf in her green dress, a fairy-like creature, as she stood against the brick wall with her hand on the wrought-iron gate; here in the firelight she was less elusive and more human.

Her lips were smiling as she looked down at the dogs in her lap.

Her eyes were downcast, and Randal could see how long and dark the lashes were as they swept against her cheeks. One day she would be lovely, he thought to himself.

It was under-nourishment which had made her seem ugly when he first met her in the south of France.

Now her cheeks were getting rounder, her elbows were no longer pointed, and the hollows at the base of her neck had filled out. Randal felt a sudden anger at the thought of what she had been through for so long.

It was intolerable that a child should have lived the life she had; and yet, in a way, he could understand D'Arcy Forest's selfishness. The life he had chosen had been an adventure for him.

He was not prepared to sacrifice adventure for any child, or for any woman for that matter.

Perhaps it wouldn't matter, eventually, Randal thought. Sorella would be the finer and the better for what she had suffered.

She would find happiness, and would value it because she had known for so long what it was to be lost and lonely.

He felt very protective towards her.

One thing he determined—that she should never again know poverty; at least he could see to that. And then he remembered that Sorella had no desire for money.

It was a home she wanted—a home and love; or at least, something or somebody to love.

"I shall try to give her that, too," Randal told himself, and instantly was besieged by a host of doubts and difficulties.

He thought of Jane. He saw again the look she had given Sorella, as she stood glittering in her diamonds with a cape of white ermine pulled around her shoulders.

Her furs might be soft, but she herself had been hard. Her eyes, too, had been as coldly bright as the diamonds she wore round her neck and in her hair.

No, Jane wasn't the person to help Sorella, Randal was sure of that.

"What are you thinking about?" he asked, surprisingly, because it was not what he had meant to say.

"I was thinking about you," Sorella stated simply.

Randal resisted the impulse to say that he had been thinking of her. It sounded too obviously like one of the answers he would have made to Jane or Lucille.

"What were you thinking?" he asked.

"I was thinking that you must have thought of your mother when you furnished this house," Sorella said.

Randal looked startled.

"How did you know that?" he asked. "I didn't say so."

"No, but you told me about her," Sorella answered, "and I was thinking that you must have loved her very much, more than you have ever loved anyone else."

Randal smiled.

"It sounds the right sort of sentiment," he said.

The mocking note which was so often in his voice had returned to it now.

"Actually I have loved a great many people in my life. It's difficult to know where one sort of love stops and another begins, or perhaps you don't know about such things?"

"I was thinking about your mother," Sorella persisted. "I think she must have wished a great many things for you, and now they are coming true—because she wished them for you. Do you understand what I am trying to say?"

Randal was ashamed then of the flippant manner in which he had spoken.

There was something in this child which stripped his pretences from him.

The cynicism he evoked when speaking of anything emotional or anything which should be held sacred was somehow out of place when he talked to Sorella.

"Of course I understand," he said quite humbly. "You're right, dead right. When I was decorating this house, I felt my mother was there, choosing many things for me, approving of what I had done."

"I was sure of that," Sorella said. "I felt her here, too."

For a moment Randal could not speak, but could only stare; and then, before any words could come to his lips, the door was opened, the lights were suddenly switched on.

"Miss Lucille Lund," the butler announced.

Blinking in the sudden light, it took Randal a moment to focus his eyes; then he saw Lucille standing in the doorway, looking exquisitely lovely and completely out of place.

She was glittering with jewellery; there were feathers in her hat; and there was a huge spray of purple orchids pinned to the collar of her mink coat.

"So this is where you're hiding, darling," she exclaimed.

Though her lips smiled, there was in her voice a hard, metallic tone which Randal recognised only too well.

With an effort he got slowly from the sofa to his feet.

Sorella also stood up, and for a moment the older woman's eyes rested on her with an expression which Randal translated all too easily.

Then Lucille's cheek was against his lips, and the warm, scented fragrance of her was pressed close to him.

"I knew I should give you a surprise, darling," she cooed. "Say you're glad to see me!"

9

For a moment Randal hated Lucille.

He felt his anger burning within him that she should have come here and forced herself upon him despite his desire to be left alone.

Then he remembered, all too swiftly, how important she was to him.

With the thought of the play and how everything depended on her good humour, his own anger sank ignominiously away and he forced a smile to his lips.

He hated himself then for his weakness and the feeling of helplessness which made it imperative that he should not annoy Lucille, and most of all because he must play the hypocrite.

He wanted at that moment to be strong, to tell Lucille to go back to London, to leave him alone.

He wanted to tell her, too, that he was engaged to Jane, that he had no intention of returning to her on the old basis of their life together.

Yet, even as such thoughts chased each other through his mind, he knew that all he would do would be to stand there, smiling and uttering some vague sentences of welcome.

He felt then that he would not have minded so much if he and Lucille had been alone.

But Sorella was there, and suddenly Randal could not bear to look into her clear, frank eyes and know that she must despise him.

He remembered what she had said about her father lying, and at the thought he felt infuriated with himself and also, quite unreasonably, with her.

"What the Hell am I to do?" he asked himself.

So much depended on Lucille, and to antagonise her now would be madness and theatrical suicide.

It was no use pretending that he didn't mind what happened to his play, he minded desperately.

He was not fool enough to think that it would not harm a young playwright if a world-famous star chucked up the main part at almost the last minute.

It would have been difficult enough to find someone to take Lucille's place earlier, but now it would be well-nigh impossible.

Well-known actresses would fight shy of a part which had been discarded after the play was in rehearsal; and though the critics had been kind to Randal up to date, he was well aware that there were many of them who would enjoy the chance to take down a peg or two a young man who swung so swiftly into fame.

Randal had an insane desire to turn round and challenge Sorella.

"Damn it all," he wanted to say to her, "what else can I do under the circumstances?"

Instead, he merely helped Lucille out of her fabulous mink coat, saying as he did so:

"What a wonderful surprise to see you. Come and sit down by the fire. You must be cold after your journey."

He threw the mink coat over a chair at the other end of the room, picked up a cigarette box and offered it to Lucille.

She took one and fitted it into her long onyx-and-diamond cigarette holder; and then, as Randal held a match to the tip, she raised her eyes provocatively to his.

"Are you really glad to see me?" she asked softly.

Randal knew the answer only too well to that sort of question, and yet once again he was embarassed by the knowledge that Sorella was listening to him.

The child had not sat down again after Lucille's entrance.

166

She was still on her feet, standing a little way from the hearth on which she had been sitting, her hand on Tweed's sleek head, the only movement she was making being with her fingers as she gently caressed the dog.

Randal felt as if her eyes drew his, and yet he still resisted the impulse to look at her.

Suddenly, with a perception that was unusual for her, Lucille became aware of the tension between the two people who had been talking so intimately when she entered the room.

She spoke again before Randal could answer her question.

"I haven't said hello to you yet, have I, Sorella?" she asked in a tone that was intolerably condescending. "I expect you're enjoying your visit to the country. Will you be a good girl and go and see that the chauffeur has brought in my suitcases?

"He is an extraordinarily dumb fellow. He'll sit outside indefinitely if someone doesn't tell him what to do."

"Your suitcases?" Randal echoed the word almost mechanically.

"Yes, of course, darling," Lucille said brightly. "Surely you don't expect me to drive back this evening? When I learnt where you were, I decided that I would throw over all my engagements and come down here to be with you. I couldn't bear think of your feeling ill and being all alone."

She spoke as though he were marooned on a desert island, and at any other time Randal might have seen the humour of it.

As it was, he felt singularly unamused.

He heard the door close behind Sorella. She had gone without a word to do as Lucille told her, and Randal felt now at least he could lie without the feeling that she was listening to him.

"As a matter of interest, how did you find out where I was?" Randal asked.

He walked across the room as he spoke and poured

167

himself a strong whisky-and-soda. He had drunk only lager at luncheon, but now he felt in need of a proper drink.

Lucille laughed.

"I've really been very clever," she said. "I've always fancied myself as a 'tec, or is it that I have read so many 'Whodunnit' stories?"

"I've no idea," Randal answered, in a somewhat bored voice. "Will you have a drink?"

"I wouldn't say no to a *crème de menthe*," Lucille answered.

It was a reply which always infuriated Randal. Why, he didn't know. It might be the fashion to say "I wouldn't say no", but to him it was a remark that invariably got under his skin, however much he tried to tell himself that he was only being pedantic.

He half-filled a liqueur glass with *crème de menthe* and carried it across to her.

"Thank you, darling." she smiled. Put it down on the little table, will you?"

He did as he was told and drew the table nearer to her.

"You were telling me how you discovered where I was," he said.

"It wasn't very difficult," Lucille replied. "When Hoppy refused to tell me and made such a fuss about your being on the verge of a breakdown and the doctor's orders and all that sort of stuff, I considered for some time where you were likely to go.

Then I remembered how much you had talked about your house in the country when you were last in America. You even rather bored me about it, so it was extremely annoying to find I had forgotten the name of the place.

"It was no use asking Hoppy, I knew that, and so, recalling what an important person you are these days, I spoke to the telephone operator in the hotel and asked her if she could find out the name of the famous Mr. Randal Gray's country seat."

"She couldn't have known it!" Randal exclaimed incredulously.

"Darling, she did! You under-estimate your importance. She said: 'Wait a minute, Miss Lund. I'm sure there was a photo of it in the *Tatler* only a few weeks ago. I'll ring down to the Hairdressing Salon and see if they've got the copy among their old magazines.' And of course they had."

Randal laughed then, although a little wryly.

"Such is fame! But weren't you taking rather a chance on coming here without making certain?"

"But I did make certain," Lucille laughed, delighted with herself. "I got my maid to ring your flat and say there was an important message coming from New York this evening, and at what number would Miss Hopkins like to take it?

"Poor old Hoppy fell for that one and she gave my maid a number. It wasn't very difficult to find out from Directory Enquiries that it tallied with your number here."

"You're too clever!" Randal said.

"I'm so pleased with my brilliance," Lucille boasted, "because Edward always tells me how impractical and inefficient I am."

"Did you tell Edward where you were going?" Randal enquired.

"Of course," Lucille replied, "and he's coming down for luncheon tomorrow."

"That will be lovely!" Randal spoke sarcastically.

After a moment he added.

"I suppose it never occurred to you that I might genuinely want to be alone?"

"We will be alone," Lucille replied with an air of surprise. "No one else is coming that I know of, except of course Hoppy, but you were expecting her anyway.

169

If you feel very badly about it, we can always put Edward off."

"I'm not referring specifically to Edward, as you well know," Randal retorted. "I wanted to be alone this weekend. I wanted to think."

"Well, you can think as much as you like," Lucille said quickly. "I shan't interrupt you; but as it happens, I want to talk to you."

"Couldn't it wait till Monday?" Randal enquired.

Lucille suddenly gave up being reasonable and stumped out her cigarette with angry fingers.

"What's the matter with you, Randal?" she enquired. "You never used to be like this."

"Like what?"

"Temperamental and ridiculous."

"It isn't being either to want to be alone, to steal a little time for creative work."

"You weren't doing much creative work when I arrived," Lucille snapped. "You were lying on the sofa chattering; and if you want to chatter, why not try it with someone of your own age?"

With a tremendous effort Randal kept his temper.

"This is being rather stupid, Lucille, and will certainly get us nowhere. You've come to stay, and of course I'm pleased to see you. The only thing is, I'm afraid you will find it very dull here."

"That depends on you, doesn't it?" Lucille asked; "and now, what about showing me your house? It looks a nice little place."

"It happens to be a perfect example of fifteenth-century architecture."

Randal couldn't prevent a bitter, satirical note creeping into his voice, but Lucille was unperturbed.

"Well, as an American I can't be expected to recognise the old dear on sight," she said. "You must take me round and explain all the most exciting points to me. You know I love antiques."

Randal said nothing for the moment.

He stood staring into the fire so that Lucille only had a view of his handsome profile silhouetted against the green walls of the room.

She looked at him for some seconds, and then with a jingle of her charm bracelets her hand went out towards him.

"Randal, darling," she called.

He turned then, slowly and a little reluctantly.

"Darling, I love you," she coaxed. "Stop being cross with me, and tell me that you haven't forgotten how much we mean to each other."

Randal took her hand and raised it automatically to his lips.

"That's better," Lucille said approvingly. "Now come and sit down beside me and tell me what is troubling you. There must be something."

Randal wished he could tell her the truth; but even as he saw how easy it would be with this opening to speak of Jane, he was aware that he dare not do so. He knew Lucille's moods only too well.

At the moment she was being ingratiating. It was the way she had of getting a man into her clutches.

Once she was sure of him, once she had him again in her power, she would no longer check or curb her temper.

She would give it a free rein and make him and everyone else with whom she came in contact suffer because for the moment she had had to humiliate herself and seek a favour rather than bestow one.

All through their acquaintance Lucille had been liable to create a scene and become intensely and passionately dramatic unless she got her own way the moment she wanted it.

It was only when Randal had the complete upper hand that she remained sweetly and gently submissive.

When he had first known Lucille, her moods had not mattered to him so far as his film was concerned. The production was entirely out of hands.

It had been bought outright by the studio and he had no further say in it.

He had stayed for a short while in Hollywood simply because it pleased him to do so, but he was free to return the moment he was bored.

He had never seen Lucille in one of her tantrums then. It was the next year, when he was writing the dialogue of his next film, that she began to be difficult.

By that time Lucille was crazily in love with him, and though he saw her rage vented on other people, it was seldom that he felt personally even the faintest breath of her anger.

But he saw the consternation and trouble she could cause in the studio; and while he was often called upon by Edward Jepson as being the one person who could soothe and placate Lucille, he did his best to avoid her when things were not running smoothly.

Now for the first time Lucille could hold a weapon over his head.

She was well aware of her own power; and Randal, after watching her work herself up into a crescendo of fury at the rehearsal, had known for the first time in his life what it was like to be frightened of a woman.

He would not admit it to himself, even, and yet he was afraid.

Afraid, not only of what Lucille could do to him publicly and to his play, but also because she was swiftly, and with what seemed to him a complete thoroughness, destroying something beautiful, something lovely and charming, which had once been an intrinsic part of their relationship.

He had made one of his characters in a play say that a woman should always bring into a man's life "something that was lovely," and fill something that had been "empty before her coming."

Lucille had inspired that idea.

She had been so very lovely, and he had admired

172

her beauty and treasured it because beauty, wherever one found it, was so extraordinarily precious.

She had, too, meant something different in his life from all the other women before her.

She had been so glamorous that it had seemed to him that she had some of those things which he had been seeking all his life.

In fact, the whole enigma of femininity had been personified in Lucille's glamour and exotic seductiveness.

She had always managed to be beautiful, Randal thought, whatever she did, whatever she said.

The grace of her movements, the lovely lines and curves of her body, thrilled him anew every time he watched her.

He believed that, even when they were tired of each other, he would still want to go on looking at her, even as one might want to go on looking for ever at a beautiful picture or a statue fashioned by a master sculptor.

Lucille was destroying that feeling when she raged and stormed and her voice rose in the high crescendo of anger.

Then she broke the spell of her loveliness. She could also, Randal found, be irritating and persistent.

This was a Lucille he had never known or else, he asked himself in all sincerity, had he changed?

Was he no longer enraptured, and therefore able to see things as they were rather than as he had wanted them to be?

As he sat down on the sofa, he tried to remember that Lucille was a lovely woman whom once he had loved very much, and that she was at the moment desperately important to him.

Because of that importance he must placate her, however hard it might go against the grain of his own feelings.

And then, even as he thought this, he was furious

173

that everything was changed, that he had lost what once had seemed so precious. Lucille was still lovely.

Her fair hair framed by her hat of blue feathers was like living gold.

He noted the lovely lines of her face, the tiny, tip-tilted perfection of her nose and the curve of her perfectly-shaped mouth, which was thrilling no doubt at this very moment billions of film-goers as they sat watching her impersonate on the screen all they longed to be in their own drab lives.

Lucille's fingers still clung to his.

Her nails, very long and lacquered a bright scarlet, made them like the ridiculous but exquisite little fingers of a Chinese maiden.

Yet, Randal knew, they were strong and tenacious, practical, and in many ways greedy. Lucille was no weakling.

It was difficult to remember, when one saw her, so fragile, so ethereal in her pale beauty, so warm and soft when one held her in one's arms, that when her passion was aroused she was rapacious and insatiable.

Once Randal had told her she was like a tiger, and because the description had amused her, Lucille had bought him a little gold charm which she had fixed to his watch-chain.

He wore it still, a tiger, its stripes made of different coloured golds.

Now, as she held on to him, he remembered that he had likened her to the tiger because he had felt she would eventually devour that which she loved.

Randal knew then that he could not tell her about Jane, not now at any rate; in fact, he dared not even hint at it.

Lucille held him in her power; and because he loathed himself for the coward he was, he could not sit beside her and play the part he knew she wanted of him.

"It's time we had tea," he said abruptly. "I can't think why it's so late."

"It was ready when I arrived," Lucille told him. "Your butler was so astonished to see me walk in that he almost dropped the tray."

"I expect Lambert has put it in the Morning Room," Randal said. "We have it there sometimes. Shall we move there?"

Lucille laughed a little softly.

"So you don't want to talk to me at this moment!"

"I haven't said so," Randal replied.

"Darling, it's so obvious. You're very transparent. I suppose all men are, but I always imagined you were different."

He knew she was deliberately teasing him and refused to be drawn.

"Come and have some tea," he invited.

"It's nearly six o'clock," Lucille replied. "You can't want tea now."

"I'm English and I want tea at any time."

"Even after whisky-and-soda?"

Randal gave up. He knew that Lucille had made up her mind to talk to him, and it was hopeless to try to go against her wishes.

With what was an ill grace, he sat down again on the sofa.

"Very well," he capitulated. "Let us talk, if that's what you want."

To his surprise, Lucille said nothing for a moment. She turned a huge diamond ring on her finger, contemplating its sparkle as though it were a crystal which could foretell the future.

"Well?" Randal prompted at length, as she did not speak.

"No, darling," she said slowly. "You're right. This isn't the time or the place for what I have to talk about. Go and have your tea, if you want it so much."

175

"Let me hear the worst, whatever it is," Randal requested. "I want to get it over."

Lucille laughed.

"Now you're being ridiculous. Go and find out about your tea. Perhaps after a meal, even one which is as insipid as English tea, you will be more amenable."

"Come with me," Randal suggested.

"If I can bring my *crème de menthe*," Lucille replied.

Holding the glass in her hand, she walked slowly across the wide hall with its big stone mantelpiece and twisted oak stairs ascending out of sight and entered what Randal called the Morning Room.

It was a small, oak-panelled room where he often wrote.

There was a big, gate-legged table in a bay window and set on this were the silver tea things and plates piled with sandwiches, scones and small iced cakes.

The tea was nearly cold; Randal rang the bell before he seated himself in one of the high tapestry-covered chairs which had been drawn up to the table.

"I must say everything looks delicious," Lucille exclaimed. "I'll try a sandwich, although, as you know, I never eat bread."

"I don't suppose one will put on much weight," Randal said.

They were talking for the sake of talking, he thought; and again a feeling of irritation swept over him that Lucille should have come to Queen's Hoo and spoilt the peace of his week-end.

"You rang, Sir?" Lambert stood at his side.

"Yes, Lambert, bring me some fresh tea, will you? I didn't know it was ready or we'd have come in before."

"It's been ready a long time, Sir, but the young lady—Miss Sorella—told me you didn't wish to be disturbed."

"Oh! I see."

Lucille laughed.

"What a tactful child!"

"I wonder why she said that?" Randal said. "It's very unlike Sorella."

"Tell me about her," Lucille requested. "I have seen her in the theatre, and Hoppy told me that you were looking after her for the time being. What are you going to do with her?"

"I haven't really thought," Randal replied.

"You'd better put her on the stage," Lucille said, "and you can write a nice little part for her in your next play; and then she'll have a chance that most girls would give their eyes for."

"I can't imagine Sorella on the stage," Randal answered.

It was true, he thought to himself. He couldn't imagine Sorella acting a part; she was so essentially an individual herself that one could not conceive her being anyone but Sorella.

He wondered where she was now.

Upstairs in her room, he supposed, and again he felt irritated with Lucille. Why should Sorella be banished just because she had arrived?

As if Lucille sensed what he was thinking, she said:

"I rather like the child. Most girls of that age don't have the gumption to run away when they aren't wanted."

"Isn't she wanted?" Randal enquired, almost brutally.

"Not by me, at any rate," Lucille replied. "I wanted to be alone with you. That, as you know, is why I've come here."

It was an hour later when Randal climbed to the top of the house and opening the door of Hoppy's little attic suite, shouted her name in a voice of thunder.

"I'm here," Hoppy called from the sitting-room.

Randal burst open the door.

Hoppy was, as he expected, sitting at her desk. He seldom came upon her in any other attitude. Sorella was in a big armchair by the fireplace, the spaniels at her feet, and a book open on her knee.

"When did you arrive?" Randal asked Hoppy.

"About twenty minutes ago," Hoppy replied. "I was coming down to see you, but I was just typing out some messages that came before I left London."

"I like to be told the moment you arrive," Randal said crossly, "and why did you disappear, Sorella?"

"I thought Lucille wanted to talk to you."

"You might have wondered whether I wanted to talk to her," Randal retorted. "You are my guest, and there is no reason for you to sit up here with Hoppy, whoever asks themselves to stay."

"How could she have found out where you'd gone?" Hoppy asked. "I could hardly believe my ears when Sorella told me she was here."

"It was your fault," Randal answered.

He explained how Lucille had tricked her into giving away the telephone number.

"Really!" Hoppy expostulated. "I've never heard anything so underhand in the whole of my life. Better not ask me downstairs or I shall give Miss Lucille Lund a piece of my mind, I promise you that."

"You're coming down all the same," Randal said authoritatively.

"Do you mean to dinner?" Hoppy asked in dismay.

"I do," Randal replied. "Both you and Sorella; and let us make this clear: I don't want to be left alone with Lucille or with anyone else. I don't want the servants told I'm not to be disturbed. I want everyone to behave normally, as if they were staying in a normal, ordinary house. Now do you understand?"

"I'm sorry, Randal," Sorella said, "but I met Lambert just as I was coming out of the sitting-room, and as Lucille was so anxious to get rid of me, I thought it would make her angry if Lambert came in with the tea. That was why he put it in the Morning Room."

"What does it matter if she is angry?" Randal's question sounded weak even as he said it.

"It matters a great deal, we all know that," Hoppy said briskly. "I was having a talk with Bruce Bellingham this afternoon about Lucille and he was saying how

178

impossible she is at times, and yet he had to speak highly of her capabilities as an actress. We dare not lose her. If she leaves the cast now, it would be catastrophic."

"But why should she leave the cast?" Randal asked. "Who ever suggested such a thing?"

"Apparently Edward Jepson warned Bruce that Lucille was threatening to go back to America, but it was only because he thought she was annoyed about something you had said or done.

"At the same time, Edward told Bruce that at times she behaved in such an unaccountable manner that even he could not restrain her."

Randal met Sorella's eyes; and then he sat down in a chair on the opposite side of the fireplace and put his hands up to his forehead.

"My God!" he moaned. "Was there ever such a mess?"

Both Hoppy and Sorella knew what he meant, and yet neither could find any words with which to console him. Hoppy left her typewriter and came to join the other two round the fire.

"I didn't realise," she said quietly, "how serious things were until I talked to Bruce today. It struck me that he was rather frightened of Lucille, or else he's afraid of having a failure."

"It's the biggest production Bruce has done so far," Randal answered. "He's mad keen to make a success of it."

"Aren't we all?" Hoppy asked drily. "Well, it's up to you, Randal."

"Do you suppose I don't realise that?" Randal replied. "The point is I'm not quite certain what Lucille is getting at. She keeps saying she wants to talk to me; and yet, when it comes to the point, she doesn't tell me anything."

"What on earth can it be?" Hoppy exclaimed. "You don't think she means to tell you she's going back to America?"

179

"No, I don't think it's that," Randal said. "Well, I shall find out tonight, but I can't stand a *tête-à-tête* dinner. You'll have to come down and talk, and for Heaven's sake try to be cheerful, even though we know our heads are all waiting for the guillotine."

Then Sorella spoke.

"I don't think Lucille means to go back to America," she said. "I don't think she means to give up her part in *Today and Tomorrow* whatever happens. It's just that she's using it as a threat for something she wants to get out of Randal."

"Maybe you're right," Hoppy ejaculated. "Lucille wouldn't have come over here if she hadn't meant to make a success of it. What can she want that you haven't given her, Randal?"

"I haven't the slightest idea," Randal replied. "I thought she might perhaps be jealous of Jane, but she hasn't mentioned her this evening."

"Jane!" Hoppy ejaculated the word so that Randal looked at her in surprise.

"What about her?" he asked.

Hoppy looked uncomfortable.

"I've done something awful."

"What is it?"

"I told Jane that she could come down to lunch tomorrow. I couldn't help it, I couldn't really, Randal. She guessed where you'd gone and she said that she quite understood your wanting to be alone, but that you'd have had enough solitude by Sunday lunch time and that she would motor down about one o'clock."

"She's going to believe in that solitude when she finds Lucille here, isn't she?" Randal asked.

"Oh, Randal! I'm sorry, but it was so difficult to refuse. She was so nice about your not going with her today and not going to the party tonight that it didn't seem terrible to let her come to lunch. It was no use my pretending you hadn't come here, when you had."

"And also, you wanted her to come," Randal said. "All right, Hoppy, I know exactly how your mind

180

works; and now having got me into this mess, you can just get me out of it, because I give up."

"But what can we say, what can we do?" Hoppy asked, almost in tears.

"I should tell her the truth," Sorella suggested.

Both Randal and Hoppy looked at her.

"The truth?" Hoppy queried.

"Yes," Sorella said. "She will find out anyway, someone will tell her. Lucille, I expect. But if you tell her, she won't mind. Ring her up now, and say that Lucille has come here uninvited, and that there is nothing you can do about it. After all, she knows how important it is that Lucille should play in *Today and Tomorrow*."

"Sorella's right," Hoppy exclaimed.

"Well, I'm not going to speak to Jane," Randal announced. "I'm tired of all this intrigue. I'm fed up with the whole thing. It seems to me ridiculous that a man can't go away quietly to his own home without having half the women in London bursting in on him with one excuse or another."

"You shouldn't be so devastatingly attractive," Hoppy retorted.

It was the first time for ages that Randal had known her snap at him.

But she looked so funny when she was disagreeable that his own ill-humour vanished and he began to laugh.

Then quite suddenly they were all laughing, Randal, Hoppy and Sorella, laughing till the tears ran down Hoppy's face and she had to mop them away with a handkerchief.

"It's all so damned ridiculous," Randal chuckled. "If I put it in a play, no one would believe it for a moment."

"You only want them both to have husbands to turn it into a French farce," Hoppy giggled.

"One thing I'm determined about," Randal said, as he stopped laughing. "I'm not going to be the only man here. Ring up Edward Jepson and tell him he's to come down at once. You'll find him at the Savoy. He is to stay the night, of course."

"There's no room in the garage for any more cars," Hoppy said practically.

"Then Edward's can stand outside," Randal replied. "That's a minor detail. I want Edward here and he's jolly well got to come. After all, Lucille is his responsibility, not mine."

"I wonder if Lucille would agree to that," Hoppy remarked, as she went towards the telephone.

As she put through the call, Randal looked across at Sorella.

"Do I shock you?" he asked.

She smiled at that.

"You made me feel rather ashamed of myself," he went on. "I'm not really a liar and a philanderer."

Then, as he said the words, he wondered why he should bother to excuse himself to a child of fifteen, a child, moreover, who had been brought up in such a manner as to make her the very last person who should criticise; and yet, as still Sorella did not speak, Randal found himself plunging into further explanations.

"It's one of those things that seem to get worse instead of better," he said.

Hoppy was through to Edward Jepson and it was impossible for Randal to say any more.

"You will come then?" Hoppy was saying. ". . . That's splendid of you. . . . Yes, be as quick as you can. I'll put dinner back to nine o'clock. . . . You'll be here long before that? . . . Thank you, we'll see you then. . . . *Au revoir.*"

Hoppy put down the receiver.

"He's coming," she announced unnecessarily.

"Well, that's one thing," Randal conceded. He got to his feet. "I'm going to go and lie in my bath for a long time. If anyone wants to see me, I'm *not* to be disturbed."

182

"What about Jane?" Sorella questioned.

"Oh, Hoppy can talk to her," Randal replied.

"Let me get through and explain and then just have a word with her yourself," Hoppy suggested. "It won't take you a moment."

"I refuse!" Randal said positively. "If anyone bullies or nags me any further I shall go to bed and sulk. I've had enough to put up with to last me a lifetime, and tomorrow is going to be Hell. You know it is.

We had better go back to London at tea time. The sooner we start work again the better. In fact, I might just as well have worked all today for all the rest coming here has brought me."

Randal spoke like a petulant, spoiled child; and then Sorella's voice reached him, very quiet and low.

"But I'm glad we did come. We had the morning and the afternoon without anyone."

The sense of peace that had been his before Lucille's arrival came back to Randal's mind. He remembered, too, that Sorella had given him the basis of a new story.

"Yes, I'm glad we came," he agreed. "We had a few hours at any rate, didn't we?"

He looked across at her as she sat curled up in the armchair.

She was so tiny, and yet she seemed at that moment to have a strength that he had not realised before. A strength, or was it resilience?

At any rate it was the power to keep at bay his worries and irritations, to soothe him and bring him a peace which no one else could give him.

"Come down to dinner," he said, "and if anyone tells you to go away, you are to be deaf. I want you there, do you understand?"

Hoppy looked at Randal in astonishment, his voice was so serious.

"Sorella doesn't want to stay up so late," she said, looking from one to the other in perplexity. "She's got to get her beauty sleep, even if nobody else wants any."

Neither Randal nor Sorella seemed to hear her. They were looking at each other.

Then after a moment Randal went from the room, shutting the door sharply behind him.

Sorella made no attempt to move; she merely sat staring at the closed door with an expression on her face which told Hoppy nothing.

"Oh dear, you've got nothing to wear," Hoppy cried. "We ought to have bought that silk dress we couldn't make up our minds about. Lucille will be in tulle and sequins, if I know anything of her wardrobe, and you've got nothing to change into but your other wool dress."

"It doesn't matter," Sorella answered in a far-away voice. "It doesn't matter at all. . . ."

10

Randal took Edward Jepson off to look at the old stables, leaving Jane and Lucille eyeing each other warily like a pair of fighting cocks.

Sorella had slipped away immediately luncheon was finished. No one in fact noticed her go, until Randal, looking round enquiringly, asked for her, and Lambert, bringing in the coffee, remarked that he had seen Miss Sorella going down the garden some minutes earlier.

"She has the most extraordinary way of disappearing," Randal said to no one in particular.

But it appeared that no one was particularly interested in his remark, for it remained unanswered.

As soon as the two women were alone, Lucille picked up an onyx cigarette box and held it out towards Jane.

"A cigarette?" she asked.

Jane recognised the gesture as a subtle act of hostility. Lucille had contrived from the moment of her arrival to make it appear that she was acting the part of hostess in Randal's house.

It was cleverly done, and a less interested person might have thought Lucille was unconscious of being aggressive, but Jane was not deceived and refused the cigarettes, with a faint air of amusement, saying:

"No, thank you. Randal always keeps my own special brand in the drawer of his desk, but I don't want one at the moment."

"You come here often, then?"

The question was almost involuntary, but Lucille felt she had to know.

"Yes, I spend most week-ends here," Jane answered untruthfully, "unless Randal comes to my father's house—Bletchingly Castle. It's rather a show place, you must come and see it sometime."

Lucille knew that the invitation to Bletchingly Castle would never be less vague as far as she was concerned, but she played Jane's game of being charming and replied with childlike eagerness:

"How sweet of you to ask me! I should love to come, of course. I must persuade Randal to fix a date for us both."

Jane leaned back in her chair and crossed her legs.

There was an air of complacency and self-satisfaction about her which made Lucille long to throw anything that was in reach.

She hated Jane with a hatred which seemed to increase every minute they were in each other's company, and her antipathy was not diminished by the knowledge that Jane was far better and more suitably dressed than she was.

Jane had arrived for luncheon wearing a tweed coat and skirt, the well-cut lines and clever severity of which were in admirable contrast to Lucille's over-elaborate wool dress and fur-trimmed cape.

Lucille was far too much of a showman not to realise when she was out-classed, and her feelings for Jane were all the more bitter because, from a feminine point

185

of view at least, Jane was at the moment definitely up on points.

But Jane was not so confident of her advantage as Lucille believed. Looking at Lucille as she sat on the sofa, the pale gold of her hair touched by the afternoon sunshine, Jane felt a sudden fear within her own heart.

It was almost impossible to believe any man could look at Lucille and not fall in love with her.

She was well aware that Randal had been, if not really in love, very infatuated with Lucille before they met.

What she was wondering now was whether his feelings for her had completely ousted Lucille from her former position in his affections.

Was it possible that anyone could grow bored with a woman so exquisite and so attractive as Lucille?

Most film stars were disappointing in the flesh. Lucille exceeded her Press agents' most glowing descriptions, and was infinitely more lovely in reality than Technicolor's most luscious projection of her.

Until Lucille arrived in England, Jane had been very sure of herself.

She was astute enough to realise that she had a great deal to offer Randal; although she knew that such things would be of no consequence to him unless his heart was engaged also.

She had believed that she had captured and captivated him too completely for there to be any necessity for her to be jealous or afraid of another woman.

Now, looking at Lucille, she was not sure.

It was one thing to watch her on the films across the footlights; quite another to see her only a few feet away and to be shocked into the realisation that her beauty was practically flawless.

Jane had spent a great deal of time grooming herself into the elegance that she knew better than most people was one of her most valuable assets, but she was well aware that she would never be beautiful in the same sense as Lucille was beautiful.

Through years of careful training and by spending exorbitant sums of money, Jane had managed to get herself spoken of as a very lovely person, and she knew that the adjective was not entirely undeserved.

She was lovely in her own way and she used her clothes-sense as cleverly as another woman might use her eyes, her hair or her lips to enchant and enchain a man.

Stretching out one hand now to shield the heat of the fire from her face, she made the gesture one of almost supreme elegance, and knew, with a sense of delight, that Lucille was annoyed.

The film star, brilliant actress though she might be, was not clever enough to hide her feelings where Jane was concerned.

She had never been very fond of her own sex, and it was always easier for a woman to get under her skin than for a man.

Now she felt that Jane personified every feminine slight she had ever received, every criticism, every unkindness which had ever been accorded her since she first became a star and knew the strength of her own beauty.

Swiftly she turned over in her mind how best to attack Jane.

How to make her lose her air of complacency and self-satisfaction, how to convey to her without actually saying it in words that Randal would never belong to her however hard she might try to capture him?

Jane gave Lucille the opening she waiting for.

"How long do you expect to stay in England?" she asked.

Lucille smiled enigmatically.

"That, of course, depends on Randal."

Jane raised her eyebrows.

"On Randal?" she queried. "You mean that you will stay in the play for as long as he wants you?"

"Actually I wasn't thinking of the play," Lucille replied.

187

There was a moment's silence; then Jane, whose expression had not changed from one of polite interest, asked:

"Are you suggesting that Randal is making other plans for you?"

"I don't quite know what you mean by that," Lucille replied. "As I have already told you, my stay in England depends on Randal; he might want me to stay on here or he might wish to come back with me to America."

She looked straight at Jane as she spoke. She had thrown down the gauntlet irretrievably.

"How interesting."

Jane's reply was concise but quite expressionless.

Then she rose to her feet. She walked across the room, and back again before stopping near Lucille.

She looked down at the world-famous film star seated on the sofa and said:

"I'm going to tell you a secret. I know I can trust you to let it go no further. Randal and I are engaged."

After a moment's silence Lucille laughed a little rudely.

"Does Randal know?"

"I suppose that is meant to be impertinent," Jane replied. "I'm sorry if it's a shock to you, but it happens to be the truth."

"I think you are making a very big mistake," Lucille said slowly and deliberately.

"In what way?"

Jane's question sounded cool and indifferent, but her eyes betrayed how tense she was.

"In assuming that Randal intends to marry you."

"I'm not assuming anything of the sort," Jane answered quietly.

For the first time she sounded angry.

"Randal and I are engaged, and we shall announce it to the public after the opening of *Today and Tomorrow*."

"I wonder."

188

Lucille also rose to her feet.

She was smaller than Jane and far more fragile in appearance; and yet, as the two women faced each other, it was obvious that she was immeasurably the stronger.

Her anger seemed almost to vibrate from her as though she was emitting sparks.

"Do you really think that I would let you marry Randal?" she asked.

"Does he have to ask your permission?" Jane enquired.

"Yes, he does," Lucille replied.

The words were snapped at Jane, and then suddenly she lost control of herself.

"You think you've been very clever," she said; "we'll see. What do you know about Randal in the short time you've known him? What do you know about any man for that matter?"

You are nothing more or less than a dressed-up doll. You haven't the experience or the cleverness to hold a man like Randal; and what's more, you won't get the opportunity—I shall see to that.

"Now run and tell him I've been unkind to you and see what he says; see whom he tries to comfort, you or me. I'm not afraid of you and you will soon learn the reason why.

Marry Randal indeed! Why, I've never heard anything so ridiculous in the whole of my life!"

Almost spitting in her rage Lucille sped across the room and made her exit with a slam of the door which seemed to reverberate through the house.

Jane was left staring after her. She had gone rather pale, she was conscious that her heart was thumping rather uncomfortably.

She longed to run after Lucille, to hurl abuse at her, to tell her what she thought of her; but her upbringing and training prevented that, and she could only stand shaking with anger, her hand trembling as she reached for a handkerchief.

She heard another door slam upstairs and knew that Lucille had gone to her bedroom.

It was then that she glanced out through the open door into the garden to see Randal and Edward Jepson approaching the house.

They were both smoking the big cigars they had lit after luncheon and the sound of their level voices seemed to Jane warm and comforting.

Undramatic, sane and sensible, it was a relief to see them after the tempestuous vituperation of Lucille.

Then suddenly Jane remembered what she had done.

She had betrayed Randal's instructions that no one was to know of their engagement, she had jeopardized the success of Randal's new play for which her father had put up an immense sum of money.

What was more, she had no excuse for her indiscretion, save that Lucille had taunted her until, as uncontrolled in her own way as Lucille was in hers, she had said the one thing she knew would hurt and wound the other woman.

For the first time for many years Jane felt apprehensive. She was usually as self-assured as she appeared; but now she felt afraid, not only of Randal, but of Edward Jepson.

The anger that she had felt in the heat of battle with Lucille was beginning to ebb away.

She knew now that all the time she had been talking she had hated Lucille with an intensity that was bitter, fiery and quite unlike anything she had ever experienced before.

She had admitted to herself a long while ago that she was jealous of Lucille, but she had never expected to feel this burning frenzy where another woman was concerned.

Edward and Randal drew nearer until, bending their heads because the door into the garden was low and they were both tall men, they came into the sitting-room.

"Aren't you coming out?" Randal asked. "It's really turned out extremely nice this afternoon."

"Where's Lucille?" Edward Jepson asked.

It was a question he had been asking ever since he had made Lucille a star and had taken upon himself the management and direction of her life.

Aged fifty-five, he looked older, for his hair was white at the temples and bald on top.

The hours he spent working but without getting any physical exercise had given him a rotund stomach and the pale, unhealthy complexion of someone who spends far too much time in close atmospheres.

It was true that Edward had once been a cowboy, but that was many, many years ago, and what he looked like now was a benign family grocer.

He was, in fact, an extremely astute, shrewd-headed business man; but he had acquired, through years of working with theatrical people, a genial, extravagant charm which made it difficult to realise just how keenly and quickly his brain was working while he mouthed endearing compliments to pretty women.

Randal liked him, even while he admitted to Hoppy that after being friendly with Edward for some years he knew as little about him as he had at the first moment of their acquaintance.

Hoppy said quite frankly she was frightened of him.

"He has a cold look in his eyes," she said, and Randal knew what she meant.

Edward might be able to say pretty things and to force to his lips a smile which was an effective disguise for ninety per cent of his feelings, but his eyes revealed his true character.

They were shrewd and penetrating, and those who wished to put something over found it almost impossible while Edward Jepson was watching them.

"Where's Lucille?" Edward asked now.

Jane found herself answering him and not looking at Randal.

"She has gone upstairs."

There was a pause. Jane hesitated and added.

"I'm afraid I've upset her."

Edward raised his eyebrows.

"Upset Lucille?" Randal repeated. "What on earth for? What has happened?"

Again Jane hesitated; then with an effort which was a credit to her pride rather than to her honesty, she answered:

"I told her our secret, Randal."

"What secret?" Randal asked sharply.

"That we're engaged," Jane said bravely.

Randal might have appreciated her courage if he had not been so astonished.

"You told her that? What on earth made you do such a thing?"

He heard Edward give a low whistle and turned to him with an air of exasperation which made Jane feel like a child who had been caught out in an act of senseless and quite unwarrantable destruction.

"What the devil do we do about this?"

"Search me."

Edward thrust his hands deep into his trouser pockets and jingled his money.

It was a habit he had when disturbed, and everyone in the theatre world knew the jingle-jangle of his coins.

"I'm sorry, Randal," Jane said almost humbly, "but Lucille was inferring that you and she were . . . well, that you were planning things together. I didn't mean to upset her, or you for that matter, but some things are too intolerable to be borne."

"Well, really, Jane, it seems rather a stupid thing to do at this moment when you know as well as anybody else the trouble we have had with Lucille at rehearsals."

"I'm afraid I know very little about your trouble with Lucille," Jane retorted; "and if what she was inferring was true, I want to hear less."

"Oh my God!"

Randal chucked his cigar into the fire and walked towards the window.

"Why must women quarrel?" he enquired with his back to Jane and Edward. "It's always the same, all this scratching and back-biting each other so that nothing gets done, except with rows, attacks of temperament and crises one after another."

"I don't think that's fair," Jane cried. "I'm not in the habit of quarrelling with anyone, as you know quite well; but as we are engaged, you can hardly expect me to stand by while another woman tells me that you belong to her."

"I really can't see that it matters," Randal said, turning to look at her; "you know it isn't true."

"Do I?" Jane asked quickly.

"The point is—what do we do now?" Randal went on, ignoring her question.

"Do you think Lucille will throw up her part?" he asked Edward.

Still jingling his money, Edward replied:

"I don't know what to think. The best thing to do is for one of us to go and find out. Are you going to talk to her, or shall I?"

"You go," Randal said quickly. "Tell her that I want to see her, that there is no need for her to be upset, that I can explain everything."

"Sure, I'll tell her that. You had better think up some real dandy explanations. You'll need them."

Whistling under his breath and jingling his money, Edward went from the room. Randal stood looking after him, a frown between his eyes.

As he said nothing, Jane spoke first:

"I'm sorry, Randal."

"What on earth possessed you to do such a damned silly thing?" he asked. "Besides, you had promised not to tell anyone."

"She made me so furious," Jane said, "and after all, what does it matter, she has got to know sooner or later."

"I suppose so, but if she throws up the play, God knows whom we are going to get to play her part."

"That appears to be all you think about," Jane said icily.

"You can hardly expect me to jump for joy when you've bitched up the whole thing. I've spent most of the week-end soothing Lucille down and then you have to go and make things completely chaotic again. I don't know what we're going to do if she packs her boxes and goes back to America."

"There are other actresses."

"You find one with the draw that Lucille has, or the ability to play the part."

Randal spoke angrily and Jane felt her own temper rising.

"If Lucille is so important to you," she said, "there's quite an easy way out of the situation."

"What's that?" Randal enquired.

"Can't you guess?" Jane enquired. "If there is no engagement between us, she can hardly be upset about it. In the words of the cheap novelettes, I can give you back your freedom, and that after all appears to be what you want."

"Now, Jane, really," Randal began, and then he stopped. "It's a good idea. Why didn't I think of it before? We can tell Lucille there is no engagement, and she will be perfectly happy and content, and everything can be as it was before."

Jane clenched her fingers together.

"So that is what you want."

Her face, rather than her words, barely spoken above her breath, made Randal realise what he had said.

"Now, Jane, don't be silly," he said. "Darling, you know perfectly well that this is only an act. You've got us into this mess, and now you've got to try to get us out of it.

"You know as well as I do what Lucille is like— temperamental, emotional, unstable, and every other adjective you may like to add to the list. But she's a big name, she's a good actress and *Today and Tomorrow* will be ruined without her.

"It's your father's money at stake and my reputation. Let us get the Opening Night over, let us get the play established, and then we can announce our engagement—in fireworks if you like, I don't care."

Jane turned towards the fire and stood staring down into the flames. Randal could not see her face, but he guessed the indecision within her mind.

He tried, for one moment, to put his own problems on one side and remember what Jane was feeling.

For the first time she appeared to him to be rather forlorn, a person who needed comforting, rather than someone riding on the crest of the wave, someone completely and utterly successful who needed no support or succour from him.

He felt almost sorry for her, and putting an arm round her shoulders, he drew her to him.

"I'm sorry, Jane," he said softly, "this is horrible and uncomfortable for you, but do try to understand that Lucille is not like ordinary people."

"I don't see why she should be treated differently from everyone else!"

Jane spoke petulantly.

"Nor do I," Randal agreed. "and yet we've got to do it. If she walks out on us now, I simply cannot face your father. But apart from that, the Press will be after me like a pack of hounds.

"Think of the scandal it will cause; and if we postpone, there are all those people to be thrown out of work, many of whom will find it hard to get another job at a moment's notice. Most of the winter productions are already in rehearsal."

"Yes, yes, I see it all," Jane said. "But can I bear to be humiliated by a woman like that? She will be so damnably cock-a-hoop at having got you back again."

Randal took his arm from Jane's shoulders.

"Very well," he said, "we'll go through with it."

"No, of course not," Jane answered generously. "You

195

can go and tell her that the engagement is broken off. I will go back to London, and I'll try to keep out of the way until after the first night."

"Will you really do that?" Randal asked. "Jane, you're marvellous."

He took her hands and raised them to his lips.

Then suddenly her arms were round his neck and her face was raised to his.

"But, darling, you do love me? Tell me you do, because, Randal, I can't live without you. I love you . . . I love you so terribly."

"Oh, Jane, my poor Jane, what a brute I am to you!" Randal muttered.

He held her close, compunction sweeping over him in a kind of flood tide.

"I love you," Jane repeated; and then, as her lips waited invitingly very near to his, she said, "When am I going to see you? We must be alone together, we must talk."

"Yes, of course," Randal replied. "The very moment I can manage it."

"You promise?" Jane pleaded.

Randal felt himself being pulled this way and that. For one moment he had felt sorry for Jane; but now he knew she was grasping out to hold on to him and he felt himself instinctively resisting her.

"We can telephone each other in the morning and evening," Jane went on; "and you must come and see me every second that you can escape from Lucille, the theatre, and the horror of those foul rehearsals. You can tell her our engagement is broken; but she can't forbid you to see me, because after all you have to see Daddy, you have to talk things over with him."

"Yes, yes, of course," Randal said soothingly.

"Oh, Randal, how I hate her!"

Jane drew his head towards her lips, and then, when he had kissed her, she sighed.

"I don't know whether I'm being a saint or a fool,"

she said. "But I'm almost sure it's crazy to agree to all this subterfuge and hypocrisy."

"If I'm any judge of what is going on upstairs, it's not a question of subterfuge, but simply the problem of how to prevent Lucille from going back to America."

"I wish to goodness she'd never been suggested for the part in the first place," Jane cried; and then, putting her hands on Randal's shoulders, she added, "I won't go on nagging; I know it is difficult for you, darling, and I wouldn't do this unless I loved you, you know that."

"I am grateful, Jane, I am really, but you've got to remember that you precipitated the crisis in the first place."

"Yes, I know," Jane nodded, "but she really was too insufferable to be borne in silence."

"Well, thanks to you I've got to bear a great deal more of it," Randal said.

Jane looked apprehensive.

"I'm going to leave you now," she said. "I don't want to be involved in any more scenes. I've had enough for one day. Will you telephone me when you get up to London tonight? Don't forget; I shall be waiting for you. And, Randal, dearest, I am sorry about this."

"So am I," Randal remarked tersely.

Jane raised her face to his again.

"Good-bye, my darling," she whispered. "It's a good thing you haven't given me an engagement ring or I would have to return it."

There was a little stab in her words which told Randal only too clearly that she would have liked a ring before now.

"You shall have one after the show has been running smoothly for at least a month," he said with a grin.

"Have I got to wait as long as that?" Jane enquired. "Well, I don't mind about the ring so long as you are quite certain that you love me."

"Haven't I told you so?" Randal enquired.

"Not often enough," Jane replied. "Good-bye again, my very dear."

He walked across the room to open the door for her.

"I'm going to get my car from the garage and drive straight home," she said. "Tell Hoppy I'm sorry not to have said good-bye to her; and let us tell her the truth, if no one else."

"All right," Randal agreed, "but really no one else. If Lucille suspects that we are merely lying to her for our own ends, it will make things worse than they are already."

"I promise not to tell a soul," Jane said. She blew Randal a kiss as she went across the hall and then she disappeared through the front door.

Randal began slowly to climb the stairs to the first floor.

11

Other diners at the Savoy turned their heads to watch Lucille.

She invariably made a dramatic entrance whenever she came into a restaurant or any place where people were gathered together.

Now, wearing a crinoline of rose-pink tulle and with a wrap of velvet and mink round her shoulders, it was not difficult for her to command attention.

As Randal followed her, he thought that in any country but England there would have been far more excitement and perhaps even a burst of applause.

He had seen a French woman, wearing a magnificent creation by some well-known Parisian dressmaker, received with cheers and claps when she entered Maxime's on a gala night.

In Hollywood it was quite a well-known thing for people to stand on their chairs to watch Lucille make her way across the floor.

But here in England people just looked—the men discreetly and with a nonchalance which nearly, if not completely, hid their interest, while the women exclaimed beneath their breath and talked excitedly to other women in their party.

Lucille, moving with her usual grace and with an air of being alone on some obscure desert island, was led by the Head Waiter to the table in an alcove which was usually kept for celebrities and distinguished visitors.

Seated, she slipped back her wrap, revealing her exquisite shoulders and a necklace of diamonds which Randal knew must have cost at least double what he could earn in a year.

"You order the dinner, darling," Lucille said graciously. "You usually know what I want to eat far better than I know myself."

Randal took the menu and did as he was commanded. He realised that Lucille was determined to be her most charming and most entrancing this evening.

He knew the signs only too well.

By the way she had since their arrival deferred several times to his opinion, by the manner in which she was leaning towards him now, giving him her undivided attention.

He only wished that he felt better able to respond to what he had often described to himself as Lucille's "ingratiating" moods.

It was impossible not to like or even love her when she set out to be charming.

She had a magnetism which seemed to draw one's very heart from one's body, and she could, if she wished, hypnotise a man, or a woman for that matter, into being spell-bound by her charm.

Unfortunately, Randal knew only too well that this mood was one which often succeeded a scene or an hysterical outburst.

When he was young, he had found in an old book-shop an amusing volume of French maxims for the young lover. He had bought it and had laughed over it with his friends.

The book had long since got lost, and yet one piece of advice had always remained with him.

It told the young gallant that, if he wished his mistress to enjoy love-making to the full, it was wise to quarrel with her first and even to make her cry. By such methods would her senses be aroused to a more ardent response.

Randal was to find out how true this was when many years later he fell in love with Lucille.

Quarrels which required to be made up afterwards were, as far as Lucille was concerned, a perfect method of ensuring that she was both loving and passionate.

Unfortunately quarrels or scenes of any type left Randal depleted both physically and mentally. He loathed upsets and what as a boy he called "a fuss."

And he found it almost impossible to switch from tears and recriminations to ardent, fiery desire.

What had taken place that afternoon at Queen's Hoo had made him so tired and so weary of anything to do with women that for the moment he would cheerfully have entered a monastery or consigned himself to the life of a hermit in the fastnesses of the Himalayas.

He had promised to take Lucille out to dinner because in the effort to calm her down, to stem the fury and vituperation which had flowed from her lips, he would have promised anything however unpleasant or impossible.

But as he changed in the flat, he had known that he wanted nothing more sensational than a meal on a tray and a book by the fire.

More than anything he wanted to forget what had

happened that afternoon. He was still acutely conscious of having behaved badly to Jane.

He was still smarting under the humiliation of his own weakness in having let her go back to London while he was forced to humble himself and to ask for Lucille's forgiveness for something which he did not in the very least consider to have been a crime.

As he tied his tie and brushed his hair, he regarded his own handsome reflection in the looking-glass above his dressing-table, and hated the charm which he knew all too well was responsible for the situation in which he found himself.

He had been involved in many difficulties where women were concerned, but never in quite such a tense and impossible situation as he was in at the moment.

Wishing to marry Jane, he dared not to break with Lucille; and he told himself, not once but a number of times, how fortunate he was that Jane at any rate was not making a scene, as she was fully entitled to do under the circumstances.

His feeling of contrition and guilt made him telephone to Jane, as he had promised to do before he left the flat to take Lucille out to dinner.

She had been very sweet and gentle to him over the telephone and it was with a feeling of gratitude that he finally said an affectionate good-night before replacing the receiver.

He came out of his bedroom to find the hall of the flat deserted.

He had half-expected Sorella to be waiting for him and after hesitating a moment he had called her name and heard her answer from the sitting-room.

She was sitting on the window-seat, looking out into the darkening night, and as there was only one light switched on in the room, it was a second or so before he saw her.

"There you are!" he exclaimed. "I'm going now. Have you had your supper?"

"I told the cook I would get it myself," Sorella answered. "She wanted to get away early. Her boy friend's home on leave from Germany and naturally she wishes to spend every moment she can with him."

"I'd no idea Ethel had a boy friend," Randal said, interested.

"It's being kept a secret," Sorella answered, "because her family don't approve. Her father wants her to marry a farmer, but Ethel and Jim have made up their minds and they expect to get married after Christmas."

"How do you learn all these things about my household?" Randal enquired. "If I had thought about it at all, I would have bet on Ethel being a confirmed old maid—I can't imagine her with a beau. It just shows how little one knows of what is going on under one's very nose."

"I expect there is an exciting story about everyone if we could only learn the truth," Sorella replied.

"Of course there is," Randal answered, "but I ought to be finding it out, not you. After all, that is my job."

Sorella smiled a little mischievously.

"You are too busy living your own life at the moment to have time to look for stories in other people's lives."

Randal appreciated the thrust and laughed at himself; then as Sorella sat looking up at him, he bent down and kissed her cheek.

"Good night, my dear," he said. "I wish I could stay at home and have dinner with you."

He felt the cool, petal-softness of her skin against his lips, and then his feet carried him from the room and he was outside in the hall.

It was only as he went down in the lift that he realised that Sorella had not said good-night to him.

She had only sat very still beneath his caress; and as he drove towards the Savoy, Randal found himself thinking of her stillness.

He had never imagined it possible for him to like

202

having a child living with him and yet he knew that he would miss Sorella if she were not there.

He remembered her laughter yesterday morning when they were alone at Queen's Hoo.

What a long time ago it seemed now! And yet it was easier to recall than anything else that had happened over the week-end.

He sighed in anticipation of what lay before him, and he sighed again half an hour later as, looking at Lucille's lovely face across the table, he wished with all his heart he could recapture the emotions she had roused in him when they first met.

It was hard to admit even to himself that she no longer had the power to excite him.

No longer did his heart beat more quickly because of her nearness, no longer did he feel that strange, mounting excitement within himself, which was the beginning of desire.

He could admire Lucille quite dispassionately. He could even appreciate the little tricks which she had used so effectively when he was not aware they were tricks.

The way she had of raising her eyelashes suddenly so that the vivid blue of her eyes was almost breathtaking; the manner in which her fingers would touch the hand or arm of the person she was with so that just for a moment contact was established and a fire ignited.

But now Randal knew the flame within him had died away, leaving nothing but ashes; and he thought that the scene she had made this afternoon had killed the last remnants of her physical attraction for him.

He would always be fond of her—there was so much that was endearing about Lucille—but he no longer wanted to hold her in his arms or to kiss her other than as a friend.

Acutely aware, however, of what was at stake, he tried now to respond to Lucille's pleasantries, and to make himself agreeable.

Fortunately Lucille had plenty to say and was ready to chatter away while Randal sipped a glass of champagne and hoped that the wine would ease some of his tiredness and perhaps even make him feel a little more light-hearted.

He was irritated at the depression which seemed to make him heavy and unresponsive, but the turbulent tempest which had passed over him that afternoon was not easily forgotten.

Lucille had said many things that he could not forget. She had raged and stormed at him; she told him many unpleasant facts about himself.

When finally her anger had passed and she flung herself sobbing into his arms, Randal felt as if he had been hit over the head not once but many times with something which had blunted every feeling except that of utter fatigue.

"We've got a lot to talk about, you and I," Lucille said softly.

They had finished the main part of their dinner and were eating *crêpes suzette* which had been prepared in front of them with all the paraphernalia of flaming brandy and special liqueurs.

"We seem to have been doing a lot of talking recently," Randal replied, "and it doesn't seem to have got us anywhere."

"I'm not talking about ordinary things. It is something very special," Lucille answered.

Randal put down his spoon and fork. He felt another mouthful would choke him.

"Do you mind if I smoke?" he enquired.

He wondered what was coming.

Lucille had been hinting for several days of something mysterious she had to say to him; but she had never come to the point, and he had imagined that it must in some way concern the play or her part in it.

"No, of course not," Lucille said.

She pushed her plate on one side where it was instantly removed by an attentive waiter.

She rested her chin on her hands and looked up at Randal with an appealing glance which a year ago would have made him want to fling himself at her feet.

"What's worrying you?" he asked, wondering to himself if she would answer truthfully or merely prevaricate as she had been doing for so long.

"Randal, dear, you're looking very fierce," Lucille replied. "It's difficult for me to talk to you when you frighten me."

Randal smiled.

"I'm not even going to pretend to believe that. I've never frightened you yet, and I don't suppose I'm going to start now. If anything, the boot is on the other foot."

"Are you inferring that I frighten you?" Lucille asked. "Darling, that's ridiculous and you know it. I grant I'm rather naughty at times and that sometimes I've made you a little bit unhappy, but you are not frightened of me, not you! No Englishman is ever frightened of a woman, if it comes to that."

"You'd be surprised," Randal said cryptically.

He waited, wondering when Lucille would come to the point.

Now she moved to lay her hand on his, a gesture which he recognised at once.

"Darling," she said in a very low voice, "how much do you love me?"

It was a question that she had asked very frequently during their association together.

Randal knew the correct answer only too well, but tonight he was not prepared to play the lover. Instead he held her fingers tightly and said:

"Let us cut the frills, Lucille. We've known each other long enough to speak frankly. There is something you've been going to say to me ever since you arrived in England. Well, now I'm waiting to hear it."

"How do you know there is something?" Lucille asked quickly. "Sometimes, Randal, you are unusually perceptive, and at other times you're so dense I could scream."

"Tonight I'm being perceptive," he said. "You're worried about something, and it is no use pretending that you're not. Well, tell me what it is."

Lucille's fingers fluttered away from his.

"It's rather hard to put to into words," she said.

He recognised her little-girl voice—young, lost, the voice she used very often in a film.

"If it's something difficult and uncomfortable, let us leave it for another time," Randal said, knowing he was running away from the issue.

"No, no!" Lucille cried.

They were interrupted by a waiter asking if they would like anything further to eat. Randal ordered coffee and liqueurs and, when they were alone again, waited for Lucille to continue.

She took out a diamond-and-platinum vanity case, looked at her reflection in the tiny glass which was released by pressing a large cabochon sapphire.

"Why did you get engaged to Jane Crake?" she asked, and then, as Randal hesitated before replying, she went on: "No, that's not a fair question, and I know the answer only too well. She's Lord Rockampstead's daughter; she is attractive and very much in love with you. You are weak where women are concerned, Randal; I've always thought so, but why not?"

Randal said nothing.

He saw too many pitfalls in this conversation and he was determined, if possible, not to run blindly into danger.

"Jane Crake did the right thing in giving you back your freedom," Lucille continued. "She realised what you should have realised a long time ago, Randal dear: that she is not the right person for you."

"I think it would be better if we didn't discuss Jane," Randal said uncomfortably.

"Just as you like. I naturally do not wish to discuss her."

There was a note of asperity in Lucille's tone.

"Then let's talk of something else," Randal invited.

"Of course," Lucille answered. "Let us talk about ourselves. That is far the most interesting subject, isn't it?"

"I think after all this time we've said almost all there is to say, haven't we?"

Lucille shook her head.

"We haven't discussed something which is actually of paramount importance."

"Which is?" Randal prompted.

"Whom you shall marry."

He looked at her in astonishment.

"I thought we decided this afternoon that I was to marry no one."

"We decided you were not to marry Jane Crake," Lucille replied: "but she isn't the only woman in the whole world, there are others."

"Why should I marry anyone?" Randal enquired.

"Not anyone," Lucille replied, raising her eyelashes suddenly, ". . . but me."

There was a pause in which Randal sat stupefied.

To say he was astonished was to understate his surprise. He had expected many things of Lucille, but never in his wildest moments had he ever contemplated for one instant that she might wish to marry him.

She had never struck him as being the marrying sort and he had never, even when he had been most infatuated with her, thought of her as his wife.

It was, perhaps, due his mother that he had always kept untouched some dream within him as to the woman he would eventually marry.

His mother had spoken of this mythical person when he was quite a little boy.

"One day when you are grown up and get married . . ." she began, and made it sound like a fairy story.

When he was in his teens, she would talk to him about women, and usually at the end of her conversation she would add:

"I hope one day you will meet a really nice girl,

someone who will make you truly happy, darling. Don't be carried away by the first pretty face you meet."

How well he could remember the anxiety on his mother's face when she said this. And it had always influenced him.

He had been carried away by many a pretty face, but not to the extent of wishing to marry them. In fact, Jane was the first person he had ever thought of marrying, and then it had been her idea.

His mother would have approved of Jane, he knew that, just as he knew that she would not have approved of Lucille.

Now with an almost terrifying clarity he saw the predicament he was in.

He did not want to marry Lucille; she was not in any way the wife he had imagined or dreamed about, nor did he love her; and yet, how could he tell her so?

How, after three years of assuring her, not once but a thousand times, of his devotion, could he suddenly say that he had changed his mind?

This afternoon, when she had upbraided and berated him for becoming engaged to Jane, he had let her assume that it was to be a marriage of convenience.

He had not said so in so many words, but he had not contradicted Lucille when she had inferred that it was Lord Rockampstead's theatrical influence and financial backing that Randal was marrying rather than Jane herself.

It was despicable in many ways that he should have acquiesced by his silence in such a suggestion; but when Lucille was raging about the room and having hysterics, it was not easy to think coherently or to speak truthfully.

Now Randal realised the position into which he had been inveigled and how very difficult it was going to be to get out of it.

Slowly, playing for time, he stubbed out his cigarette and then with a faint smile which took all the harshness out of his words he asked:

"What on earth are you talking about, Lucille? It all sounds crazy to me."

"Crazy, that you and I should get married?" Lucille enquired, and she laid her hand on his arm. "Darling, this is not an impulse; I've thought about it for a long time. We will announce our engagement very shortly, perhaps next week; and then, when once the play is going well, we'll get married.

"We might go to Paris for a short honeymoon before we go back to America. Edward was saying today that he thought the studio would want to make a film of *Today and Tomorrow*. We'll go back to Hollywood together and make it together.

"That would be a story in itself; the publicity boys would like that, wouldn't they?"

"But . . . but, Lucille . . ." Randal began to stammer.

"There are no buts, darling. I've got it all worked out in my mind," Lucille interrupted. "We've loved each other for a long time; we know each other well, and therefore it isn't likely that we should be making a mistake. I could make a few more films, not many, just one or two, and then we'll go into production together.

"We'll produce your plays and your films and when they make millions, which of course they will, we'll keep the money ourselves instead of letting someone else take it from us. Edward's made a fortune out of the last two things he backed.

"You're going to be a very great success, Randal. There's no sense in your being the goose that lays the golden eggs and letting someone else always keep the eggs, don't you agree?

"Darling, I know this is a surprise to you, and I know that you are going to put forward all the usual objections. First of all, you are going to say that we shan't see enough of each other.

"But that is why I'm telling you that I intend to go into the production side of films and plays.

"I think I've acted long enough. I've enjoyed it and I've made a great deal of money; but there is no

209

reason why we shouldn't go on making money, and a great deal more when we are working for ourselves rather than for other people.

"And secondly, there is the difference in our nationalities. You're English and I'm American. Darling! What could be nicer?"

"We shall have a home on both sides of the Atlantic. I love your little house in the country; it's a sweet little place, and I know what you feel about my home in Beverly Hills.

"It never seemed the same to me after you'd gone away. I missed you, Randal, I missed you more than I thought it possible to miss anyone.

"I used to look out through that big window of the sitting-room and think I should see you lying by the swimming pool."

"The place seemed kind of lonesome when you weren't there, and it was then I made up my mind that we had got to be together, you and I, not just occasionally, but for the rest of our lives.

There was a little throb in Lucille's tones, which would have moved Randal more if her speech had not seemed half familiar to him.

He remembered that various sentences had been lifted almost complete from a film she had done the winter before last.

He could see her now, standing in shimmering satin before a booted and spurred cowboy for whom she had been "kinda lonesome."

"You're a very sweet person, Lucille," Randal said quickly, "but you are making a mistake over this. We are neither of us really the marrying kind. We've been happy together, terribly happy, and I shall always be grateful to you for that happiness.

"But if we were tied together by wedding ceremonies, rings, licences, and all the other paraphernalia, we'd both hate it.

"You've lived your own life far too long to want

210

anyone interfering, and husbands are interfering people, you can take it from me."

Lucille laughed, a spontaneous, girlish laugh.

"Oh, Randal, you are stupid!" she exclaimed. "Do you really think you are frightening me? The truth is, darling, that I want to be married, and I shan't miss my single blessedness in the slightest.

"I want to marry you, and it's no use your telling me now, at this late hour, that we're not united to one another, for I just shan't believe you."

Randal took a deep breath. He realised that there was nothing for it but to tell Lucille the truth.

She would have to know now, once and for all, that he did not intend to marry her, that there was no chance of his ever doing so, however inexorably she had made up her mind.

Before he could speak, however, Lucille put up her hand and laid it against his lips.

"I don't know what you are going to say," she said, "but I am not going to listen to any more arguments against our marriage. I know that you are thinking of me and imagining that I shall regret it.

"That is where you are so wrong. I have loved you for a long time, Randal, and I know that I shall be very happy and very content as your wife. I think this is why I felt so restless and so upset over the play.

"I was waiting for us to get things settled; and now they are settled, I can really get down to making the very best of that lovely part you wrote for me.

"You know, Randal—better than most people—that if I am not happy in my own mind, if I haven't got what I want in my private life, then I'm hopeless on the stage or in a film.

"It's silly, I know, to allow's one private affairs to interfere with one's public appearance, but I can't help it, I'm just made like that."

Lucille made a little eloquent gesture to illustrate her own weakness; and then, taking Randal's hand in hers, she said:

211

"Oh, darling, I'm so happy. I'll give the best performance of my life now and you'll be so proud of me."

He was completely and absolutely silenced. There was nothing he could say, nothing at all. He knew that the threat beneath her words was intentional.

There was nothing ingenuous or naïve about Lucille, and she had been, he must admit it, completely frank as to her intentions.

Randal did not need to be very perceptive to know all too clearly what Lucille intended him to know.

She had said as clearly as if she had said it in so many words that if he did not promise to marry her, she would not act in the play. It was just as much an ultimatum as if it had been set down in black and white.

For a moment he could not think how to answer it.

There was nothing he could say, nothing he could do; he could only sit at the table, Lucille's hand in his, and wonder for how long he could go on saying nothing without her becoming angry with him.

She appeared not to notice his silence.

"It's all so wonderful!" she chattered on. "I'm so happy now that it's settled. I've thought about it for a long time. It isn't an easy thing for someone like myself to make up her mind to give up her freedom, you know that.

"I've always enjoyed knowing I could do what I liked, and go where I wanted and not be beholden to anyone; but now I feel quite different about it all.

"But what will be such fun will be to think that I haven't got to plan only my own future, but yours too; I can be a tremendous help to you, darling—you know that."

Lucille took out her vanity case again and reddened her lips.

"I think we'll be married in London," she said. "I want a Church wedding and your Churches here are quite divine. Some of our special friends can fly over for it, and then we will have a big reception for the rest when we go home to Hollywood."

She put her vanity case back in her bag.

"But before we make too many plans," she said, "we've got to remember the play. Because I was rather naughty to you last week, I'm going to be specially good from now on. That last scene as you've written it is superb. I will say the words over to myself as I go to sleep, and I shall know them all in the morning. I don't suppose anyone else will be word-perfect."

Lucille looked round for her stole and pulled it round her shoulders.

"For your sake, darling, I'm going to bed early to-night. I don't want to go, I want to stay here talking with you, and we might even have danced a little. Do you remember how we used to dance to the radiogram when we first knew each other?

"We'll do that again one day. Tonight I'm going to bed with my lines, which I've got to know by nine o'clock tomorrow morning. Isn't it fine and dandy? Aren't you proud of me?"

Lucille smiled at Randal, a flashing, fascinating smile, which film-goers knew only too well; then she rose to her feet.

"I must drag myself away, darling," she said. "It's only one of the many sacrifices I make for you, one way and another."

Hastily Randal told the waiter to bring him the bill, and then he followed Lucille across the restaurant floor.

Once again heads were turned in her direction, and the people whispered and chattered about her as she passed.

As they went up the steps of the vestibule, the same attention was paid her, glances of admiration, exclamations of excitement that were all very familiar, but still the breath of life to Lucille.

They reached the lift and here, to Randal's surprise, she turned and gave him both her hands.

213

"You are not to come up, darling," she said. "You look tired and I have told you how good I'm going to be, just reading and rereading those lovely lines of yours until I fall asleep."

Automatically Randal raised her hands to his lips, and then she was gone.

The lift doors closed behind her, and he walked slowly across the vestibule out to where the Bentley was parked in the courtyard.

He felt dazed and was so bemused at his own thoughts that he forgot to tip the Commissionaire. Slowly he edged his car into the traffic in the Strand, hardly knowing where he was driving, seeing only Lucille's face raised to his, hearing only the tones of her voice as she planned their life together . . . together.

Lucille herself was well pleased with the effect she had achieved. She was smiling as she stepped from the lift and walked down the corridor towards her suite.

As she opened her door, the fragrance of the great baskets and bowls of hot-house flowers was almost overpowering.

She drew her velvet-and-mink stole from her shoulders and threw it on her bed; but she didn't, for the moment, telephone for her maid. Instead, she sat down at the dressing-table and stared at her reflection.

Her eyes were shining. The looking-glass told her that she was still very young and beautiful.

Then she gave a little laugh.

She had been well aware of Randal's surprise, and she knew she had been extraordinarily clever in not allowing him to speak, in preventing his protests from being voiced as they rose impulsively to his lips.

By tomorrow he would have had time to think cautiously and sensibly over what she had said and over the alternative that she had made very clear.

He would agree to marry her or she would not appear in *Today and Tomorrow*.

Not for one moment did Lucille think it mattered that Randal was reluctant to be her husband.

214

She was so certain of her own attractions that she believed and was completely convinced that any reluctance he might have was due, not to his lack of love for her, but simply because he wished to remain single and untied.

She had been furious and incensed that he had for a moment contemplated marriage with anyone else; but it had been all too easy to believe what her vanity had suggested, that Jane had been only a stepping stone to further Randal's ambitions.

Lucille was jealous of Jane; she had, indeed, disliked her from the first moment she had seen her, because she had recognised certain qualities in the English girl that she knew were missing in her own character.

But the years of adulation and success were not easily forgotten or set aside for one small, jealous heart-ache.

She was Lucille Lund, she was the most fabulous, most alluring and by far the most scintillating star in the whole of Hollywood.

She had no reason to doubt Randal's love for her last year, or the year before, but it never occurred to her that his feelings might have changed.

Hers might alter, she might grow bored or tired of men, but they remained adoring for as long as she desired their adoration.

Only when she had discarded them were they free to find other women, more out of pique than because other charms could possibly be more alluring than hers.

It was a simple, self-satisfied creed; but Lucille's life was, actually, though no one would have believed it, a very simple one.

Her beauty had brought her an outstanding, tumultuous, world-wide success. So long as her beauty remained, she had nothing to fear.

The men who loved her in the past had not been very clever or subtle; they too had been simple in their desires. It never struck her for one moment that Randal might be different.

He was a man and was therefore in love with her.

She wished to marry him, and therefore it was obvious from all that had happened before that any reluctance on his part must be entirely superficial and quite unimportant.

Lucille had, however, a certain shrewdness which had come to her through having to struggle in the early part of her life.

She had sensed that Randal might say something they would both regret, and therefore by a consummate bit of acting and by an ingenuous volubility she had glossed over the awkward moment and remained complete and absolute mistress of the situation.

"I am very clever," she told herself aloud and smiled again at her own reflection.

Her loveliness seemed to excite her.

The glitter of diamonds at her neck, the low-cut bodice of rose-pink tulle made her fragile fairness seem almost ethereal in the soft lights on either side of the dressing-table.

She stretched her arms out a little voluptuously. She wished now she had not sent Randal away so impetuously.

As he had known when they first met tonight, she was in the mood for love.

She felt soothed and relaxed after the hysteria of the afternoon. She wanted to feel the warmth of Randal's mouth against hers; she wanted to feel the strength of his arms around her and hear his voice murmur sweet words in her ear. She could feel a flame flickering within herself at the thought of his strength and his attractions.

She knew so well the ecstasy of surrender, the moment when her whole being seemed to fuse with his. She knew the joy of being conquered.

Yes, she wished now she had not sent him away—for a moment she glanced towards the telephone by her bed. Should she call him back?

In another few minutes he would be home in Park Lane, and the thought of his returning to the loneliness of his flat decided her. She put out her hand towards the telephone, and even as she did so, it rang.

She was sure it was Randal telephoning to tell her how much he loved her. Hastily she snatched up the receiver.

"Hello!"

"There's a gentleman downstairs who wishes to see you, Madame."

"A gentleman?" Lucille queried.

She wondered if it was Randal, or perhaps Edward. It would be too late for anyone else, she thought. And then she glanced at her pink quartz travelling clock and saw it was only a quarter to eleven.

"Who is it?" she enquired.

"The gentleman would rather not give his name, Madam; but he says he must see you on very urgent business."

"Of course I must have his name!" Lucille said impatiently. "And anyway, it's too late to do business at this hour."

"Will you hold on a moment, Madam?"

The operator's voice was cool and disinterested. Lucille waited impatiently. She wanted to talk to Randal; she had no time for other people at this moment.

The operator spoke at the other end:

"The gentleman would rather not give his name, Madam, but he says you will remember Jakestown, and that will be sufficient introduction."

There was a long pause.

"Are you still there, Madam?"

"Yes, yes," Lucille answered. "Ask the gentleman to come up."

"Very good, Madam."

Lucille put down the receiver.

She stood staring at it. Her face was very white, and after a moment she turned and went from the bedroom into the sitting-room.

As if her legs would no longer support her, she sat

217

down on the sofa, staring straight ahead of her, her fingers unconsciously twisting and retwisting themselves together.

Jakestown! She could remember it only too well—the one long, ugly street; the houses with their wooden shutters; the gasoline station which had the radio turned on full blast all day and most of the night; the saloon which might have stepped straight out of a Wild West film with its swinging doors and ugly, creaking sign.

She could remember it too well. The shops which had little to buy in them; her lodgings with the permanent smell of stale food and badly designed drains; and the theatre—would she ever forget the theatre?

The rough, uneven stage, the draughty, ill-lit dressing-rooms, the iron staircase twisting up by the stage door, a death-trap for those who were in too much of a hurry; the audiences, bored or drunk; and the stage manager who never spoke to any of them without a foul oath or a word of almost obscene blasphemy.

Jakestown? No! No, it couldn't be, not after all these years!

There was a knock at the door. Lucille wanted to answer it, but the words died in her throat.

The knock came again, and then she heard the key—which she had left there when she had come into the room—turn in the lock.

She couldn't move, she couldn't speak, she could only sit very still, her eyes fixed on the door as it slowly opened.

12

He stood there, looking, Lucille thought, like some terrible caricature of himself.

For a moment she could only stare at him, unable to

utter a single word. He closed the door behind him and walked slowly towards her.

"Surprised to see me?" he asked.

The tone of his voice, jaunty and cocksure, was more horrible than she had believed it possible for any voice to be.

"You!" she said at last, and the monosyllable seemed to be strangled in her throat.

"Yes, me," he replied mockingly. "Bit of a surprise, eh? Well, you seem to have done well for yourself."

He glanced round the room.

His eyes rested on the extravagant baskets of orchids and carnations, on the many small objects which Lucille carried everywhere with her and which were obviously not the property of the hotel.

An onyx-and-platinum cigarette box, the pink quartz ash-trays, the crystal-and-silver photograph frames, the cushions of satin and brocade, which she fondly believed made any room look more furnished and more individual.

His quick, appraising eyes missed nothing; then they lingered lastly on the table by the window, on which stood the drinks—a fabulous array of bottles which Lucille offered generously to her guests.

"Since you are so pressing, I'll help myself to a Scotch," he said with a twisted smile which mocked her inability to speak.

He threw his soft hat down on a chair and she was startled to see that he was nearly grey.

For a moment she had thought it was only debauchery which made him look so different; but now she saw that it was also age. She made a rapid calculation in her mind.

Good Lord, Beau must be nearly sixty! It was incredible.

She could hardly believe it, and yet she remembered all too vividly that he had been well over forty when she first knew him.

She remembered how flattered she had been that he,

219

a so much older man, should take such an interest in her. She hadn't realised then what he was like.

She was to learn later that he liked his women young. She had been flattered, poor, silly, little fool, when he singled her out of the chorus and invited her to have supper with him.

The others had warned her.

"Beau is no good to a girl," they said. "You keep away from him."

But Lucille hadn't listened. Beau Brittain! The name seemed magical enough in itself, and she had thought him by far the most attractive man she had ever seen.

She was to learn later what the pouches under his eyes meant, what the slight shaking of his hand foretold as he reached for yet another double.

But she was in too much of a hurry, too infatuated to heed anything save Beau's voice whispering in her ear, Beau's eyes devouring her freshness.

She could remember even now the thrill of his first kiss, the ecstasy within herself because she thought she had captured him—captured Beau Brittain, the most important actor she had ever known in her life.

Even now Lucille could almost cry at the pathos of it. She had been so gullible, so absurdly, ridiculously unsophisticated.

She even believed it when Beau told her that he had taken the part in a touring company to help a friend, and that because of it he had refused a lead on Broadway!

Yes, she had even swallowed that, poor, gullible little idiot that she was.

She thought him wonderful and she had made no secret of her feelings.

She had been flattered, and perhaps her all-too-obvious adoration had helped him for a short while to stick to his pledge to keep away from the drink which had got him kicked out of every decent theatre by every decent management.

Only rotten, down-at-heel, shoddy companies, like

the one which had engaged Lucille, would have taken on Beau Brittain at that moment, with a reputation of lost performances and a dozen police charges for being drunk and disorderly.

To give both the Producer and the Stage Manager their due, they had tried to warn Lucille, but she wouldn't listen. She had believed Beau instead when he told her that they were jealous of him.

She had walked willingly and eagerly up the street of Jakestown to the house of the Minister.

It was only after they had been married that she began to realise that it was not Beau who had trapped her, but her own innate respectability.

The conscience which she had inherited from her father had committed her to a life of degradation and misery such as she had never believed possible.

Beau hadn't wanted to marry her, she realised later. All he had wanted to do was to seduce her; but if a wedding ring was the price she put on seduction, then he was prepared to pay what she asked.

It was only on looking back over those first weeks and months, when Beau was, as she thought, courting her, that Lucille clearly and without any glamour attached to it saw what he had wanted.

If she had slept with him for perhaps a week or two, that would have been sufficient; Beau would have tired of her and would have gone off hunting for someone different.

Women were by no means his main interest in life; they played a very second place to his love of drink; but when he was not drinking, he had to have a palliative of some sort, and women were easier to obtain than most things.

It was only because she resisted him, or, rather, failed to understand his insinuations that he became seriously interested in her.

There was something about his debonair, debauched features which attracted women as easily as rats are attracted by aniseed.

He looked a wicked man, and they shuddered with delight and ran after him, almost pleading with him to show his wickedness. Actually, he was neither worse nor better than most men of his type.

He was just a drunkard, and the fact that he did not drink all the time was due to lack of funds rather than to any high-souled ideas of being reformed.

When he had spent his last penny, Beau would go on the water wagon until he had accumulated enough to get comfortably and nauseatingly drunk.

He would save towards his bouts of drunkenness as other people saved for a car or a home where they could settle down and be happy.

It took Lucille three years to discover the truth of this.

Three years when she put him to bed, cleaned up after him, lied to protect him and wept bitter, miserable tears because she felt so helpless, utterly unable to cope with a man who was completely impervious to anything she might say or do to alter him.

And yet she loved him.

She wondered now, as she watched him pour himself out a drink, how she could have gone on for so long loving this insensitive clot who had always, even at the very beginning, preferred a bottle to her.

She noted almost dispassionately that his shoes were cracked and worn; that his suit was threadbare, although it was typical of Beau to wear it with an air and the creases of his trousers were as sharp as razor edges.

Except when he was unconscious he always had a certain smartness about him. It was part of his incredible vitality that, even when he had drunk enough to make most men completely incapable, Beau could still keep on his feet, still crack a joke with that extraordinary raffish air of his, which could when he wished charm a hard-boiled theatre manager into giving him yet another chance.

Beau filled his glass half-full of whiskey and squirted

222

a suspicion of soda on the top of it. Now he raised it to Lucille mockingly.

"God keep you," he said. "I wish I could!"

It was his favourite toast and one which usually brought a shriek of laughter from the women to whom he made it. It was those words more than anything else which enabled Lucille to pull herself together.

The sense of paralysis, which had seemed to imprison her with horror so that she was unable to move, vanished and she got to her feet.

"What are you doing here?" she asked, "and where have you come from?"

"One question at a time, my dear," Beau replied, and seating himself in a comfortable chair, he crossed his legs.

"You've improved," he went on. "You're a damn' sight better-looking than when I first knew you. Who's responsible for the evolution of the chrysalis into the butterfly?"

Lucille gave a little stamp of her foot.

"Why are you here?" she demanded.

It was almost inconceivable, but she could feel coming over her the same weakness that had always been hers when she came into contact with Beau.

He had always dominated her, always forced his will upon her, so that she was powerless to defy him.

Now, because she was afraid, her voice rose shrilly.

"I demand that you answer my questions!"

"Why not?" Beau replied. "The story of my life since we last met won't take long. I've been in prison!"

He grinned as he said it, and she knew that not only was it true, but it was, of course, the obvious explanation of why he had left her alone for so long.

"I thought you were dead."

"It's surprising, but I'm not. I've had many adventures since our paths last crossed. Now let me see— you left me in Tankeville, didn't you? I don't remember your leaving, but they told me you'd been gone some time when I came round to asking for you."

"It is only surprising that I'd stayed so long," Lucille said in a hard voice.

"My dear, don't think I blamed you; I should have done the same in your place. You stuck it nobly. I should indeed be grateful that you could tolerate me for as long as you did."

"Why have you come back now?" Lucille shot the words at him and knew the answer even before he smiled at the question.

"Must I really tell you?" he asked. "I'm in my usual state of penury. You must be a very rich woman!"

"If you think you are going to get anything out of me you are much mistaken."

"Am I?" Beau raised his eyebrows. "I was reading an interview you gave to the *Evening Standard* last night. I enjoyed the bit about how Edward Jepson discovered you the first time you appeared on a stage. *"From the Schoolroom to Stardom"* I think that particular paragraph was headed.

"It's funny, but I remember your twenty-third birthday quite well, or was it your twenty-fourth? We were playing in Mertown and you persuaded me to buy you a paste brooch that had taken your fancy.

Two dollars fifty it cost me, I remember it distinctly, and you kissed me for it. It was, you told me, the one thing you really wanted."

"Don't!" Lucille's protest was muttered almost beneath her breath.

"I think actually it must have been your twenty-fourth birthday," Beau went on. "I wonder if the Sunday newspapers would be interested in my memoirs? I wouldn't ask too high a figure for them!"

Lucille drew a deep breath.

"How much do you want?"

"For my memoirs?"

"To get out and stay out. I believed you were dead. I must have been an idiot to imagine that you wouldn't turn up sooner or later and try to make trouble!"

"Is it making trouble to return to your wife? You are still my wife, I suppose?"

"I told you that I thought you were dead. If I had thought you were alive, I would have divorced you, and quickly."

"Surely that would have rather spoiled the poise of being the dewy-eyed schoolgirl, the little innocent whose first appearance on the stage was attended by the brilliant good fortune of being selected by Edward Jepson. He must be a shrewd picker. Has he any idea of your real age?"

"You be quiet about my age," Lucille said furiously. "I've asked you how much you want. You'd better name your price before I call the police and have you chucked out for blackmail."

"Why waste your breath saying things that you know as well as I do would do you far more harm than it would me?" Beau asked. "Sit down, relax, and let me learn a little more about my famous wife."

"How did you discover who I was?" Lucille asked.

Beau Brittain chuckled.

"That in itself is a good story. If I thought of looking for you after you had abandoned me at Tankeville, I would of course have looked for Maria Schmidt. But actually I never was one for trying to keep a woman who was tired of me.

"I was broke when I left the hospital and I shouldn't have known what to do with myself if I hadn't been taken up by a cattle rancher who was in the next bed.

"I was as weak as a kitten and I could remember nothing that had happened since I started to break up the drinking saloon because that damned music the pianist was making got on my nerves.

"It was Ted, my rancher friend, who told me how I got the cuts on the back of my head and a broken leg which kept me on crutches for over three months.

"He took me back to his ranch; and because he was an ardent teetotaller himself—converted by one of those

225

blasted Revivalist chaps—he wouldn't let me drink either.

"As soon as I was well, I helped myself to the money he'd got stored away there in what he imagined was a secret cache under the floor-boards and made a quick getaway for the coast.

"Unfortunately I learned that the police were on my heels, so on an impulse I took a passage on a tanker sailing to South Africa.

"It's a long story for me to tell you what happened on that tanker and the various uncomfortable situations in which I found myself in one place or another.

"Anyway, I ended up in Ireland, looking for my relations, the ones who used to write to my father long after he had emigrated across the Atlantic. I found them right enough, and they gave me a warm welcome.

"I expect you always knew my name wasn't Brittain, or Beau for that matter. I was christened Michael O'Grady.

"The O'Gradys welcomed me back amongst them, so I settled down to see a bit of the Ireland I've sung about so often and sentimentally."

Beau paused to take a deep drink of his whiskey.

"Interested?" he asked.

Lucille's face was as hard as granite.

"Go on," she said. "I might as well hear the rest of it."

"There's not much else to tell," Beau went on. "I crossed to England with some cousins of mine who believed that the streets were paved with gold and that it was as easy to gather money there as it was to pick up potatoes in their mother-country.

"They were disappointed, and so was I. We decided to part company, but unfortunately we gave a party first at which we swore undying friendship and pledged our brotherhood in Irish whiskey.

"Then I left them; but having no money for my

train fare, I borrowed a car from a stranger who had left it outside the local pub.

"It wasn't his fault or mine that I was used to driving on the right-hand side and with a right-hand drive. It was on my way towards London, or what I imagined was the route to London, that in swerving to avoid a lorry I hit a cyclist.

"I killed him, and the judge, blast him, brought it in as manslaughter.

"I got fifteen years, but good conduct got me out a year earlier, and I found myself loose in a country which had passed through the hell of a war without my knowing much about it."

"The point of this story was to tell me how you learned about me," Lucille said coldly.

"Of course, you must forgive my being preoccupied with myself; I have rather grown out of the way of thinking about other people," Beau said. "It was in prison that I first learned what happened to Maria Schmidt. We had visitors occasionally, prison visitors.

"If you want to be bored, I can tell you there is nothing more boring in the world than sitting for half an hour with a prison visitor.

"As it happens this one wasn't so bad. She was a hatchet-faced old hag, but she talked about more interesting things than most.

"She was very taken up with some film she had been to see the night before. I can't remember the name of it now.

"She told me how pretty the leading lady was, raved about her in fact; and when she heard that I had been on the stage, she told me she'd try to get me some stage and film papers to look at.

"She agreed that the literature in the prison was deadly in the extreme.

"The week after her visit I received a small bundle of magazines. To tell the truth, I wasn't particularly interested in them; contrary to most people's beliefs,

227

one doesn't lie in prison ruminating about one's past or making plans for one's future.

"One just lives from day to day and from meal to meal.

"Still, I suppose I was interested in seeing what had happened to the stars I had known before I got locked up; and there, slap on the front page, was a picture of you.

"It was you all right, although at first I couldn't believe my eyes. I might have been mistaken about your face, but not about your legs. I was the first person, I think, who discovered how good your legs are.

"Do you remember how angry you used to be with me for making such a fuss about them to the Managers? Well, I wasn't likely to forget those legs; and there you were, 'Lucille Lund—Star of Universe Super Features'."

"And there and then you decided to blackmail me as soon as you came out."

"As a matter of fact I decided nothing of the sort," Beau replied; and surprisingly Lucille believed him. "If you hadn't come to London I didn't suppose for a moment I should be talking to you now.

"To begin with, it costs the devil of a lot of money to cross the Atlantic; but since you are here and since I have a partiality for comfort, it is very pleasant to remember that we are legally married. I slept last night in a Salvation Army Hostel."

He looked toward the open door of the sitting-room which led into the bedroom.

The pink, shaded lights by the bed seemed at that moment to Lucille obscene rather than inviting.

"I have already asked you how much," she said.

"I haven't yet decided," Beau replied coolly. "May I help myself to another drink?"

"No, you may not." Lucille snatched the glass from his hand and slapped it down on the table. "If you think you are going to get sodden and incapable here,

you are mistaken. A nice scandal that would cause.
I'll give you some money and you can go right now.

"Tomorrow we'll draw up a contract of some sort. I'll
pay you so much a month or a week to stay away from
me."

Beau laughed.

"What a clever business women you've become!" he
jeered. "I remember when I had to do the accounting
as you found it so difficult."

"That's not true," Lucille flashed at him. "You were
always hopeless where money was concerned. I remember having to force you to hand over a part of
your salary, otherwise you would have drunk it all
away before we had even paid the rent."

" 'The evil men do lives after them', " Beau quoted,
and suddenly Lucille could see him saying those very
words on a ramshackle stage out in the West, while the
audience, tough cow-hands and settlers with their wives,
listened open-mouthed. They had toured together with
a Shakespearean company for nearly eight months.

They would never have lasted so long as that if
their salaries had not been so meagre that it was almost
impossible for Beau to get a drink on them.

Then he had one glorious bust when they reached
Gettesville, and the Shakspearean company had gone on
without them.

Lucille could remember only too vividly how desperate she had been that week and the week after.

Beau had finished his bout of drinking by smashing
up the saloon in which he had been served.

It was what invariably happened; and when he came
out of hospital, there was a police charge awaiting him
and a fine, which meant they had to pawn even their
clothes in order to pay it.

Even as she had asked Beau how much he wanted,
she could hear herself saying the same words under
very different circumstances.

"How much?"

She had asked, not one saloon keeper but a dozen,

when they brought her a bill for breakages, for damage caused to furniture, for compensation for their own black eyes and bruises and sometimes broken limbs.

"How much?"

She could hear her own voice, hard and metallic, and at the same time frightened—frightened because she had no idea how they were going to pay the charge.

There was another occasion on which she had asked "How much?"—a moment which even now had the power to hurt after all these years.

She could see the girl now, whimpering as her father spluttered with rage and her mother sat tight-lipped and sharp-featured, saying very little.

There was no doubt of the facts; the girl, who was a stage-struck little fool of about seventeen, had hung about the stage door the whole week they had been in town.

She had sent Beau presents—flowers which he chucked into the waste-paper basket, cigarettes which he smoked and a cheap tie which he had used to tie up the leg of a broken chair.

He had laughed about her, as he invariably laughed about all his fans; and, as Lucille knew too well, there were quite a number of them.

If she hadn't felt it quite impossible for her to go out to supper after the show, that she must get home to bed, it would not have happened.

But the girl had been waiting, and Beau, because Lucille, with a temperature of a hundred and two, had not been there to look after him, had taken her out to supper.

Unfortunately she had a little money with her and Beau had used it to get drunk.

It was not enough to make him incapable, and he had seduced the girl, though, as Lucille pointed out somewhat bitterly to her parents, she was obviously willing enough to be seduced.

The next evening Lucille was better and Beau had no further use for his inamorata.

Stung by his indifference, the girl had first of all made a scene and then gone home to tell her parents. As usual, when things got too uncomfortable, Beau had left Lucille to face the music and discreetly disappeared.

The father had started by storming, raging and uttering violents threats to evoke the law. Gradually his anger subsided as he found there was nothing to be gained by it.

They were quite reasonable people, Lucille decided, and though she despised the whimpering girl whose romantic yearnings had got her into trouble, she was sorry for the father and even for the far less amenable mother.

They had worked hard to bring up their child decently.

The evidence of that was there on the lines of their faces and their hands rough and red from toil.

And in the way that, despite their distress and anger at what had occurred, they spoke proudly of the progress their daughter had made at school and the people she had got to know in town.

It was because she could feel herself becoming sorry for them and because she knew she must defend Beau from the consequences of his thoughtless action that Lucille asked the one question which she knew would bring the whole interview into its right perspective.

"How much?"

She had known, even as she said it, that these were not the type of people to ask for money.

The compensation they wanted was justice and punishment for the man whose offence against their daughter could never be undone and would never be forgotten.

"I'm not asking for money," the father said fiercely. "There's no dough in the world as can put right the wrong as has been done to our Sarah. I came down here to make that flash actor marry her; but if he's married to you he can't do that, though God help you with the kind of husband you've saddled yourself with."

"I think I'm more capable of dealing with him than your daughter would be," Lucille said. "Shot-gun marriages are not likely to be successful. If you take my advice, you'll bring up your girl with a standard of decency which prevents such drastic methods from being necessary."

Her words seemed to sting the mother, who had been silent for a long time, into speech.

"We don't need your advice, thank you," she said sharply. "Come, Clem, there's nothing to be gained here, and well you know it. I'll talk to Sarah when I get her home. This won't happen again, you can be sure of that."

"It wasn't my fault," Sarah whimpered like a snared rabbit.

Her face was puffy and stained with tears and any pretension to looks she might have had was lost beneath the strain of her own misery and her parents' anger.

"Next time you write notes and send presents to a man I should find out first if he is single or married," Lucille told her.

"You can't be very old yourself," the father said suddenly. "It's sorry I am for you, Ma'am, married to a blackguard like that, and you can tell him from me if he has a whole skin tonight, it's due to the fact that he's got a wife to speak for him and defend him, though the Lord knows why you should want to."

"That's my business," Lucille replied.

She watched them file from the room, the girl crying again, the father making a last, awkward movement as though he would have liked to shake her by the hand.

It was only when they were gone that she felt a weakness within herself and a sudden desire to crumple up and cry even as Sarah had cried. She could understand how the girl had felt.

She had lost something, not only her virginity, but her dreams of romance.

It had all come down to a lot of sordid recriminations, fruitless anger and the knowledge that what had been done could never be undone.

Alone, Lucille had covered her face with her hands.

She had loved Beau when she married him, she still loved him; that was the worst of it, that now after all that he had done she still loved him.

She would be angry with him, she would hate him when he was incapable or when he behaved as he had last night.

Yet he had only to touch her, to seek for her lips and she would find herself weak in his arms, surrendering herself to him as easily and unprotestingly as any stage-struck little fool like Sarah.

This was a humiliation almost more unendurable than the knowledge that the man she was married to was a drunkard and a cad.

Lucille had been brought up with decent standards. Her father had been a good man and she knew that if Hans Schmidt was to meet Beau he would find him rotten through and through.

Yet she loved him.

It was a love that had nothing mental about it, nothing fine and nothing spiritual. It was a love physical and earthly, the need of her body for Beau's, the undisguised need of a woman for a man.

Not once, but a hundred times Lucille had told herself that she must leave him.

Sometimes when he had been carried back to their lodgings and she had managed with almost superhuman strength to get him up the stairs and on to the bed, she would stand looking at the besotted, inebriated oaf whom she called her husband.

He would be an unprepossessing sight at such times. The smell of the drink he had consumed was almost overpowering, his clothes soiled or torn from some fight in which he had indulged before they had got him home.

Lucille would turn away from him with an expression of disgust.

"Tomorrow I will go," she would tell herself.

When the morning came, Beau would need her.

Sometimes he was too ill to do anything but lie in a darkened room with ice on his forehead and a thirst which nothing could quench—nothing that she would bring him at any rate.

At other times he was morose, talking despairingly of suicide and of being no use to anyone in the world. More frequently he was just helpless and dependent on her.

"Hold my hand," he would plead. "I'm feeling damned ill. I can't play tonight, you know I can't."

"You've got to, Beau," she would say. "If I tell them you're ill, they will know why and they'll chuck us out this time for certain. We were warned last week and the week before that. You can't fail them tonight, they would never forgive you."

"My head is splitting in two," Beau would groan. "I don't care if they do chuck us out, I won't go down to the theatre, not if Sam Goldwyn himself was waiting for me."

But usually he'd manage it.

With ice and black coffee and showers every hour or so, Lucille would get him sobered up.

Then after a painful performance in which he would forget or muff his lines, he would borrow enough money from someone for a drink and it would start all over again.

And yet she could not bring herself to leave him. They spent three years of hell together.

Three years in which Lucille was young enough to believe that death was far more desirable than life; until at last, so slowly and insidiously that she was not certain when it happened, she found herself free from him.

The spell by which he had held her was broken and she knew that she no longer cared.

Even then, it was hard to make the final decision to pack her box and go.

Only when Beau was taken to the hospital after a fight in which he had damaged one man really seriously, did she know that the psychological moment had arrived and she need stay no longer.

She had left him without a word, without a note or a message; and when she was gone, she wondered to herself why she had lingered so long, why it had always seemed too difficult to get away.

Exactly a year later Edward Jepson had seen her and a new chapter in her life had begun.

Looking at Beau now, dissolute, down-at-heel, and old, Lucille wondered what would have happened if he had still been with her when Edward Jepson had come along.

He might not have let her go, or at any rate he would have made things so difficult that Edward might have lost heart or felt it was not worth the trouble.

Beau had been very jealous of other members of the cast, Lucille remembered. He had not been jealous of her as an actress because he had no reason to be.

She was young and immature, and although Beau had very little acting ability, he had at least experience, and he could if he wished and was sober enough put on quite a creditable performance.

But he had been jealous of her as a woman; that perhaps was understandable, but his jealousy was not quite normal.

He was not afraid that she would be unfaithful to him, but he was afraid of her ceasing to be useful to him.

He wanted her, Lucille had often thought, not so much because she was attractive or because her body ached for his, but because he liked to be ministered to.

It was as though some instinct of self-preservation within Beau made him realise that he must have someone on whom he could depend, as an invalid might depend on a trained nurse or a child might depend on its mother.

That, Lucille thought, was what Beau really wanted her for, so that she should mother him and in many ways protect him from the consequences of his own behaviour.

Sometimes, when she had been sorry for him, she would try to find some psychological reason for his dependence on her.

But before she had really sifted the truth from the many highly-coloured tales he told her, she had got to the stage when she no longer thought him pathetic, but merely disgusting.

And yet now, after all these years, when he had come back to disrupt and disturb her life, Lucille could still find him pathetic.

It wasn't anything he said or even anything he did, but just something about him.

His hair, thin and grey where once it had been dark and luxurious; the tiredness of his eyes which had once seemed alive with virility; the sagging of his jaw line; the droop of his shoulders.

With a start Lucille pulled her thoughts together. This was not the moment for weakness.

Suddenly she thought of Randal. It was Randal she was going to marry, Randal who was going to be her husband, and the sooner Beau was out of the way the better.

She couldn't divorce him, she couldn't do anything which would cause publicity, scandal or talk; and yet somehow he had to be disposed of.

"I shouldn't if I were you," Beau said suddenly, his voice high and mocking.

"Shouldn't do what?" Lucille asked, a little startled.

"Murder me!" Beau replied. "You'd have a great deal of difficulty in disposing of the body. I know all

236

about it; my fellow convicts used to talk of the different methods they had tried; and none of them, I regret to say, had got away with it."

"I wasn't thinking of murdering you," Lucille said, but her voice didn't sound convincing.

Beau laughed.

He always had a disconcerting way of being able to read her thoughts and she had imagined it was due to her being so much younger than he, but now she wondered.

It had been one of his opening gambits with a woman to whom he wished to make himself pleasant that he should offer to tell her fortune.

It involved holding her hand for a long time, and Lucille, who had fallen for this move herself, was always very sceptical when she watched Beau trying it on someone else.

Yet now she wondered if in some ways he was genuinely clairvoyant.

She could remember, although it was nearly twenty years ago, exactly what he had told her when first he looked at the lines of her hand.

They had just met and he knew nothing about her past and yet he had described her family fairly accurately.

He had told her that her mother was dead and that she had not been happy at home because of another woman—a stepmother most likely—and then he had gone on to speak of her future.

There would be many men in her life, but only two would really matter to her.

She would marry one of them and she would achieve success, great, glittering, exciting success in the profession she had chosen.

She had laughed at that. When one is earning sixteen dollars a week the greatest success one can visualise is being offered eighteen or twenty.

Once or twice when she had reached Hollywood she had remembered Beau's words. Now, because she was afraid of what he might read in her mind, she got to her feet.

"We've got to think this over very carefully," she said. "You'd better come back and see me tomorrow. In the meantime, you are to speak to no one about me, nor let anyone know that we are even acquainted."

"You'll have to make it worth my while," Beau said with a smile.

"I'm quite prepared to do that," Lucille answered sharply. "I've already asked you several times how much you want."

"I should think something like a hundred thousand dollars" Beau replied casually.

She gaped at him for a moment, her breath entirely taken from her; and while she was still gaping at him, he walked to the table and helped himself to another drink.

"You're mad!" she said at last.

"On the contrary, I'm quite sane and comparatively sober," Beau grinned. "I've just been working out what you must have saved these past twelve years. Even allowing for newspaper exaggeration as regards your earnings, you must have made a tidy fortune one way or another."

"If I have, there's no reason why I should give it to you," Lucille answered.

"I don't know, I can think of a lot of reasons why you should," Beau contradicted. "I reckon one of the Sunday papers over here would give me a couple of thousand—pounds, not dollars—for the story of my marriage with one of the world's most famous film stars.

"Can't you see how it would hit the headlines? 'Secret Marriage of Lucille Lund. The years on tour. Nights when she struggled with a drunken husband.' "

"Have you no decency?" Lucille flashed at him.

"Not much when it comes to money," Beau replied. "You ought to know that. I always had a respect for money, but I learned a great deal more about it in prison. I can tell you that men will do anything to get it.

"They will not only break every one of the ten commandments a dozen times over to lay their hands on a bit of spare dough, but they will do other things, filthy, dirty, obscene things.

"They will prostitute not only their bodies but their minds, and all for money."

Beau's voice had deepened as he had been speaking, and now he gave a little shudder as though he thrust away from himself the memory of some horrors almost too terrible to be recalled.

Then he drank off the whiskey he held in his hand.

"One hundred thousand dollars," he said, "and then, if it pleases you, I'll get on a boat for China."

"You can't be serious," Lucille exclaimed. "We'll talk this thing over. I'll give you some money, quite a lot of money, but not my entire fortune."

"You've got a good deal more than that salted away, and well you know it," Beau replied. "But we'll talk all you like. If you ask me to a meal tomorrow, I shan't say no; but I've rather made up my mind and I somehow don't think you will be able to coax me into altering it."

"I'll kill you rather than give you everything I've worked for all these years!" Lucille cried hotly.

Beau chuckled.

"I thought you were thinking of murder, but it isn't easy. And they tell me that either swinging or the chair is a singularly unpleasant way of dying."

Lucille picked up the velvet handbag she had been carrying when she came into the room.

"It's time you went," she said. "How much do you want tonight?"

"Enough to get me a decent lodging," Beau began, and then, as she opened her handbag, he moved with almost incredible swiftness and took her note-case out of her hand before she could open it.

Helplessly Lucille watched him count the notes and chuck her case down on the sofa.

"Ten pounds," he said. "Well, it might be worse! I'll see you tomorrow night, my pretty, and you had best have the hundred thousand waiting. You better bring me some sterling to be going on with—fifty or a hundred pounds might keep me till the end of the week."

"Get out of here before I kill you!" Lucille stormed.

Her rage was almost uncontrollable, but Beau continued to laugh at her.

He picked up his hat and set it on his head at an angle she remembered as being characteristic of him; then with his hands in his pocket, he stood looking at her for a moment, watching her rage impotently at him, noting the sparkle of diamonds round her neck, the furious gestures of her bejewelled fingers.

"You're still a darned pretty woman," he said at length. "I don't know how you've managed to keep looking so young, but you've managed it right enough. It's unfortunate I'm getting to be an old man.

"Fifteen years ago I should not have walked out to look for other lodgings tonight; I should have stayed here and you wouldn't have wanted to stop me, but prisons are mighty sterilising.

"I've only one sweetheart now—that's money and what it will buy me. Sleep well, honeybunch."

He bent towards her and she smelt his whisky-laden breath as he pressed his lips lightly against her cheeks.

But before she could cry out against him, before she could even formulate the angry abuse which seemed to rise in a crescendo to her lips, he had saluted her mockingly and gone from the room.

The door slammed behind him and she was alone.

For a moment Lucille stood trembling with rage, her breath coming in quick gasps; and then slowly her anger died away from her and she felt the tears gather in her eyes.

It was years since she had cried and now she wasn't

quite certain why she was weeping. She wasn't crying
because she was angry, of frightened, or sorry.

Perhaps really she was crying for her lost youth,
for she knew now that it was gone for ever, the youth
in which she had wasted three precious years in loving
a wastrel like Beau.

13

Everything was at sixes and sevens.

Randal was used to things going wrong just before
an Opening Night, but it seemed to him that he had
never known rehearsals be so consistently difficult.

What made it worse was that there was nothing one
could put a hand on.

It was just a general impression of tangled ends and
bad timing, of roughness and a lack of that smooth
polish which makes all the difference to a first-class
production.

He regretted not once but a thousand times that he
had let himself be persuaded by Lord Rockampstead
into having the Opening Night in London rather than,
as was traditional, in Manchester or Glasgow.

It was not only Randal who had been over-per-
suaded in this matter, but everyone else connected
with the production of *Today and Tomorrow*.

Lord Rockampstead had been adamant on this point
despite everything anyone could say to the contrary. It
was in fact a kind of fetish with him.

He had believed in the play, he had backed it, and
he wanted his friends to see the very first night of its
showing.

He could not bear to wait for the usual rather slower
process of an opening in the provinces and six weeks
or so on tour when the rough ends could be pared off

and the whole thing polished to the highest state of perfection.

He believed in *Today and Tomorrow;* he thought it would be the sensational, outstanding play of the year, and he was determined to enjoy the Opening Night, surrounded by the people he liked best and whose opinion he valued.

He had no patience, and Randal told himself now that impatience was not usually successful in the theatrical world.

But the die was cast; *Today and Tomorrow* was to open on October 25th and tremendous preparations had been made to make the Opening Night as colourful, exciting and successful as a film première or a command performance.

It had been publicised up to the hilt and already had a waiting list of bookings, which all sounded excellent from the box office point of view.

But Randal was almost in despair.

If only he knew what was wrong, he felt he would have been happier. The point was that he didn't know, neither did Bruce Bellingham.

They had all been working so hard this past week that none of them had had time to think of anything but rehearsal after rehearsal.

When they got home at night, it was to flop into bed too dead tired to do anything but sleep until they were called in the morning—to rise hurriedly and post down to the theatre for yet another rehearsal.

There was some undercurrent of disruption which Randal sensed and yet he could not put his finger on it.

He was sure that Lucille was at the bottom of the trouble, whatever it might be; and yet it was difficult to find fault with her acting.

She was word-perfect in her part; she did exactly as she was told; she looked lovely, and she had managed to receive so much advance publicity that no one,

242

however prejudiced, however envious, could complain that she at least was not pulling her weight.

And yet, Randal thought, when he had time to think about her as a person rather than as Marlene, the heroine of *Today and Tomorrow,* she was not her usual self.

Since the night when she had told him that she wished to marry him they had hardly been alone for more than a few seconds; and when they were she had said very little to him that was not the ordinary, commonplace chatter of the theatre.

Sometimes he thought she was looking strained.

Then he told himself there was every likelihood of that, considering she was working sometimes twelve hours a day and finding, as they all found, that it left one utterly exhausted.

No one would have minded being tired if rehearsals had been good; but they were disappointing.

Randal had to face the facts, and as he watched Lucille rehearsing the last scene of the play, he asked himself savagely what was wrong.

Lucille was acting her part competently and with a cool assurance; she was never for a moment at a loss as to what to do or how to carry on, and yet something was missing.

What was it? Randal wondered. He knew that Bruce Bellingham was as perplexed as he was.

Bruce's hair was in a permanent state of mop-like untidiness these days, and yet, like Randal, he was not certain why he felt so distracted and worried.

There was nothing wrong with the play itself, Randal told himself. He was as certain of that as he had ever been certain of anything in his life before.

With the alterations he had made to the second act at Sorella's suggestion the play was very near perfect. It was impossible to see where one could improve on it.

It must be Lucille who was at fault, Randal thought,

watching her as she said good-bye to the man she loved and was left alone on an empty stage.

It was a curtain which should have brought tears to the eyes and yet Randal felt peculiarly dry-eyed and tight-lipped about it.

Bruce was speaking to the leading man; and while he was talking to him, Randal noticed that Lucille was standing a little apart, her hands hanging limply at her sides, her eyes staring straight ahead of her.

There was a look almost of desperation on her face, he thought, and then he laughed at the very idea.

What had Lucille got to be desperate about?

He glanced at his watch; it was half past ten, and suddenly Randal felt that he could stand no more.

He didn't wait to say good-night to anyone, but made his way round the back and, going out through the stage door, told the door-keeper to tell Mr. Bellingham he had gone home.

"Have you finished for the night, Sir?" the old man asked.

"I hope so for everybody's sake," Randal replied. "If they are as tired of this play as I am, they will want to get to bed quickly and forget it."

The door-keeper chuckled.

"Now don't you be feeling like that, Sir," he wheezed; "it'll be all right on the night."

Randal didn't bother to answer him, but walked down the street to where his car was parked.

How often he had heard those words, "It will be all right on the night"! It was a catch-phrase, a slogan of the theatre, and people repeated it automatically with a conviction in their voices which came entirely from wishful thinking.

"What is wrong? Damn it, what is wrong with it?" Randal muttered to himself as he got into his Bentley.

Then, as he drove away, he had a longing to talk to somebody.

Not Lucille, nor Bruce, nor Edward, nor anyone

who was too besotted with the play and its production by now to have an original thought left in their heads about it, but somebody outside it all, someone whom he liked and trusted.

Jane of course was the obvious person.

She had kept her word, she hadn't been near the theatre since, to save the show, she had broken off their engagement and to all intents and purposes gone out of his life.

He had a sudden longing for her now. She was so lovely, so elegant.

She would, he thought, put the play in its proper perspective. For the last week it had overwhelmed him and everyone else who was acting in it.

They had lived with the play—it had been food, drink and sleep to them—it had become their gaoler from whom they could never escape.

Randal put his foot on the accelerator and broke all speed records down the Mall. Luckily there were few people about, for it was raining hard.

He reached Hyde Park Corner and turned down Chapel Street into Belgrave Square. Jane wouldn't be expecting him, but he hoped she would be alone.

Even if she was with other people, he thought, he would make her come away with him somewhere quiet where they could talk, where he could tell her how worried he was, where he could enjoy the comfort of her sympathy and be sure of her understanding.

He got out of the car and hurried across the wet pavement to the protection of the portico over Lord Rockampstead's front door.

He rang the bell and it was only a few seconds before it was opened.

"Is Miss Crake at home?"

"Good evening, Mr. Gray," the butler answered with a smile. "It's nice to see you, Sir. You're quite a stranger."

"I'm afraid I am," Randal said, entering the hall, and letting a footman help him out of his overcoat.

"The play is progressing favourably, I hope, Sir?" the butler asked. "We're all getting very excited about the first night. His Lordship has booked seats in the Upper Circle for most of the staff."

"I only hope you won't be disappointed," Randal replied.

"I'm quite certain we shan't be that, Sir," the butler answered.

As he followed the man across the hall to the lift, Randal wished that he felt equally confident.

"Miss Jane is in her own sitting-room, Sir. His Lordship is out. He will be sorry to have missed you."

Randal could not reply that he was glad to have missed his Lordship, which was the truth. He wanted to see Jane and no one else. It took only a few seconds for the lift to glide up to the second floor.

Jane's sitting-room was a symphony in egg-shell blue and silver, and it was lit by candles, a conceit which Randal found amusing and extremely soothing to over-tired nerves.

It was also very flattering to feminine beauty; and as Jane rose from her writing-desk when Randal was announced, he thought he had never seen her look so lovely.

She was wearing a dinner gown of pale gold chiffon, caught at the waist with a jewelled belt of multi-coloured stones and she had long ear-rings of different coloured sapphires to match hanging from her tiny ears.

"Randal!"

She exclaimed his name in delight. Then she ran towards him holding out both her hands.

"Darling, I was just thinking of you; why are you here?"

"Isn't that rather obvious? To see you," Randal replied.

He heard the door shut behind the butler, and putting his arms around Jane, he held her close.

"I'm tired and worried," he confessed, his cheek against hers.

246

"Poor Randal!" Jane's tone was caressing. "Come and sit down and tell me all about it. I'll get you a drink."

He allowed her to lead him to the sofa by the fire, and then he watched her as she walked across the room to press the bell.

"We are going to have a bottle of champagne," she said. "It will do you good, and I feel now you're here I want to celebrate."

She took command of him and Randal was only too glad to let her do as she wished.

He drank the champagne when it was brought, and after a second glass he felt some of his worries slipping away from him.

It was one thing to be over-wrought and distressed in the theatre, and another to recapture that feeling of frustration when sitting in front of the fire, with a lovely woman doing her best to make one feel comfortable and happy.

"Darling, tell me all about yourself," Jane said. "How is that beastly woman? How I hate her!"

"Do you mean Lucille?" Randal asked rather feebly.

He knew quite well of whom she was speaking. Then, he didn't know why, the desire to talk went from him.

After all, it wasn't so easy to tell Jane what was worrying him. She would think he was exaggerating the troubles which always seemed to pile one on top of another just before an Opening Night.

"I'm tired of myself and tired of the theatre," he heard himself saying. "What have you been doing?"

"Thinking about you," Jane answered. "I can't tell you how much I've missed you. I loathe Lucille Lund more every day of my life. If it wasn't that I thought she was so valuable to your play, I should pray that she might fall from a window and break her neck or something equally horrible."

"Don't think about her," Randal insisted, "and above

247

all, don't let's talk about her. Have you been to a lot of parties? Whom have you seen?"

Even as he asked the questions he realised how little he was interested in the answers.

There was only one thing with which he was concerned at the moment—his play. He found himself thinking of how the rehearsal had gone that day. It hadn't been right. They had taken that final scene too quickly; and the first act appeared to drag. He must speak to Bruce about it.

Jane was talking and he hadn't the least idea what she was saying.

He knew suddenly that he must go back, back to the theatre; or, if they had all gone, to Bruce's lodgings. They must get together and talk things out.

This wasn't something he must decide by himself, he must have someone to help him.

". . . it really was terribly amusing," he heard Jane say.

"Was it?" He asked the question because he felt that she was waiting for him to say something.

"If you could have seen Diana's face, she really didn't quite know how to take it. For one moment she thought she ought to be angry, and then she decided to treat it as a joke. Of course, everyone knew it wasn't what he intended."

"Of course not," Randal murmured.

"Darling, your glass is empty!"

"I don't want any more."

"Nonsense, there's nearly half a bottle left. You can't waste good wine like that!"

Jane poured him out another glass. Randal began to feel light-headed.

He remembered now that he had had nothing to eat since luncheon and then he had only snatched a sandwich in a bar behind the theatre.

If he went home, he thought, Sorella would cook him an omelette and there would be coffee, that fragrant, delicious coffee which only Sorella could make to his satisfaction and which had spoiled him for everyone else's brew.

Perhaps he had better go home and get Bruce to come round to the flat.

"Darling, you're tired!"

"Yes, I am, I had better be getting home to bed," Randal answered.

He would have got to his feet, but suddenly Jane sat down beside him and putting her arms round him, drew his head on to her shoulder.

"My poor Randal, you work too hard," she said softly.

He felt the tips of her fingers caressing his forehead. She pressed them against his weary eyes and he felt them move down his cheek until they touched his neck.

Then her lips were on his, warm and hungry, inviting his kisses with a passion that he had never known from Jane before.

For a moment he resisted both the touch of her fingers and the invitation on her lips. He was too tired, too weary, far too preoccupied at this particular moment.

Then insidiously she awoke in him a desire for her.

This was Jane—Jane who had often seemed so cool and aloof; Jane who had been for a short while out of his reach. Almost instinctively his arms tightened around her, and as he did so, he felt Jane press herself closer to him.

A flame seemed to pass between them and their passion mounted higher and higher till Randal felt himself floating away into an ecstasy of desire in which everything was forgotten save the aching need of his body for . . . Jane. . . .

Two hours later Randal walked softly down the stairs. There was no one in the hall, although the lights were on.

His overcoat was lying on the chair; he picked it up, put it on, and almost surreptitiously let himself out of the front door, pulling it to behind him with a little clang.

He got into the Bentley, started up the engine and drove slowly round the Square. It was then he knew that it had happened to him, knew it with a clarity which there was no denying.

For a moment he hated Jane, hated her because she had destroyed yet another illusion, broken and shattered yet another dream.

He had thought she was different. There had been something special about her which had attracted him, apart from her more obvious attractions.

He had thought he had found in her something for which he had always been looking; something he could not put into words; something he could not explain even to himself, and yet he had been seeking it all his life.

Now he knew only too surely that he had been mistaken.

Jane was a very lovely, very attractive young woman; but she was not unique in any way, not different from all the other lovely and attractive women he had possessed far too easily, who had loved him not for himself, but for his virility.

If only he knew what he wanted, Randal thought; if only he could put it into words; but it was as elusive as a plot which had not yet formulated itself in his own mind.

He only knew it was there, this something that he wanted, this thing which could not be expressed. It was like that excitement within himself when he knew the first stirring of a plot in his mind.

There was a thrill and wonder in that which was in some way comparable to what he sought in a woman and yet could never find.

He could never feel that same stirring, that same inexplicable breathlessness when he met someone or when he was suddenly fully conscious of their presence.

Then all too soon it would vanish, leaving him

homesick and miserable because it was gone, leaving him unsatisfied and disappointed.

Yes, those were the right words, and then he remembered who had used them before.

"If you marry Jane, you will be disappointed," Sorella had said.

He could hear her saying it, and remembered his own sense of annoyance that she should be so silly; but she had been right. He knew that now. He was disappointed in Jane—she had failed him.

It was Sorella, too who had said:

"People are so unsatisfying."

That was true. Jane was unsatisfying. He had expected so much, much more of her; and now he knew that it was not hers to give.

He felt detached from himself and from his own yearnings. He could see them only as if he were reaching out his arms towards something intangible; perhaps spiritual was the right word, he was not sure.

There was something wanted, something he craved for and yet could never find.

He saw his life as if it were a pilgrimage. He was traveling along a winding, twisting road which he knew he must follow however far it went, however long the way.

Every so often he would think he had come to the end, that he had found what he wanted; but after resting for a short time he would know only too clearly that he had been mistaken.

He was a pilgrim, finding his way to some uncharted, unexplored Mecca, of which there were no maps and to which there were no signposts.

A mirage—that was what Jane had been, and that was what many others had been before her.

"Unsatisfying; disappointing."

The words seemed to haunt him; as he got into bed they seemed to repeat themselves over and over again in his mind.

He fell asleep whispering them and when he awoke next morning they were still in his mind.

Hoppy came into the room before he had even begun his breakfast.

"I'm sorry to brother you so early, Randal," she said, "but you must sign these letters for me. I wouldn't worry you if they weren't urgent."

"Give them to me."

Randal opened the folder and scrawled his signature without even glancing through the letters. It was something he never did unless he was unduly rushed or worried, and Hoppy looked at him anxiously.

"Is there anything wrong?" she asked.

"Why should there be?" Randal enquired snappily.

She knew then that something was very wrong; but being tactful she said nothing, merely gathering up the signed letters and going from the room.

When Randal was dressed half an hour later, he found Sorella waiting for him in the hall. She was wearing a new overcoat and on her head she wore a little green velvet beret to match her green dress.

"Can I come with you this morning?" she asked a little wistfully.

"If you want to," Randal said ungraciously.

They went down in the lift in silence and only as they got into the car did Sorella say quietly:

"It's the dress rehearsal today, isn't it?"

Randal grunted a reply and driving somewhat aggressively edged the car into the traffic which was moving slowly, with frequent stops, down Park Lane.

"May I say something?" Sorella said after a moment.

"About the play?" Randal enquired. "If you're going to tell me something's wrong, I know that already."

"Of course you do," Sorella said. "I was in the theatre yesterday afternoon. I stayed there till nearly six and then Hoppy wanted me to go home with her— that was why I came away."

"And what conclusion did you come to?" Randal asked.

He was speaking sarcastically, in the voice that he had not used to Sorella for a long time. She glanced at him under her eyelashes, but otherwise she appeared to take no notice.

"Lucille is worried unhappy."

"Well, if she is, it isn't my fault," Randal replied.

He thought back over the past week.

No, there was nothing that he could accuse himself of doing which might be responsible for Lucille's unhappiness, if that was what it was. He had been nice to her; he had been affectionate and considerate.

No, Randal told himself, if Lucille was unhappy, he was not to blame. Sorella must be mistaken, but he knew that was unlikely. Sorella was so seldom at fault.

"Perhaps Edward could find out what is the matter," Sorella suggested. "I think he knows that something is wrong, for I heard him say to someone yesterday: 'I wish to Heaven I knew what was troubling Lucille. She's quiet, and when she's quiet it's serious.'"

Randal recognised instantly the truth of this. Lucille had been quiet. She was usually flamboyant, overpowering, impossible to ignore or forget.

She would seem to dominate everything, the whole stage would be full of her, the theatre would seem to contain nothing and nobody else.

Now he knew what was wrong with the play.

He had expected Lucille to dominate it from the beginning to the end. He had written the part of Marlene for a dominant character.

He felt that sub-consciously he must have had Lucille in mind when he wrote it, even though he had not expected her to play it.

It was only by completely dominating all three acts that the effect he wanted could be achieved.

That was what was wrong, that was what was perturbing him.

Lucille was acting the part and saying the words and giving precisely the right action at precisely the right moment, but she was not dominating each scene.

It was as if she had withdrawn from the stage, leaving her body behind, but the spirit of her was missing. And only the spirit and fire of Lucille could make *Today and Tomorrow* into the success it ought to be.

Sorella was right—how right she was! And yet something perverse and disagreeable in Randal was not prepared to say so at this moment.

With hardly a word they arrived at the theatre, and he left her as they went in at the stage door. He supposed she would go through the wings and into the front of the house.

He didn't really think about it as he ran upstairs to Lucille's dressing-room.

Her dresser was there, old Maggie, whom everyone loved, but who could be a devil when she was annoyed or when Lucille was not getting the attention Maggie thought she ought to have.

The lights were on, the fire was burning brightly and there was the fragrance from a dozen vases of hot-house flowers mingled with the aroma of Lucille's special scent.

"Is Mr. Jepson here yet, Maggie?" Randal asked.

"Good morning, Mr. Gray," Maggie replied. "Yes, he was here a moment or two ago. I don't suppose he's gone far."

Even as Maggie spoke, Randal heard a step in the passage and saw Edward Jepson coming from another dressing-room.

"Edward, I want to speak to you," Randal cried.

"Of course, old man. There's an empty dressing-room here and I've annexed it for myself. You know what a lot of people I have to see when the play's in production, and Lucille gets annoyed if I talk business in her room. She says it ruins the atmosphere.

Edward led the way into the spare dressing-room. which was very unlike the one Randal had just left. Here was a plain deal table, two hard chairs, reflected and re-reflected in the undusted mirrors which covered the walls.

"Haven't got round to furnishing it yet awhile," Edward said with a grin, "but I haven't forgotten this."

He took a bottle of whisky from the cupboard and put two glasses on the table.

"Help yourself," he suggested.

"It's too early for me," Randal replied.

"Oh, I can do with a tiny one," Edward said, pouring himself out two fingers and swigging it down neat. "Now, what's the headache?" he enquired.

"That's for you to tell me," Randal said. "What's the matter with Lucille?"

For a moment Edward raised his eyebrows, then he decided not to prevaricate.

"I wish to God I knew."

"Well, you'd better find out," Randal said. "We open tomorrow night. If the show goes like it did yesterday, we'll shut at the end of the week."

"What do you suggest is wrong?" Edward asked cautiously.

"Lucille's wrong," Randal replied. "She's playing the part as it's written and you know as well as I do that's not good enough. Marlene is meant to be tremendous, sensational. She's a personality one can't ignore. Lucille has not only got to sweep those who act with her off their feet, she's got to sweep the audience, too, or they will sweep themselves out. Have you got it?"

"Do you know what's troubling her?" Edward asked.

"If you mean by that, is it my fault, the answer is no. I have agreed to everything she suggested—everything."

Edward's eyes narrowed as he looked at Randal.

"Would you like to elucidate what you mean by everything?"

"Lucille can tell you that herself in due course," Randal replied.

"I see." Edward poured himself out another drink.

It was then they heard Lucille coming down the passage. There was no mistaking the sound of her footsteps. She went into her dressing-room and the door slammed behind her.

Edward finished the whisky in his glass and put the bottle away in the cupboard.

"You'd better get round to the front and leave this to me," he said.

Randal watched him go down the passage and enter Lucille's room without knocking.

After a moment Maggie came out into the passage and stood propped near the door with a disagreeable expression on her face.

She hated being called from Lucille's room—always took it as a personal affront. Randal waited a few minutes and then he walked past her and down the stone steps which led to the stage.

There was about a quarter of an hour of the first act to be got through before the heroine appeared.

It went smoothly, but Randal found himself tense, waiting for the moment when he would see Lucille, wondering if she would be any different, if Edward would succeed in finding out what was wrong and in putting things right.

Then when her cue came, there was no Lucille. They waited for a moment and from behind the stage they could hear the callboy shouting:

"Miss Lund, please! Miss Lund, please!"

The rest of the actors who had been keyed up into giving a smooth performance seemed to slump. Randal could sense the fall in the atmosphere. Bruce ran his fingers through his hair and chucked his script down on the stage.

"Where's Lucille?" he asked angrily.

There was no reply. Everybody seemed to stand waiting. It was as if a great machine had been checked suddenly in the very moment of its revolving.

"Where's Lucille?" Bruce turned towards Randal.

"I'll go and see what has happened," Randal answered.

He started to walk along the front row of the stalls

256

to reach the door on the stage. At the end of the row Sorella was sitting.

She was watching the stage and did not see Randal approach until he was almost beside her. She looked up at him and hastily got to her feet.

As she did so one of the men from the Manager's office came down the gangway.

"Are you Miss Forest?" he asked. "You're wanted on the telephone."

"Am I?" Sorella asked in surprise. She looked at Randal. "I wonder who it can be?"

"Hoppy, I should think," Randal answered.

"Of course." Sorella smiled at him, and then went up the gangway as he went behind the stage.

The Manager's office was full of people; the man who had fetched her indicated the telephone lying on a table with its receiver off. Sorella took it up. As Randal had anticipated, it was Hoppy at the other end.

"Is that you, Sorella?"

"Yes, Hoppy is anything the matter?"

"I want you to come back to the flat at once. At once, do you understand? It's important. There's someone here to see you."

"Who is it?" Sorella asked.

It was difficult to hear what Hoppy was saying owing to the noise in the room.

"I can't tell you on the telephone," Hoppy said.

Her voice sounded strange, Sorella thought.

"I'll get a taxi and come back at once," she promised.

She put down the receiver and thanked the man who had fetched her. As she went towards the door, she glanced back at the stage. Everyone was still waiting with a look of suspended animation.

Only Bruce was moving, striding up and down angrily, running his fingers through his hair.

Sorella gave a little sigh.

She wanted to stay and see what happened. She knew how important it was to Randal that Lucille should do what was expected of her; but something was wrong, very wrong, Sorella thought.

She sighed again.

It was no use waiting; Hoppy had told her to come at once. Her voice had seemed different, quite perturbed and sharp as it was when she was put out about something.

"I must do what she wants," Sorella thought, and turned determinedly towards the exit.

She wished Randal was there—she would like to have had one last look at him before she went.

14

As Edward walked into the dressing-room he made a gesture which told Maggie that he wanted to be alone with Lucille.

"There's no time . . ." she started to say, but Edward interrupted her.

"Scram!" he commanded.

Maggie, muttering beneath her breath, went out into the passage, shutting the door behind her with an energy which spoke volumes.

Lucille looked at Edward and raised her eyebrows.

"Anything the matter?"

"Yes," he answered briefly.

She put down the stick of grease-paint she was holding in her hand.

"What is it?"

He thought there was a strange apprehensive note in her voice.

"To speak straight from the shoulder, honey, it's you," he replied.

He thought in surprise that he detected an expression of relief on Lucille's face.

"Sweetheart, your playing is lousy," he went on, "and I'm not the only one to notice it."

"Lousy?" Lucille got to her feet angrily. "They can't say that. I'm word-perfect, I'm doing exactly what Bruce and Randal ask of me."

"But that's the lot," Edward said. "You're giving them what they ask and not another darned thing. You know, and I know, it's not enough. We know it, and the British public will know it tomorrow night."

"You're talking rubbish," Lucille said aggressively.

Edward sighed and his hands deep in his trouser pockets jingled his money.

He waited. He had learned that silence was often far more effective than talking when he was dealing with Lucille.

She was so used to people talking and so used to hearing her own voice that silence commanded her attention where even a loudspeaker would leave her unmoved.

She walked across the dressing-room and back again.

She was wearing the white linen robe which she invariably used to make up. It was freshly laundered and in its severity gave her an unusually young appearance.

"She might," Edward thought suddenly, "be a young girl going to her confirmation."

Then, as she turned towards him, he saw a look of worry and anxiety on her face as he had never seen before in all their long acquaintance.

"Lucille, baby, what is it?" he asked, his voice low and tender.

She looked up at him, then clasped her hands together with a curious movement as though she wanted to wring them.

"I can't tell you, Edward."

"Now see here, honey, if you're worried or in any trouble, that's where I come in. It's what I'm here for, to look after you, to keep the wolves at bay—whatever sort of wolves they may be."

Lucille made a sound that was between a sob and a laugh.

"It's not that sort of thing, Edward."

"I thought maybe that Randal . . ."

"No, no!" Lucille almost shouted the words. "It isn't Randal. It's nothing like that."

She was almost hysterical, and Edward putting out his big arms drew her close to him.

"Now listen, baby, you've just got to tell your big Daddy what's troubling you. It doesn't matter what it is, I'll put it right, I'll promise you that. There's mighty little I can't do when I set my mind to it."

"You can't put this right," Lucille answered.

For a moment she seemed to surrender to the comfort and strength of Edward's arms.

She laid her head against his shoulder; then with a sudden nervous movement she pushed him away from her and, walking to the dressing-table, flopped down in the chair and stared at her reflection in the looking-glass.

Even in her distress and anxiety she looked lovely.

She somehow expected to see herself haggard and distraught; instead her usual pink-and-white beauty stared back at her.

Her eyes, large and luminous, registered only the facile, cardboard gravity of a film heroine; and her mouth, rather than being twisted with some inner pain, appeared to pout provocatively.

"Well?" Edward's voice prompted from behind her.

Lucille suddenly seemed to make up her mind.

"If you want the truth, you shall have it. . . . I've killed a man!"

There was the jingle of Edward's money before he said:

"And how did you do that, honey?"

"I murdered him. Do you understand, I murdered him!"

Edward took one hand out of his pocket to scratch his nose.

"Any guy that I know?" he enquired.

Lucille's lips tightened for a moment.

"My husband."

This time she succeeded in making Edward look astonished.

"Your husband?" he repeated slowly. "Suppose we go back to the beginning, sweetheart. Where did you get him and what's his name?"

And then Lucille told her story. She was no longer reluctant to talk; in fact the words seemed to pour from her lips as if she could hardly control them.

She told Edward how she married Beau when she was twenty. She told him how much she had loved him and the hell she had found awaiting her after the ceremony was over.

She told the tale simply and without exaggeration, and Edward could understand all too clearly the misery she had experienced as she and Beau toured together with cheap companies in small, unimportant towns.

He knew without Lucille's explaining what the journeys had been like, sitting up all night on hard seats and waiting for hours at draughty junctions. He knew, too, the conditions of the lodgings which were the best they could afford.

He could understand Lucille's feeling of depression and misery; but he could understand, too, why Beau had sought consolation in the drinking saloons.

Then Lucille, continuing her story, told Edward how she'd imagined that Beau must be dead, only to have him turn up unexpectedly at the Savoy.

"He asked me for a hundred thousand dollars," she said, "and when I wouldn't give it to him, threatened that he would sell his story to the newspapers. He knew my age right enough and he knew what harm it would do me to let the public learn the truth.

"He had got me where he wanted me and he was determined to turn the screw.

"I sent him away the first night. He took what money

261

I had in my note-case and said he would be back the following day. I was desperate, Edward.

"Even if I gave him the hundred thousand dollars, which was practically everything I've got saved, there was no guarantee that, having got it, he would keep his mouth shut.

"He would talk at any time, if it suited him, or if he was hard up for money. I lay awake all that night thinking, and then when the morning came I decided what I would do."

Lucille paused, and Edward saw that her hands were clenched together so that her knuckles were white.

"It was wrong, it was wicked, it was bad, I see that now; but at the time I could think of nothing except getting rid of Beau and silencing him once and for all."

"What did you do?" Edward asked curiously.

Lucille gave a little shudder.

"I hardly dare to tell you," she replied. "I think I must have been crazy, but I wanted to be quit of him. It wasn't only that I was afraid of him, it was also because I hated him.

"He stood for everything that had been sordid, horrible and bestial in my life, everything I had got away from, everything I thought forgotten and buried in the past.

"He brought back the memories of all the horrors I had suffered.

"He made me feel again, as I had felt when I was married to him, helpless and ineffective, a bad actress and a rotten wife who couldn't do anything right.

"When you came along, you altered everything for me. You altered me. I couldn't bear to slip backwards, to be what I was before, unsure of myself, unsure of everything."

"What did you do?" Edward repeated.

There was a sudden loud rapping on the door.

It was the callboy. They heard his voice high and shrill outside. Neither Edward nor Lucille paid the slightest attention.

262

For a moment Lucille was silent, but only as if she drew a deep breath so that she might have the strength to continue her story.

"There was a chemist called Hausmann who was in love with me during the war," she went on at length. "I don't expect you will remember him. I didn't see much of him, but he was crazy about me and he was crazy about a lot of other things, too.

"He had escaped from Poland just before the Germans invaded it. He had been through some pretty grim moments in his life and they had left their mark on him.

"He was convinced that sooner or later the Germans would try to invade America. He told me that when that happened I wasn't to try to escape, but to kill myself.

"He used to talk for hours about the horrors the Nazis would inflict on us when they were the conquerors of the world, and in the end he gave me a little phial of morphia which he made me swear I would always carry about with me.

"There were six little tablets in it. He told me that two were enough for a lethal dose, but he gave me the rest in case there was someone I cared about with me at the time and I should want to take them with me.

"I think he was thinking of himself, but he was really such a bore with his talk of tortures and castrations and I don't know what else that I got tired of him and wouldn't see him any more.

"But I kept the morphia in my jewel case. It was where I had put it for safety when he first gave it to me, and I wouldn't chuck it out. You never know when a little morphia might come in useful."

"Was that what you gave Beau?" Edward asked.

"That was what I gave him," Lucille replied. "I crushed up all six of the tablets and put them in a half a bottle of whisky. I shook it up well. It seemed to mix all right."

"And Beau drank it?" Edward enquired.

263

"I don't know," Lucille answered. "When he came round for the dollars, I told him I was making every effort to get them for him. I gave him fifty pounds to be going on with and told him that he could come back at the end of the week. He wanted a drink, of course.

"He never could sit still for a moment unless he had a glass in his hand, and I poured him out a stiff one. It was all that was left in the bottom of the bottle—I had seen to that.

"When he had drunk it, he wanted another. I went to the cupboard and took out the half-bottle in which I had put the morphia.

"'I've got someone coming to see me and they mustn't find you here,' I said. 'You had better go; and if you must drink, take the bottle with you.'

"Beau never had any pride where drink was con-concerned. He stuck the Scotch in his pocket.

"'I'll be back,' he said, as he reached the door, and then he was gone.

"At first I could only think of how clever I had been; and then I suppose it was my upbringing and the Church-going I had to endure as a child. I began to get upset.

"I kept thinking of Beau opening that bottle and drinking it off. I wondered what he would feel like when the morphia first began to work on him. I went on thinking and thinking."

Lucille put her fingers up to her eyes.

"I can't sleep, Edward," she said. "I haven't slept since that night. I keep remembering that I've murdered Beau."

Edward put his hand on her shoulder.

"You poor child, why didn't you tell me before?"

"I was afraid," Lucille answered. "Afraid and . . . ashamed."

"Now listen to me . . ." Edward began briskly.

There came another loud knock at the door.

"Miss Lund, please."

"To begin with," Edward went on, as though he had

not heard the callboy's interruption, "I don't believe that morphia taken in whisky would kill a man. That we will have to find out; but in my opinion alcohol would, to a very great extent, prove an antidote."

"Then you think Beau isn't dead?" Lucille cried. "Oh, Edward! If he isn't, I'll be glad, yes, wonderfully glad not to have this horror haunting me, not to have the thought that I am a murderess on my conscience."

"All this talk of being a murderess is just poppycock," Edward said sharply. "Now I'll tell you honey, what I am going to do. I am going to ring up a friend of mine at Scotland Yard and ask him to find out what has happened to Mr. Beau Brittain.

"Or maybe they know him as Michael O'Grady, who has recently been released after serving a charge for manslaughter.

"They're pretty smart in keeping track of their criminals over here, and you can bet your bottom dollar that the police have had Beau Brittain taped from the moment he came through the prison gates.

We'll find out what has happened to him. If he's dead or alive the police will know or they will be able to find out within a few hours."

"Oh, Edward! If only he's alive!" Lucille said. "I'll give him the money; I'll do whatever you suggest, so long as I don't have to lie awake suffering as I've suffered this last week."

"You poor, silly, little baby," Edward said.

His hand was on her shoulder. Lucille reached up her own to pat it.

"You're a good friend, Edward. I feel different already. Something heavy that was weighing me down inside has lightened."

"Don't you think about it any more for the moment," Edward admonished. "Go on to the stage and give a decent performance. You owe it to Randal. The boy's worried stiff about you."

"I can't act; I can't do anything but think about Beau," Lucille replied. "When you know for certain, perhaps I'll feel different; but at the moment I feel just as though I was an automaton. I can say the part, I can remember to do what I've been told, but I can't feel anything that Marlene would feel. I can only remember that I have murdered a man I once loved and who for three years was my husband."

"Stop it!" Edward's voice was peremptory. "You'll make yourself ill. Promise to leave this to me. I'll handle it. I promise you that nothing you are imagining is true or likely to be true. Men don't die as easily as that."

"And if he's alive?" Lucille said slowly. "What then?"

Edward glanced at her sharply.

"That's a real question, isn't it?"

"If he's alive I want a divorce."

"That isn't going to be easy," Edward replied, "not without publicity."

"I know, but I want it just the same," Lucille replied.

"Because of Randal?"

"Because of Randal!"

With his hands in his trouser pockets Edward walked across to the window. For a moment he stood with his back to the room looking out on the dingy, weather-beaten houses opposite.

"I somehow never thought of your marrying anyone but me," he said after a moment.

"Edward!"

There was undisguised astonishment in Lucille's ejaculation. There was a smile on Edward's lips, a rather bitter one, as he turned round to face her.

"I've loved you ever since I first saw you," he said. Didn't you know?"

"But you never told me; you never even hinted at it," Lucille cried.

"Well, we seemed to get along quite happily as we were and I thought that, seeing that I was so much older than you, it might be a good thing to give you your head; but now I'm not so sure that I am so much older."

"Oh, Edward!"

There were tears in Lucille's eyes as she got to her feet and walked across to him. For a moment they stood looking at each other, then she slipped her arm through his.

"You stupid old thing," she said unsteadily. "Why didn't you tell me? I must have hurt you so often and in so many ways. All those different men, and now . . . Randal."

"Yes, now Randal," Edward repeated, and his tone was sour.

"I thought of going into production when I was too old to play the parts I've always played," Lucille explained. "I thought how suitable it would be to marry him—he is the coming playwright, a young man with a brilliant future; but I always thought of your being there. You know as well as I do, Edward, I couldn't do without you."

"Couldn't you?"

He was pleased and to Lucille there was something pathetic in his pleasure.

"Why do you let me talk like this?" She turned away from him suddenly. "You're trying to make me feel better. You're lying to me so that I shan't remember Beau is dead and that I've killed him. I'm a murderess, Edward, whatever you may say. How can you or Randal or anyone else love a murderess?"

Lucille was crying now, tears running down her cheeks.

Edward, who had seldom seen her cry, went down on one knee beside the chair into which she had thrown herself and tried to mop away her tears with his pocket handkerchief.

"Now, now, honey, don't you take on so."

The door opened and Randal came into the room.

"What's the matter, Lu . . ." he was saying, then stopped abruptly.

Edward looked round at him.

"Lucille's sick," he said. "She can't go on for a little while."

"But we're all waiting," Randal said. "Look here, Edward, you know how important this rehearsal is."

Edward got to his feet.

"I know just how important this rehearsal is," he said slowly, "and what Lucille means to the whole play; but give her time."

And then under his breath he added so that only Randal could hear.

"Get out you young fool, and leave us alone!"

The day which had begun badly went from bad to worse. The whole cast was upset by the delay caused by Lucille's non-appearance.

They hung about waiting; and then at last, when she did send a message to say she was ready, it was difficult to create any atmosphere other than that of resentment or to make the sequence of the play anything but disjointed.

The emotional crisis, whatever had caused it, appeared to leave Lucille limp and absolutely spiritless.

She went through her part mechanically, making no mistakes, but letting Marlene be a lifeless, uninteresting personality, which made one wonder why the story of *Today and Tomorrow* had ever been written.

"I can tell you one thing, old boy," the Stage Manager said to Randal half-way through the afternoon. "We're in for the biggest bloody flop this theatre has ever seen. I'm not saying it's your fault. It's that damned film star.

"You take my advice—another time you leave them as belongs to the films where they belong. You want beef and guts when it comes to a stage show and that Yank's got neither."

It was no use denying that the Stage Manager spoke the truth.

Beef and guts were exactly what Lucille did want for the part of Marlene, and at the moment she was as limp as a piece of paper that had been left out in the rain.

Eventually the dress rehearsal came to an end. There was no doubt that everyone's feelings about it were unanimous.

Small-part actors and actresses stood about whispering in corners, the Stage Manager could be heard behind the scenes voicing his opinion in a very blasphemous and virulent manner.

As the orchestra shuffled into their overcoats and hurried towards the stage door, Randal heard one of them murmuring the ominous words, "Three weeks."

Bruce, with his hair standing on end as if he had seen a ghost, called a rehearsal for the following morning.

"It's no use going on; everybody's tired," he said, "but we'll have to run through it tomorrow and see if we can speed up the whole production before the evening. I'm not going to say much more now, but I think you all know what is wrong."

They all knew what was wrong, right enough, but there was nothing any of them could do about it.

They could only look at Lucille as she went from the stage without a word and up the stone stairs to her dressing-room.

Randal made as though he would follow her, and then he changed his mind. He felt he could not stand any more. He was tired, hungry and completely and absolutely dispirited.

The whole thing was finished, as far as he could see. He had got a monumental flop on his hands and there was nothing he could do to save it. He put on his coat and hat and made for the stage door.

As he went out, he bumped into Edward coming in. The latter was smiling as if something pleased him.

"Hello, old chap," he said to Randal as they met in the doorway. "How's it gone?"

"There's only one word for the whole production, and that's 'lousy'."

Randal almost spat the last word at Edward as though it was a relief for the violence of his feelings.

Then he strode away into the autumn dusk without waiting for a reply. He thought he heard him call his name, but he didn't look back.

He thought as he went that he loathed Edward at that moment as much as he loathed Lucille. He wished he had never written such an ambitious, impossible play as *Today and Tomorrow*.

As he drove back through the wet streets, Randal played with the idea of postponing the Opening Night.

Suppose he persuaded Lucille to say she was ill; suppose he said some structural alteration had to be done to the theatre; suppose he thought of any excuse, however fantastic, rather than let the critics tear him limb from limb tomorrow night.

The more he thought of it, the more depressed he was; and then, as he went up in the lift to his flat, he wondered why Sorella had not come back to the theatre.

He had not thought of her before, but now it annoyed him that she should not have been there. Perhaps she would have thought of a solution.

She had helped him in the past; perhaps even this tremendous, horrifying problem would not be too much for her.

It was with a feeling of being badly used that Randal put his latch-key into the flat door and let himself in.

Neither Sorella nor Hoppy had been seen the whole afternoon and he felt aggrieved that they should have deserted him when he needed them both. He wanted their sympathy and understanding.

He wanted, at any rate from Sorella, some practical, sensible advice, though why a child should solve a problem that was far beyond his own ingenuity he was not prepared to explain, even to himself.

Hoppy was in her office as Randal entered the front

door. He heard the click of the telephone as if she had put down the receiver on hearing him come in.

He took off his coat and, as he laid it on the chair, turned to see Hoppy standing in the doorway of her office.

He was about to ask her where she had been all the afternoon, when something in the expression of her face stopped him.

The words on his lips were replaced by the almost instinctive question:

"What's wrong?"

"Have you seen Sorella?"

"No, of course not. Isn't she here?"

"You haven't seen her in the theatre? I telephoned and they told me she wasn't there, but I thought she might have spoken to you."

"No, I haven't seen her. What's all this about? What has happened?"

"Come into the sitting-room," Hoppy said.

Wonderingly Randal followed her. The sitting-room looked warm and cosy with the red curtains drawn and the fire blazing on the hearth.

There were sandwiches waiting for him in a silver dish on the table, which also held the drinks.

But Randal had forgotten his hunger, forgotten everything save a sudden feeling of fear as he said to Hoppy:

"What is this about Sorella?"

"Oh, Randal! I'm worried, desperately worried, and it's all my fault. I shall never forgive myself, never, if anything has happened to the child."

"What do you mean, if anything has happened to her?" Randal asked almost angrily. "What could have happened to her? Where is she?"

"I'll try to tell you from the beginning," Hoppy said in a tired voice.

"Tell me anything you like," Randal replied, "but first of all, where is Sorella? Isn't she here?"

"No, she's gone."

"Gone, but where, and why?"

"That's what I want to tell you," Hoppy answered. "Oh, Randal! I can't think why I was such a fool."

Hoppy's very real distress gradually indicated itself to Randal, and in a gentler voice than he had used before he said:

"Tell me everything in your own way, but first of all I'm going to give you a drink, you look all in."

"I'm so worried," Hoppy muttered. "I can't think where she can have gone."

Randal poured out a drink for Hoppy.

"Drink it," he commanded and stood over her while she took two or three sips. "Now, tell me what has happened."

"You hadn't been gone to the theatre long this morning," Hoppy began, "and I was just finishing a few letters and deciding I would follow you, when Norton came to say that there was a gentleman to see you. I went out and found a little, elderly man in the hall. I guessed at once he was a lawyer. He had that look.

"'Mr. Gray's at the theatre,' I said, 'It's the dress rehearsal today for his new play which opens tomorrow night.'

"'A new play?' the little man enquired. "I had no idea; dear me, how interesting. My wife saw one of Mr. Gray's plays when it came to Leeds and enjoyed it very much.'

"'Is there anything I can do for you?' I asked. He seemed to hesitate.

"'You're Mr. Gray's secretary, I suppose,' he said at length.

"'Yes, his confidential, private secretary,' I replied, and felt that somehow it had given him confidence.

He glanced at Norton, who was waiting, and I realised that he would like to speak to me alone.

"I took him into the office and shut the door.

"'Now, how can I help you? I asked, rather impatiently I'm afraid, because I wanted to get down to the theatre.

"'I came to ask Mr. Gray,' the lawyer said 'if he

could give me any news of Miss Sorella Forest, who was, I understand, with him in the aeroplane some weeks ago when her father was killed.'

" 'Yes, of course,' I replied, 'Sorella is living here at the moment.'

" 'Good, good,'—the little man seemed delighted. 'I'm afraid you'll think we're very remiss,' he went on, 'not to have got in touch with her sooner; but tell the truth the news of the accident, though I believe it was in many papers, escaped my notice.

" 'I'm afraid I never read any papers except *The Times* myself, but I must have been particularly hurried the day Mr. D'Arcy Forest's death was reported, because I never saw it. Anyway, better late than never, and I'm anxious to see Miss Forest as soon as possible, as I have very good news for her.'

" 'Good news!' I exclaimed. 'Would it be indiscreet to ask what it is?'

" 'Not at all,' the man replied. 'My firm, Lucas, Robinson and Manners, are executors for the Will of the late Mr. Bathurst, who I expect you know was Miss Forest's grandfather.'

" 'I had no idea, as it happens,' I remarked; 'but I hope he has left her some money.'

" 'Not a very large sum,' the lawyer replied, 'but something a little over £800, which I fancy will be acceptable to a young lady who I feel sure had no expectations from that quarter.'

" 'Why do you say that?' I asked.

"The little man looked at me with a faint smile.

" 'The late Mrs. D'Arcy Forest was cut off from her family when she ran away from home to marry an actor,' he said, 'Mr. Bathurst was a very strait-laced, puritanical sort of man, who believed anyone who went on the stage was heading straight for perdition.

" 'He altered his Will, as I remember only too well, immediately after his daughter's marriage, excluding her from participating in any part of his estate.

" 'Everything was left to his son, and then, at the

273

very end of the war, Mr. Bathurst's only son was killed in action.

" 'It was a terrible shock to the old man. He had a stroke soon after the news came to him. He recovered from it, but he was never quite the same again; and then, six months before he died, he changed his Will.

" 'He had not a considerable amount of money to leave, but he was determined that none of it should at any time find its way into the pockets of D'Arcy Forest, whom he hated as strongly as on the day he had run away with his daughter.

" 'He therefore left a legacy in trust for his grandchild, to be paid to her when she was eighteen, provided her father was dead. The rest of his money went to found a number of scholarships in memory of his son in schools in and around Leeds.' "

Hoppy took a deep breath. Then she went on to tell Randal how pleased she had been at the news.

"Eight hundred pounds!" she had exclaimed. "Sorella will be delighted; but of course she can't have it for some years. Is there any chance of her anticipating some of it to pay for her education or something like that?"

The lawyer looked puzzled.

"I don't understand," he said.

"Well, apparently the child has no money at all," Hoppy explained. "Her father left nothing, in fact he seemed to own only the clothes he stood up in. Mr. Gray feels in some way responsible for Sorella and is perfectly prepared to keep her here; but I think any girl would like to have a little money of her own until she is old enough to earn her own living."

In answer the lawyer took out his spectacles, and drew from the despatch case he carried in his hands.

"No, I am not mistaken," he said after a few moments" perusal of the papers. "Miss Sorella Forest was eighteen six weeks ago, and curiously enough, her father's death must have preceded the date on which she could receive her legacy by only a few days."

"Eighteen!" Hoppy exclaimed. "But surely we can't be talking about the same person?"

"I imagine so," the lawyer replied. "The young lady to whom I am referring is Miss Sorella Forest, only child, as far as I am aware, of Mr. D'Arcy Forest, one-time actor, and the late Mrs. Forest, formerly Margaret Bathurst, one-time ballet dancer. I have here the birth certificate, registered in Manchester, where Miss Forest was born."

"Eighteen!" Hoppy exlcaimed. "I can't believe it."

And yet she did. She understood now so many things which had perplexed her before.

Hoppy had telephoned to the theatre; had sent someone to find Sorella; and when she came to the telephone, had asked her to return to the flat immediately.

It was while Hoppy was waiting that she had begun to be afraid of what this might mean to Randal.

She had known for a long time, although she had tried to ignore the fact, that Randal was becoming increasingly interested in Sorella.

With a feeling almost of despair Hoppy saw her treasured plan of marriage between Randal and Jane slipping away from her.

She had thought about it so much that she almost felt as if she were an ambitious mother scheming for Randal's happiness and security.

It seemed to Hoppy so advantageous in every way that he should marry Jane.

Lord Rockampstead's millions would be at his disposal, he would have a wife who would not only entertain all the best and most important people in the land, but who already knew them well and intimately.

It had always been important to Hoppy that the gates of Society as well as of the theatre and the film world should be open to Randal.

She loved him and therefore she wanted him to have everything; and Jane was able to give him all those things which, at the moment, he lacked.

But now, just when Jane and Randal were secretly

engaged and only Lucille and the production of the play stood between them and a public announcement, Sorella must come along and muddle things.

It wasn't that Randal was likely to consider her seriously as a person.

It was just that he was fond of the child and liked having her about, and what woman would stand for that? Jane had already made herself very clear on that point.

She wasn't jealous. Hoppy would not attribute such a commonplace emotion to the feelings that Jane had about Sorella.

It was just that Randal's attention was divided and instead of giving all his interest, all his love and all his adoration to Jane, he spared some part of himself for the little waif whom he had brought to the house after the tragic accident in which her father was killed.

"If only D'Arcy Forest hadn't been killed," Hoppy thought, "they would have vanished from Randal's life as swiftly as they came into it!"

But D'Arcy Forest had died and Sorella was very much alive.

Hoppy was conscious how much Randal liked to be with the child. That week-end at Queen's Hoo had brought her the realisation that there was a close affinity between them.

Even in the theatre, when rehearsals were in progress, she was aware that although Sorella and Randal might sit apart, they always seemed to be conscious of one another.

When something went well on the stage, Randal would glance round as if for Sorella's approval; and if things went wrong, he would look at her, too, as if he pleaded with her for some suggestion or solution to set things right again.

There were so many moments now that Hoppy could see vividly had been important. At the time she had dismissed them as mere incidents.

Moments when Sorella's face had lit up at the sight

of Randal and she thought there had been a reflection of that light in his too.

Moments when she had heard his voice calling Sorella the very instant he entered the flat; when she had heard the child's joyful cry in response and had listened to them going together into the sitting-room talking eagerly and intimately.

There was danger here! Danger to Jane, and to Randal's happiness which he would find with Jane!

When Sorella came back to the flat, she had come straight into the office where the lawyer was waiting, and for a moment Hoppy thought she must have been mistaken and that the whole thing was ridiculous.

Sorella looked very immature in the green dress which Hoppy had helped her choose—a young girl's dress, plain and straight with its narrow leather belt, rounded neck and short sleeves.

Sorella looked exactly as if she should be carrying a satchel on her way to school.

Then, as Hoppy watched her listening attentively to the lawyer, her face curiously expressionless as she learned first of the legacy and then the truth about her age, she knew there was no mistake. Sorella was not a child!

It was just that she was so tiny. Her exquisite little features and small bones, which must have been characteristic of her mother, had combined to hoodwink them all into believing what D'Arcy Forest had wanted them to believe for his own ends.

Perhaps unconsciously, too, she had acted the part which was expected of her—the little child whom D'Arcy could use to extort money from stupid women, the young girl of fifteen whom Randal and Hoppy had believed in.

She had altered enormously in these past few weeks, Hoppy thought, and yet they had not really noticed. They had gone on believing what they had been told to believe and seeing what they expected to see.

How often Randal had said that the whole art of acting was to believe in the part you played!

Sorella had believed in her part and so had everyone else with whom she came in contact. Hoppy had felt her heart throb at the thought.

Yes, now it would be different. Sorella was grown up and a young woman.

It was then she felt herself grow panic-stricken. She heard the lawyer bidding them both good-bye. She had let Sorella take him to the door and she had waited until the girl returned.

Sorella came back into the room very composed and very quiet, but with her eyes suddenly alight as if she could not hide some secret, inner joy.

"So you are eighteen!" Hoppy's voice was harsh.

"Yes, isn't it wonderful? I always felt I was older. I felt I knew things I should not have known at that age, and yet I had met no children with whom to compare myself. I remember my fifth birthday. There were five candles on the cake. I must really have been eight, because after that I could count.

"I used to say to Daddy,

" 'I shall be nine next week.'

" 'And he would reply:

" 'For God's sake don't make so much song and dance about it. We'll tell everyone you're seven. There's something rather winsome about a seven-year-old.'

" 'He always tried to put me back, but when we were alone I would make him stick to the truth—at least, I thought it was the truth. But now I see he had been cleverer than I was. He had already put me back three years.' "

"I can't think how we were ever deceived into thinking you were anything but your right age," Hoppy said sourly.

"It's because I'm so small," Sorella replied. "I only come up to Randal's shoulder."

It was then Hoppy hardened her heart.

278

"Well, now that you're eighteen, we had better make plans for your future, because you can't stay here."

"Why not?"

"Because we know you're eighteen. My dear child, you can't be so unsophisticated as not to understand that," Hoppy said sharply. "It won't do Randal's reputation any good if people learn you've been living here so long unchaperoned. A girl of fifteen was questionable enough, but at eighteen!" Hoppy raised her eyes to the ceiling in horror.

There was a little pause, and then Sorella asked:

"You really think it can do Randal harm?"

"Of course," Hoppy replied. "People are only too eager to make mischief and to believe the worst. Also we have to consider Jane and her feelings. I can't think what she will say, especially as she suggested to me a long time ago that you should not be here alone."

"Jane suggested that?" Sorella questioned.

"Yes, of course she did," Hoppy snapped; "but I told her Randal felt responsible for you and it could not possibly matter if you stayed until they were married. What am I to say to her now? It's an extraordinarily uncomfortable position for everyone."

She stopped a moment as a thought struck her.

"I only hope Randal won't feel he has got to be quixotic in the matter!"

Even as she said the words she wished them unsaid.

"You mean he might feel he ought to marry me?" Sorella queried.

"No, of course I meant nothing of the sort—that's too ridiculous to contemplate," Hoppy replied.

But it was too late. The idea was there and both of them were acutely conscious of it.

"At least I have twenty-five pounds of my own," Sorella said in a very small voice.

"Did the lawyer give you that?" Hoppy enquired curiously.

Sorella nodded.

"I was going to buy some presents for everyone."

279

"Well, the best thing you can do is to find somewhere to lodge," Hoppy said. "I dare say there is a room available at the top of my building. If you would like to run round and ask the porter, he'll tell you right away."

Hoppy didn't mean to be unkind.

She had merely been concerned with Randal. Deep down in her heart she knew instinctively that Sorella's age was going to make a tremendous, overwhelming difference to everything, and yet she would not admit it to herself.

She was running away from the knowledge, striving to stem off the moment when she must face the fact that Randal's life could never be exactly the same as it had been before Sorella came into it.

Sorella had gone from the office and shut the door behind her.

Angrily Hoppy had begun to type some quite unnecessary letters. She felt at the moment that she could not go down to the theatre.

She could not bear to see Randal, she could not talk to anybody, she just wanted to think, to wonder what was going to happen, and to be afraid.

It was lunch time before she realised what the time was. She heard Norton come into the room and glanced up at the clock to see that it was after one o'clock.

"Are you in for lunch, Miss?" Norton asked. "Cook expected you to be down at the theatre; but she says there's a nice bit of Irish stew for the staff, if you fancy it."

"No, thank you, Norton, I'm not hungry," Hoppy replied, "but I would like a cup of tea, if it's no trouble."

"I'll get it at once, Miss," Norton answered and went towards the door.

"It's real sorry I am about Miss Forest," he remarked conversationally, "We shall miss her, all of us."

"Yes, I suppose we shall," Hoppy said, and then

added quickly: "What do you mean? Has Miss Forest found somewhere to go?"

"She didn't say where she was going, Miss," Norton replied. "She just collected a few things and I took them to the lift for her. There wasn't more than she could get into a suitcase.

" 'Tell Mr. Gray to send my other clothes to the place where he sent my father's,' she said. 'They'll find a good use for them there.' And then she gave me a pound, Miss.

" 'I felt ashamed to take it, I did, seeing as how we've always known she had no money of her own; but she insisted.

" 'Thank you very much for all you have done for me, Norton,' she says, as nice as nice, and gave me her hand. I don't know why, but I felt real upset to see her go."

"But where has she gone? She must have left some address!" Hoppy exclaimed.

"I don't think so, and I thought you must have known, Miss. To tell the truth, I didn't know as how you were here, seeing as you said you were going down to the theatre first thing this morning."

"She must have left a note for me or for Mr. Gray."

Hoppy ran down the passage to Sorella's little room. She burst open the door.

On the bed were lying two of the dresses Hoppy had helped Sorella choose. There was nothing else in the room. The drawers were empty—there was no note, no address, nothing.

Hoppy had stood there, suddenly stricken, and then she panted back to the telephone. She rang up the Head Porter where she herself lived. Had a Miss Forest been asking for a room?

No, the porter had not seen her. It was then that the realisation of what she had done swept over Hoppy, and with it an overwhelming sense of horror.

She was far too honest to deceive herself into pretending it was not her fault, or into making excuses.

It was she who had driven Sorella away, and it was she who must break the news to Randal.

Her voice died falteringly away as she finished the story. Hoppy sat trembling in her chair. There was no mistaking the nervous tension under which she had lived the whole afternoon.

She had telephoned everywhere she could think of, even to the shops where she had gone with Sorella to buy the clothes which Randal had paid for.

She had known, even while she did so, that it was hopeless.

She had known quite well that Sorella had left her dresses, except the one she was wearing because they were out of date. They were the trappings of an episode which was past. She would buy more clothes now, more suitable ones for a young woman of eighteen.

Hoppy suddenly put her hands up to her face.

"I can't think where she can have gone," she said. "I've thought and I've thought, Randal, and I can't think where she can be."

For a moment Randal said nothing.

Hoppy's story had been told with an honesty which left him in little doubt as to exactly what had been said and the hurt that she had inflicted on Sorella.

He understood even better than Hoppy had done why Sorella had gone away. He knew that it was for his sake and that it was because of her love for him that she would do anything, however hard, if it could be of benefit to him personally.

He sat still for several minutes. Then he rose to his feet and pulled back the curtains from one of the windows.

He looked out over the darkness of the Park, at the street lights glittering below on the moving traffic, and remembered how often he had seen Sorella sitting in the twilight looking out.

He knew then that if he was never to see her again his life would be utterly and completely empty.

He knew, too, exactly how much she had come to

mean to him and how impossible it would be to go on without her.

He knew that she was all that he was looking for, all that he had wanted, all for which he had yearned.

His pilgrimage was at an end, he had found what he sought, he had come to the end of the road.

For a moment the sheer wonder, the very miracle of it held him speechless.

He could feel a surging joy within his heart leaping upwards; and then he remembered that Hoppy—poor, white-faced, trembling Hoppy—was waiting for him to speak.

He turned towards her, a kindness and generosity born of his love for Sorella making him more gentle than he would have been on any other occasion.

He put his hand to Hoppy's shoulder and felt her tremble a little at his touch.

"You're not to blame yourself, Hoppy," he said quietly. "You couldn't know, because I have never told you, and I have not told Sorella either that I love her with all my heart. I love her as I never believed it possible to love anyone, and if she will have me, I'm going to marry her."

15

Hoppy covered her face with her hands and Randal saw that she was crying.

He stood looking at her, at her greying hair and shaking shoulders, and then she raised her face and said through her tears:

"I'm sorry, Randal, I didn't know, I didn't understand."

She looked very ugly when she cried, and it was her

ugliness which struck Randal as being more pathetic than anything else.

He felt a sudden warm affection for her.

He knew how fond she was of him and he understood, how all she had done and all she had planned had been solely because of her love for him—a love which made her want to mother him and do always what was in his best interests.

"Don't cry, Hoppy," he said. "You've got to help me. I need your help now as I've never needed it before."

It was the one appeal that was guaranteed to make Hoppy pull herself together. Randal needed her.

She pulled a handkerchief from her pocket—a sensible, large, plain, white linen square. She rubbed her eyes fiercely and blew her nose noisily.

Then she was ready for work.

"What do you want me to do?" she asked.

"We have got to find Sorella," Randal said; "but there is something I must do first."

"What is that?" Hoppy enquired.

"I've got to tidy up my old life. I've got to tie up the ends, so to speak."

He walked resolutely to the telephone. Hoppy gave a little cry:

"Randal, what are you doing?"

He picked up the receiver and before he dialled the number he turned to look at her. There was an expression on his face that she had never seen there before.

"I'm going to do the right thing at last, Hoppy. I'm going to Sorella with clean hands."

He dialled a number and Hoppy stood watching him helplessly, until as he spoke she was suddenly galvanised into action.

"I want to speak to Miss Lund," he said.

Then Hoppy was beside him, one hand on his arm which was holding the receiver, the other over the

284

mouthpiece so that whoever was at the other end would not hear what she said.

"Randal, are you mad?" she asked in a low voice. "If you tell Lucille now that you love Sorella, anything might happen. She may refuse to go on with the part, she may have hysterics; she may walk out of the theatre. Wait until after tomorrow night. For Heaven's sake, wait till then."

Gently but firmly Randal freed himself from Hoppy's restraining hands.

"You don't understand. I've behaved like a cad long enough."

His voice changed.

"Is that you, Lucille?" he asked.

Hoppy knew that she was defeated. Without a word she turned and walked away from him. He heard her cross the room and heard the door slam behind her.

"Hello, Randal."

It was Lucille's voice at the other end of the line.

"Lucille, I've got something to tell you . . ."

"And I've got something to tell you, Lucille interrupted. "Oh, Randal, I'm sorry for the way I've behaved, not only this afternoon, but all last week. I've been worried, desperately worried, and, darling, I really haven't been certain what I've been doing or what I've been saying. You've got to forgive me."

"Yes, yes, of course, Lucille," Randal remarked impatiently; "but I want to tell you . . ."

But Lucille was talking too fast for him to be able to stem the flood.

"Some day I'll tell you, Randal dearest, just what I've been through," she continued, "and then perhaps you'll understand. But now everything is changed. I shall be able to do my best in your really wonderful play."

There was a murmur behind her and she paused for a second.

"Edward says I don't sound sorry enough, but I am, really and truly sorry. It was only because I was so desperately worried. You see, I thought a great friend

285

of mine was dead and he isn't. No, he isn't dead, he's in prison."

"In prison?" Randal repeated incredulously.

He didn't understand what Lucille was trying to tell him. He wanted to speak about himself, but for the moment there was no chance of getting a word in.

"Yes, in prison," Lucille said again and laughed. "It sounds a funny reason for rejoicing, doesn't it? But I thought he was dead and instead he had just got involved in a fight because someone broke a bottle of whisky he was carrying.

After he had hit a man for breaking it, he hit the policeman who came to find what the fuss was about.

It seems that's a terrible thing to do over here, and my poor friend's got a two-year sentence. Two years! But I'm glad about it, yes, glad."

Lucille sounded quite hysterical, and Randal realised that the only thing for him to do was to agree with her.

"Well, I'm glad too if it makes you happy," he said. "But listen for a moment, Lucille. I've got something to tell you which may upset you."

"I don't believe anything would upset me at the moment," Lucille replied.

"I hope it won't then," Randal went on. "The truth is that I am in love, Lucille. I'm in love with Sorella and if she'll have me I'm going to marry her."

There was a pause, and then Lucille said slowly:

"You're going to marry Sorella—but how can you, she's only a child?"

"She's eighteen," Randal answered. "There's been a mistake about her birth date, but now we know the truth I'm going to marry her."

He said the words defiantly and waited for the storm to break. But strangely enough Lucille's voice was quite quiet when after a moment she said:

"So there was a . . . mistake about her age. . . . It seems funny somehow, your wanting to marry a little thing like that."

"Well, I do," Randal said defiantly, and added with

286

a touch of his old diplomacy, "I would like you to be the first to wish me happiness, Lucille—that is if Sorella will have me!"

"Haven't you asked her yet?" Lucille enquired curiously.

"Not yet," Randal replied.

He was going to add that he had lost Sorella and then thought better of it.

It was all too long and complicated a story to relate to Lucille now. Besides, he was anxious to get on with the task of finding Sorella. That was more important than anything.

But he had done the right and the brave thing in telling Lucille.

Although he had anticipated that she would take it very differently from this, he knew, that he could not go to Sorella besmirched with all the hypocrisy and pretence of the last weeks.

For the first time for a very long while Randal faced himself frankly and was disgusted with what he saw.

He felt as though he must wash himself clean, whatever the cost, whatever the punishment he must endure to do so.

Yet surprisingly Lucille was behaving in a very different manner from what he had expected.

"I do wish you happiness," she said at length. "I thought for a long time that we should get married, but now I'm not so sure. As a matter of fact, I don't think I shall marry anyone for some years at any rate."

She giggled as she spoke, and Randal thought that it was at some private joke that he didn't understand.

"I must go," he announced hastily. "Bless you, Lucille, for being so sporting about this."

"I'll see you tomorrow," Lucille replied, "and, darling, you're going to be very, very proud of me. I'm going to make your play just the biggest success ever."

"Thank you, Lucille."

Randal put down the receiver. So that was that.

He could hardly believe that he had told Lucille that everything between them was over and she had taken it quietly, without a protest, without a scene of any sort.

It was all so incredible that for a moment he could hardly believe it was true, that he had not been dreaming the whole conversation.

He could only imagine that Edward was somehow concerned in this, that he had talked to Lucille and had made her see sense, or that he had persuaded her, in some way of his own, that a career was more important than marriage.

Whatever the cause, Randal was thankful, sincerely and deeply thankful.

He had always hated the thought that a love affair must end in tears and recriminations.

And it would have seemed worse on this occasion than on any other, because Lucille was a lovely person and had brought so much beauty into his life.

Well, it was over, and he was free of one entanglement which he believed must keep him spiritually, if not physically from Sorella. There remained one more.

Slowly, and with a reluctance that he had not shown in telephoning Lucille, he took up the receiver again.

He knew now that he had never really loved Jane; but he had meant to marry her and she had been, for a short time at least, very desirable as a woman.

Now he felt ashamed, both for himself and for her, when he thought of the easy, facile passion with which she had surrendered to him a few nights ago.

He wished with all his heart that she had never come into his life.

He wished that Hoppy had not put into his mind the idea that he must marry her, and that it had not been all so easy, such a primrose path into Jane's affections.

He blamed himself for having been led away as easily as any boy might have been by the gaiety, the laughter and the brilliance of Jane's social connections.

He had, in fact, been dazzled by the "Magic Circle".

He had been as bemused and enraptured by them as any stage-struck teenager who hung about the stage door asking for autographs.

It was a phase through which he ought to have passed many years earlier.

But he supposed, when he thought about it, that the years when he should have been caught up in the social whirl had been spent in Burma, where he found life a serious, strenuous business, with little time for light relief.

"At last I've grown up," Randal thought.

Having dialled Jane's number he heard the bell ringing at the other end.

The butler answered the call and told Randal that Jane was at home and that he would connect him with her private sitting-room.

There was a few moments' wait and then he heard Jane's voice.,

"Hello, who is it?"

"It's Randal."

"Randal, darling! I was just thinking of you."

"Jane, I want to talk to you—are you alone?"

"Yes, quite alone. What is the matter? Has anything happened?"

"Yes, something has happened."

"What is it? Something bad for the play?"

"No, the play is all right," Randal replied.

He remembered that he would not have been able to say that half an hour ago.

"That is a good thing. I thought Lucille might have thrown a temperament."

"No, what I have to tell you has nothing to do with Lucille."

"Who then?"

"It is about Sorella."

"Sorella?"

"Yes, there has been a mistake over her birth date. She is eighteen."

There was only a short pause before Jane said:

"I guessed it. I knew all along she was not what she pretended to be."

"It wasn't her fault," Randal answered quickly. "She genuinely believed what her father had told her. It is only today that we have found out the truth."

"So what?"

There was something hostile in Jane's question which told Randal all too clearly that she anticipated what was coming.

"I hate to hurt you by saying this, Jane," he said after a moment. "But I think perhaps you've guessed already that I love Sorella. I want to marry her."

There was a silence—a long, horrible silence. Randal felt his mouth go dry; then at last Jane spoke.

"I knew it that night I came to the flat and found you talking so happily together," she said. "You made me feel an intruder, unwanted. Yes, I knew then."

There was so much pain and bitterness in her voice that instinctively Randal cried out:

"Don't Jane! Don't!"

"Yet I was fool enough to think I could hold you!" Jane went on, as if he had not spoken. "That was why I made you love me the other night. After you had gone, I knew I had failed. I thought it was my last chance. It was stupid of me, wasn't it?"

"Jane, I'm sorry," Randal said. "I hate to hurt you like this, but it would be worse if we went on pretending. You'll find somebody else far better and far more suitable than I am.

"The son of a Bank Manager from Worcester can't really gate-crash into your world. You know that, and I know it. I would rather be a big fish in my own little pond. But don't let us forget or decry the happiness we have had together.

"I shall always be grateful for having known you. Will you remember that?"

"Yes, Randal, I'll try to remember it. Perhaps in the future it will help a little." Jane's voice broke suddenly.

"Good-bye, darling . . . and God bless you."

She put down the receiver.

There was a click and she had gone. Randal felt a shame such as he had never experienced in the whole of his life before.

He felt despicable and he hated himself because he had the power to inflict such suffering on anyone as charming and as sweet as Jane.

Then, as he rose from his desk, he felt a sudden complete and utter relief that he was free of it all, free of everything save his new-found love for someone utterly different from both Jane and Lucille.

He walked across the room to the hearth-rug and he remembered how Sorella had sat there, her little face raised to his, her hands still in her lap, her eyes deep and serious.

Fool that he had been not to realise then how unique she was, how different from any other woman he had ever known!

That peace and quietness about her, that strange instinctive wisdom which had never failed him when he most needed it.

She had come into his life so unexpectedly, a waif without home or background, that it was to be understood that he could not at first assess her true worth.

Yet he thought now that he must have been blind and very dense not to have realised sooner what she was or what she meant to him.

Slowly and insidiously she had become a part of his life, so that it was only now when she was gone that he realised how completely she had filled it.

The flat seemed empty and dead without her and he thought that he could never go to Queen's Hoo again without seeing her there.

He was trying to think what he must do first to find her when the door opened and Hoppy came in. She was very pale, save for her eyes, which were red and swollen from the tears she had shed.

There was a look of enquiry on her face and Randal

realised that she was waiting tensely to hear what had happened.

"Come and sit down, Hoppy," he said kindly.

She obeyed him mechanically and he noticed that her hands were trembling as she smoothed her worn black skirt over her knees.

"Everything is all right, Hoppy," Randal smiled reassuringly. "Lucille is going to make the play the greatest success there has ever been, so you needn't worry on that score."

"And Jane?"

Randal's eyes would not meet Hoppy's.

"I'm sorry about Jane."

"I'm afraid a lot of it was my fault, . . ." Hoppy began.

Randal stopped her.

"All that is past. Don't let us talk about it any more. Everything one does in life has its repercussions, every action leaves an impression and perhaps a scar behind. We none of us can help that.

I'm sorry for a great many things, Hoppy—I'm also ashamed of them; but they are done, I can't undo them. And now we've got to find Sorella."

"Yes, but how?" Hoppy asked.

"That is what I'm wondering," Randal replied.

"If only I hadn't said what I did!" Hoppy murmured.

"It's done and it can't be undone," Randal said quickly. "We have got to remember that about everything, Hoppy. It is the future that counts."

"But where would she go?"

"If only she had some relations or friends," Randal sighed.

"She had no one but us," Hoppy whispered hardly above her breath, and Randal felt the implication even as she did.

They had both of them failed the child.

Then even as he thought of Sorella as a child Randal remembered that she was a woman; but he added to

292

himself it didn't matter what one called her—child, girl, woman—she was all three and most of all herself.

A unique, distinct, original personality which was Sorella—someone so different in every way from anyone he had ever met, and yet the embodiment of everything he had looked for, wished for and sought.

"Where would she go?"

Randal strode across the room and back again, as if in action he might find the answer to his own question.

"We might ask the police to help us," Hoppy ventured.

"No, not that unless we absolutely have to," Randal replied. "Sorella would hate to be hunted and interrogated. I could not bear that for her. Besides, I have a feeling that it is up to me to find her.

"I know that sounds absurd and romantic, the Prince in the fairy tales; and yet this is a kind of testing. I've been with her so long that I ought to know what she would do."

He walked across the room again before he went on:

"You know, Hoppy, that if it was the other way about, Sorella would know where to find me. She is always so sure, so convinced of what is right.

"If ever there was a problem, she would solve it, if there was a difficulty, she would find a solution. Because I love her, I ought to be able to find her now. Do you understand?"

Watching him as he spoke, Hoppy felt a sudden constriction of her heart. Never in all the years she had known and worked for him had she seen him like this.

This was a different Randal, one who had suddenly shed everything that was tawdry, everything that was pretentious.

She was suddenly very proud of him—this new Randal, this man who was striving to be honest and straightforward, truthful and good.

"What an old-fashioned word that is," Hoppy thought, "and how often we forget it!"

"I have got to find Sorella," Randal went on, "and I believe somewhere, in something that she has said at one time or another, there is a clue which will set me in the right direction."

He walked to the door.

"I'm going out."

"Where to?" Hoppy enquired.

"I don't know," he replied. "I'm going to walk about, thinking of where Sorella can have gone when she left here. Even to wander through the streets may give me an idea. Don't worry about me, go home and go to bed."

Hoppy didn't reply. A few minutes later she heard the front door slam behind him. She made no attempt to go home. Instead she made up the fire and sat in front of it.

She felt cold and old, and she did what so many women have done before her—she sat in judgment upon herself.

She saw how she had failed Randal even as the other women who had loved him had failed him.

They had all of them, she included, made little effort to inspire him or to ask of him anything that was not very easy for him to give; that, Hoppy saw, had been where their failure lay.

Randal was so talented, he had so many qualities, so much charm, that it was difficult to remember that he was capable of giving so much more, of being, in many ways a far finer person than he was already.

That was where Sorella had been different.

She had never flattered Randal; she had only expected from him the finest and the highest of his capabilities.

She had inspired him simply and solely because there was that same greatness within herself which lay latent in Randal.

There was indeed, Hoppy thought, something intensely spiritual about both of them, only that Randal's

294

soul had been hidden for so long by a material veneer of success that one had forgotten it even existed.

She saw now how she, like Randal, had been blinded by the worldly goods which Jane could bring him, and had been bemused and bedazzled by all the grandeur which was an intrinsic part of her background.

Hoppy had thought that Jane could give Randal so much. She saw now how infinitely more valuable were the gifts that Sorella could bring him.

Humbly Hoppy faced her failure and then smiled as she thought of the future.

Randal and Sorella would be very happy. They would find new worlds to conquer; better and greater things to do together. Both of them had been through strange and varied experiences which would in the future stand them in good stead.

"I will help them," Hoppy thought to herself, and she fell asleep smiling.

She awoke with a start some hours later to find that the room was very cold, for the fire had gone out, and she was stiff from sleeping in the chair.

She yawned, rubbed her hands together, then looked at the clock.

It was three o'clock in the morning. She wondered if Randal had come in and, thinking she had gone home, had gone to bed.

She opened, the sitting-room door, only to find the light still on in the hall and that Randal's hat and coat were still missing.

She knew that he had not returned, and she thought of him walking the streets and felt herself ache for the misery that she knew he was experiencing.

"Why not go to the police?" she thought. "They would be far more successful than Randal is likely to be."

At the same time she understood that this had become a kind of Crusade with him, the end of the pilgrimage that he had spoken of so glowingly and with an inner emotion that she had not suspected in him before.

She knew then that she must go home.

She could not help Randal any further at the moment. This was something he must face alone, something he must do for himself and without assistance.

Feeling old, tired and helpless, Hoppy put on her coat, and tying a handkerchief over her head, she went out of the flat and set off for home.

She was round at the flat at eight-thirty the next morning.

It was earlier than she usually arrived; but she had been unable to sleep and knew that the only salve for her anxiety was to see Randal and find out what had happened to him.

As she came in at the flat door, she met Norton carrying a pair of mud-stained trousers down the passage towards the pantry.

"Mr. Gray awake?" Hoppy equired.

"Awake, Miss?" Norton replied. "He's awake all right. Hasn't been to bed for that matter. He didn't get in until six o'clock this morning. Had to wake me up, as he had gone out without his latchkey; and a nice state I finds him in, I can tell you. Look at his trousers!"

"What had he been doing?" Hoppy exclaimed.

"That's what I'd like to know!" Norton exclaimed. "Soaked to the skin, he was, and his shoes that damp he might have been paddling in the river. Crazy, I calls it, if you ask me!"

Hoppy waited to hear no more, but walked into the dining-room. Randal was having breakfast, a newspaper propped in front of him.

He was wearing a silk dressing-gown of maroon velvet with cuffs and revers of royal blue. His initials were embroidered on his pocket and he had told Hoppy when he bought it it was the essential garment for any successful playwright.

Now, this morning, it seemed to Hoppy, it appeared

quite alien on him. He was looking tired and there were dark lines under his eyes.

At the same time, he seemed to look fitter and more alert than he had for a long time. It was as though the years of soft living had seeped away from him overnight.

"Good morning, Hoppy," he smiled. "Will you have a cup of coffee?"

"No, thank you," Hoppy replied. "Where have you been?"

"I thought that was what you were going to ask me," Randal answered, "but I don't know."

"But you must know," Hoppy said incredulously.

"I can remember a good many places," Randal replied. "The Embankment, Shaftesbury Avenue, St. Paul's, the Houses of Parliament . . . but I don't expect you want me to tell you much about them. I walked a great many miles last night. I was thinking, Hoppy, thinking as I haven't thought for a very long time, and it has done me a power of good."

"Have you thought where to find Sorella?" Hoppy asked practically.

"Yes, I think so."

"Oh, where?" Hoppy exclaimed.

"I don't know the name of the place, yet," Randal replied. "I'm waiting for Cook's to open. I've an idea they might be able to help me. If they fail, I must try every travel agency in London."

"You think she's gone abroad?" Hoppy equired.

"No, I'm sure she hasn't. That is one thing of which I am certain. She told me she wanted to get to know England, so I'm convinced that she is in England.

"Last night, as I walked, I tried to remember everything she had ever said to me, and after a while two things came back to me.

"First, when we talked about the last act of the play she said that if she had been in Marlene's place she would have wanted to go right away from everything she knew.

297

"That we both know, was Sorella's idea, yesterday, to get away. She thought she was hurting me by staying here, so she would want to get right away.

"She wouldn't remain in London, so it will be useless to look for her here. That leaves more or less the whole of the British Isles in which to search for her.

"But I have remembered that when we were talking she told me that once she had been to the country with her father.

"They had gone to a little hotel in Yorkshire and Sorella had said she was happier there than she had ever been anywhere else in her life.

"She said she used to go up on the moors, lie in the heather and listen to the birds. She had not felt alone, she had felt very close to God.

"Now, Hoppy, think of Sorella leaving here yesterday. She would not have been happy to go, at least I like to think that she wouldn't have been, and in going away she had the whole world to choose from.

"But because she was unhappy. I believe she would choose the only place where she had ever known happiness, the place where she had not been alone because she had been very close to God."

"But where is it, Randal? Where is it?" Hoppy asked.

"I only know that the hotel is in Yorkshire and that there was an old mill near it."

"An old mill?" Hoppy said excitedly, "that at least gives you a clue."

"That is why I'm going to Cook's," Randal replied, "to ask for a hotel that is near a mill. They will think I'm mad, but if they or any other agency can't tell me where it is, I shall just search Yorkshire till I find it."

He glanced at the clock and got to his feet.

"Cook's open at nine."

"Randal, let me go for you," Hoppy begged. "You've got your rehearsal at half past."

"Rehearsal?" Randal repeated, and then he laughed.

"Why are you laughing?" Hoppy enquired. "Aren't you going to the rehearsal?"

Randal put his hands on her shoulders.

"Listen, Hoppy, and try to understand what this means to me. I'm looking for Sorella and nothing and nobody is going to stop me looking. I am not going to the rehearsal today.

"I am not going to the Opening tonight. I don't care what happens one way or another. There is only one thing I am interested in, and that is Sorella, whom I love."

Randal bent and kissed Hoppy's cheek.

She gaped at him in astonishment, he hurried from the room, running down the passage with the energy and agility of a young boy.

She heard him singing in his bath, heard him shout good-bye a few minutes later as he hurried across the hall.

Even as he left the flat, the telephone began to ring, and Hoppy with a bewildered shake of her head went to cope with the tangle of affairs that Randal had left behind him.

It was over two hours later when Randal, driving the Bentley, turned her nose northwards.

There was a suitcase in the back of the car and a packet of sandwiches beside him. Norton had insisted on his taking both and Randal had chafed with impatience at having to wait for them to be got ready.

He had, in fact, not had to wait more than a minute or so, as by the time the Bentley was ready for the journey, and he had collected the maps he required, Norton's sandwiches and the luggage were ready too.

Hoppy had come down to the front door to see him off.

"You have the name of the place with a mill?" she asked.

"I have the names of three," Randal replied as he got into the car. "Good-bye, Hoppy—wish me luck."

"Good luck and God help you," she said quietly.

She had waved until he was out of sight, although he did not look back.

She knew then that Randal loved Sorella as he had never before loved anybody or anything. There had never been anyone in his life for whom he would put aside his work and not think it a sacrifice.

Bruce Bellingham had rung at ten o'clock to ask why Randal was not at the rehearsal and had been absolutely incredulous when Hoppy had said he wasn't coming to the theatre.

"Is he ill or mad?" Bruce enquired.

"Neither," Hoppy replied, and found it impossible to say more.

Bruce had rung off in disgust, but Randal had only smiled when Hoppy told him how many people had telephoned from the theatre.

Bruce was not the only one. There was the Manager, Edward, several officials from the front of the house, Randal's publicity agent and half a dozen Press representatives.

They were all as astonished as Bruce had been when Hoppy said he could not be contacted.

But as she watched Randal set off for Yorkshire, Hoppy realised that he had forgotten their very existence. Randal had wiped the slate clean of all but one name.

It was true enough that, as Randal drove along, hurrying through the traffic and travelling as fast as he dared, he had no thought for all that he had left behind.

Once again he had that sense of travelling down a long road which was leading him to the goal which he had sought all his life. He felt that he must hurry, that every moment was precious, every moment vital.

He drove faster and faster, forgetting everything save his desire to find Sorella and tell her how much she meant to him.

Late in the afternoon, as he ate one of the sandwiches which Norton had provided for him, he realised that at last he was in Yorkshire.

The moors stretched up on either side of the road and the air seemed clearer and fresher, as if he had come to the top of the world and the valleys lay far behind him.

He had chosen to visit first a place called Bendale Mill.

It lay down unfrequented roadways, past mountain streams and over ancient grey stone bridges which seemed hardly wide enough for a modern vehicle. It was a clear day with occasional bursts of sunshine and at times the sky was very blue and at others overcast with cloud.

The lights on the hills were very lovely and everywhere the autumn tints, orange, brown, gold and bronze, seemed to cover the world with glory. Randal drove faster down the twisting roads.

He was not feeling in the least tired and the same urgency which had spurred him when he first left London seemed to be intensified as the day wore on.

It was then, suddenly, that he came upon Bendale Mill.

A few cottages nestled round a small hotel, the moors stretching away behind the Mill, just it seemed to Randal as Sorella had described it to him.

He drew up at the hotel, and as he got from the car he was conscious for the first time of feeling stiff.

It took him a moment or two to find the proprietress; but when she came, a sturdy, apple-cheeked woman with a friendly smile, he enquired if Miss Forest was staying there.

"Indeed she is, Sir," was the reply. "The young lady arrived last night. Were you wanting to see her?"

Randal felt his heart leap so swiftly that for the moment he could not reply.

He had expected a refusal. He had expected to be told that he had come to the wrong place and that Sorella was unknown.

But she was here, and he could find no words in which to answer the proprietress because of the joy within his heart. At last in a voice curiously unlike his own he said:

"Yes, I would like to see Miss Forest. Can you tell me where she is?"

"I saw her with my own eyes climbing up the moors after lunch. There's a wee path through the garden. Follow that and you'll come to the top of Bendale Hill. There's a rare view from there, as I expect the young lady has already found."

The last words were spoken to the air. Randal had already gone, hurrying through the garden almost at a run.

The proprietress watched him climbing the path; then she smiled to herself a little knowing smile and went back to the kitchen.

The path was steep and Randal was breathless by the time he reached the top. There was a flat piece of ground and then the moor rose again.

He looked round, but there was no sign of Sorella, so he must go on climbing. It was not easy going, and the wind, which he had not felt till now, seemed to do its best to hinder him.

But still he hurried on until at length, as he came to the top of yet another climb, he saw Sorella.

She was sitting with her back to him looking out over a magnificent vista of moor, river and sky which lay beyond her. Randal stood very still.

He had come at last to his goal.

He felt then as though he could hardly breathe, as if the wonder and the excitement burning within him were almost too great to be endured.

And as he stood there, not moving, not speaking, but just looking at Sorella, it seemed as if the intensity of his feelings communicated itself to her wordlessly and with some magnetism that had always existed between them.

Slowly she turned her head and, seeing him, rose to her feet.

Then, as her eyes met his, she did not move, but waited for him to come to her.

Slowly, Randal advanced, and when at length he

stood beside her, he looked down into her small face raised to his and knew that to find her he would, if necessary, have walked bare-footed over the whole earth.

They stood looking at each other, until in a voice deep and low with emotion, Randal spoke.

"Sorella, my darling, how could you go away and leave me?"

"I thought it was best for you," she answered.

Her eyes seemed to search his face a little anxiously.

He did not put out his hands towards her, for he knew that he must not touch her until he had said what he had come to say; and yet even that seemed unnecessary.

Already they knew that they were one, they belonged to each other, they were undivided, and yet for convention's sake, he must tell her what he felt she already knew.

"I have come to find you, Sorella," he said, "because I can't live without you, because I love you, because I want above all things, if you will have me, that we shall be married.

He drew in his breath.

"I have told Lucille and I have told Jane why I have come here, to ask you to be my wife. But, darling, if you send me away, I can tell you now that there will be nothing left for me in the whole world save an emptiness and a loneliness beyond words."

He waited, his eyes on her face.

Then he saw with a wonder as if he watched a miracle the colour come into her cheeks and the light into her eyes. It was as if he watched the dawn, and a dawn so beautiful, so tender and so young that there were no words to describe it.

He knew it to be the dawn of happiness—a happiness in which they were each dependent utterly and completely on the other.

It was then, as she did not speak, that human nature broke beneath the strain of waiting.

With a cry that was half of joy and half of triumph, Randal put out his arms and drew Sorella close to him.

"Tell me you love me," he demanded. "Tell me, for I can wait no longer. Sorella, I love you so!"

She smiled then, and with the parting of her lips he knew her to be more beautiful and more lovely than any woman he had seen in his life before.

There was, in fact, at that moment, an almost angelic beauty about her, as if her very soul shone through the transparency of her body.

"I love . . . you Randal," she answered.

Her voice was low, yet clear and serious as if she made a vow before the altar.

"Sorella!" He could say no more.

His lips sought hers; and at that moment the sun came out and shone through the clouds, enveloping them with a warmth and glory which was like a blessing from Heaven itself.

Randal's lips held Sorella's and in that first kiss he knew an ecstasy that had in it something of the Divine. Man and woman made one.

He felt Sorella respond to the joy and wonder within himself. He felt her tremble, and yet he knew she was not afraid.

In that moment Randal knew that nothing in life could ever be more poignant or more perfect than this.

And when at length Sorella's head fell back against his shoulder and he looked down at her face in the sunlight, he saw there were tears shining in her eyes for very happiness.

"I love you, Sorella," he cried again. "I love you. Oh my precious darling, my little love, tell me that you will never leave me again—that you are mine—mine for ever."

"For . . . ever, Randal," she whispered.

He knew then, as he had known so surely as he hurried north, that his goal was reached, his pilgrimage was over.

He had found what he sought and it was his for eternity. . . .